CLUMSY FOOT

by

Karl P. Warden

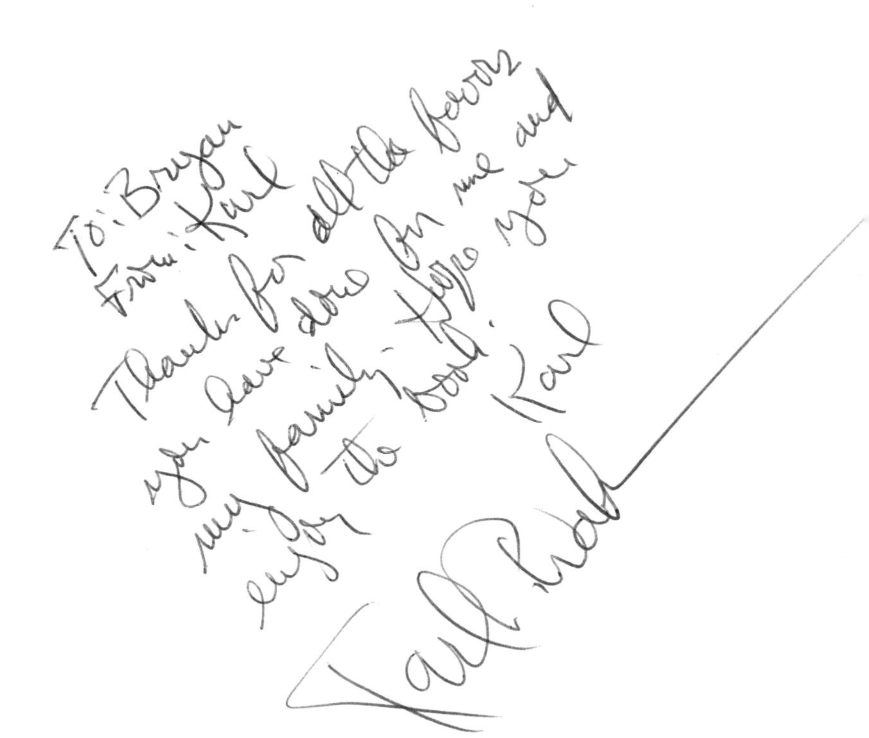

ISBN 978-1-60145-395-2

Printed in the United States of America.

Booklocker.com, Inc.
2007

Acknowledgement

To my editor and friend, Mary Wilder, who, once again, labored through my punctuation problems and saved my bacon. Thank you Mary. Thanks also to Jim who read it and said he liked it.

Dedication

To Betty and Cindy and K.D. who lived it all with me. Those happy days will be with me forever. I love you all more than you'll ever know.

Prologue

On the afternoon of October 17, 1980, in the Rare Manuscripts Room of the Hamilton Drayton Memorial Library in Ann Arbor, Michigan, a scholar, working with 16th Century unclassified documents, part of a large collection donated to the library by the Bolton Foundation, translated the following short manuscript:

"I, Enrique Juan Folques de Rojo, being mindful of the frailty of man's life and of the multitudes of blessings for which the Everlasting God doth jealously claim, Amen, do pen this statement for that my posterity not judge me harshly.

"As a member of the party of Lucas Vazquez de Ayllon viewing the shores of Carolina, I became separated from my party in a region called Chicora. There I wandered for many months in the wilderness. I followed the setting sun across great cloudy mountains, thence across a flat and woodless plain and thence across mighty rivers and wasted lands until, after many days, Amen, by the Grace of the Master of all that be, I arrived at a valley in that desert which was abundant with water and food. There, in Seven Towns, were multitudes of savages who accepted me as they would one of their own. I became a brother to these kindly people. I have dwelt here for many seasons and have taken unto myself a wife. I call her 'Liawu' because in their language this means 'the fair one'. Over the years we had many children, the eldest of whom was a boy whose name must always remain a secret. We called him Israel, for he had been born of a wanderer in search of his own land. On an occasion an evil man appeared from the South. He saw our valley, its seven villages and the plate and blue stones that decorated our world. He proposed to return to the South and to tell other men of his kind what he had seen. Though he was of my race and spoke the language of my youth, which I could barely

remember, I did not like him and I feared that he might bring disaster to our land. When we could not persuade him to remain with us in peace, and when we then perceived his plan to bring more men whose only purpose would be wicked, we destroyed him. Upon council it was decided to make a great change so that in the future no such visitor would tarry long, and no invader would have reason to bring violence to our cities or to our way of life. Accordingly it was done in a place that was marked in a peculiar way. I was chosen as the keeper of this secret place to be succeeded by the eldest male child of the body of Liawu and, in turn, by his son and his sons forever. All these things and more I do for the greater glory of God and my immortal soul. Amen."

The scholar returned the manuscript to the document collection and did not catalogue it, for it was of no importance to his research project. It was later badly damaged by a water leak in the library. Together with a small number of similarly damaged documents, it was incinerated.

PART I

THE ASSIGNMENT

Colonial University
Macon, Georgia

Professor Andrew J. Duval
August 18, I978
Room 107 Law School

Dear Dr. Duval:

First let me express to you the appreciation of the Board and the Alumni Office for your willingness to share in the development of this important enterprise.

I believe that Dean Trondheim has given you most of the details, but I would like, for the record, to fill you in on the big picture.

The late Mr. Okey P. Smith is not an alumnus, or should I say--was not an alumnus of our school. Truthfully, we are not certain where he obtained his schooling. That may prove to be a part of your assignment, to see if you can find out--but I'm getting ahead of myself.

Okey P. Smith passed away several weeks ago in the crash of a private airplane in New Mexico. He was a resident of Santa Barbara, California and, as far as we are now able to determine, was a widower without surviving relatives. His wife, Dorothy, predeceased him by several years. They had no children. He was a man of very considerable wealth. His fortune was accumulated in Central America from the operations of a mineral exploration company named "Clumsy Foot Enterprise," which he founded, and was substantially augmented by investments in California real estate through a company called "Black Bear" which he also wholly owned. His estate has been guesstimated at over fifty million dollars. According to the attorney who contacted me, it may be substantially in excess of that figure. I needn't remind you that such an amount of money would be a significant addition to the resources of Colonial University.

Okey P. Smith's will established a trust fund under which his attorney, as trustee, is to divide the entire estate between certain Indian aid organizations in the Southwest, several organizations devoted to the assistance of jail and prison inmates, and Colonial University where his father-in-law the late Professor Roscoe P. Lamb had served as a faculty member. This testamentary directive was written in such a way that the lawyer trustee has complete control over the actual division and disbursement of the moneys. To put it bluntly, any of the beneficiaries could receive ten cents or tens of millions of dollars, and the decision will be that of the attorney.

Now to the point, naturally we wish to maximize Colonial University's share of the Smith estate and this is where your services are needed. It seems that among the effects of Okey Smith is a manuscript in the form of a diary. The attorney feels that it is autobiographical and that our University Press should publish it as a memorial to Smith. He has suggested that we assign a professional scholar to the task of determining whether this writing is a work of fiction or whether it is, as he thinks, the life story of his client.

Because of your background of knowledge of the American Indians and also because you are a distinguished teaching lawyer, we feel you are the best man to investigate and classify the document.

Naturally we cannot allow the University's imprimatur to be placed on a publication which is in the least suspect or which does not reflect the high degree of scholarly and historic accuracy for which Colonial University has justly become world renowned. On the other hand, we must never lose sight of the responsibility of the university to remain financially stable so that we can continue to produce first-rate scholars and scholarly papers.

Therefore, on behalf of the Board, I request you to fly to Santa Barbara and contact the attorney, a Mr. Raymond L. Ryan of the firm of Ryan, Hill, and Lincoln. He will turn the diary, manuscript or what have you over to you for your inspection and preliminary investigation. As soon as you have read it, let us have your ideas as to what our proper course of conduct should be. Thank you for your efforts on your behalf.

With kindest regards,

J. W. Tuttweiler. Chairman of the Board

PART II

THE MANUSCRIPT

Chapter One

November 1958 brought three uninvited visitors to the streets of Chicago--Eisenhower's recession, ice-cold rain, and me. The recession came from the District of Columbia. The cold rain came from North Dakota. I came from West Virginia.

As soon as my feet hit the big city streets, winter oozed up my legs and into my body. In feeble protest, I hauled up the moth-eaten collar of my pea coat. There must be some kind of special warm heaven for the poor bastards who die hunched in a Chicago doorway while the wind off Lake Michigan hunts the streets. No place on earth is as miserable as West Madison Street in the winter.

I huffed into my cupped hands, stomped my numb feet, and thought about how life had been only an hour earlier riding into town on the "No Passengers Allowed" side of a big Diamond-T Rig.

I had aired my thumb for five hours on the highway outside of Wheeling, West Virginia, before that good Samaritan teamster came by and put the air brakes to his truck. At first he claimed he picked me up because I looked like a buddy from his World War II army days. I told him it wasn't me. I had been in the Korean police action navy. He didn't give a damn. He just wanted someone to chin with when the country music on the truck radio faded into static. Between trashing gears and honking air horns he laid a bunch of lies about the war on me. I pretended I hadn't heard them a hundred times before. Like any other ex-G.I., I've told every one of them myself, with me, of course, as the hero. Anyway, shooting the breeze with him in a warm truck cab was easier than walking to Chicago.

Seventy-five miles west of Massillon, Ohio, he announced it was time for a rest break, and wheeled us into a neon-trimmed truck stop called "Big Ruby's Bar-B-Q." Inside, the jukebox caterwauled that "It wasn't God who made honky-tonk angels." As we slid into a booth, a real live angel hustled over with thick black coffee in thick white mugs.

"What's In Chicago for an ex swab jockey like you?" he asked as he stirred a half pound of sugar into his coffee.

"Work, I hope, They tell me you can still find jobs up there."

"Yeah, you hillbillies would hitch-hike to hell if you heard they were handing out jobs, wouldn't you? Well, I hate to tell you the facts of life sailor boy, but things are tight up in Chicago too. If you had any sense, you'd go back in the Navy."

"No way! The Navy and I made a deal. When they finally agreed I could go home, I agreed I wouldn't come back. I won't renege on that bargain."

"What did you do after you got out?"

"Oh, I got ambitious and went to school on the G.I. Bill. Then my old man got real sick and I quit and went back home. After he died, an undertaker and a pettifogging damn lawyer, between the two of them, took what little he had left. Since then I've just drifted."

"Too bad. Them sonsabitchin lawyers are nothing but bad news. You been to Chicago before?"

"I went through Boots at Great Lakes."

"How'd you like it?"

"I didn't."

"Like the man says, if they was gonna give the world an enema, they'd stick it in at Chicago. Ain' t that right?" he snickered.

Since he was buying the groceries, I laughed out loud.

Ten hours and five gift cups of coffee later we rolled into Chicago. He didn't bother to ask me where I wanted out. Of course he didn't need to. There are only three places in Chicago for immigrant Appalachians, south of 63rd, west of Halsted, or on Madison Street. He dumped me on the far west end of Madison, and wished me luck.

Chapter Two

So there I was-end of the line, sleet falling and the temperature fifty degrees below absolute zero. On Madison, you stand or you walk. I pulled up my socks and elected to walk.

By mid-afternoon, I was almost downtown and the sleet had slowed. Other inhabitants had begun to creep out of the woodwork. Among them was the Chicago Police Department's umbrella squad.

I knew what was coming as soon as I saw that beat-up blue and white Plymouth splash through the slush at the curb line. It hit the puddle opposite me and stopped with the engine running. The fat cop, riding shotgun, rolled down the mud-splattered window, poked his head out and nodded me over to him.

"New in town?" he asked, without curiosity.

"Yes, sir. I'm just in from Wyoming. I'm here to visit some relatives." That was a stupid lie. I plastered a big phony smile on my face to try to cover it up.

"Wyoming, huh?" O.K., cowboy, tell me your relatives' name and address". He knew damn well I wasn't from Wyoming and that if I had any relatives in Chicago they probably wouldn't claim me.

"She's my cousin. I forget her married name; she lives in this end of town. Somewhere," I added lamely.

"Alright, hillbilly, hear this, and hear it real good. The deadline for bums like you is LaSalle Street. You stay on this side of LaSalle. If you move across LaSalle or mooch anywhere in Chicago, we'll run your ass in so fast it'll make your moonshine filled head swim. Got that?"

"Yes, sir!"

"Don't forget it. Now move on!"

He looked me over again and made a note on his clipboard, one more hard look and they splashed on to dispense equal protection to some other good citizen.

I figured that little scene was played on West Madison a hundred times every day. Maybe if a rookie cop had performed it, it would have sounded tough. Tough or not, one lesson I got from it, the cops know every bum on the street. Well, why shouldn't they? The population doesn't change that much on any skid row. Before long, I would know all their ugly faces too.

When the fat John Law and his buddy finally got out of sight, I searched my pockets and discovered that if I just had ten more dollars, I'd have ten dollars and thirteen cents. It was time for heavy economic planning. Eight cents would buy me a sack of tobacco and some cigarette paper. On the other hand, ten cents would get three fingers of Sweet Lucy or two cups of coffee in any joint along the row.

The smoke sounded best if I could manage to get one rolled. That would leave me five cents for one cup of coffee for supper. The truth is I never developed a taste for Sweet Lucy. As the old man said, "Liquor ain't my particular problem."

Before I found a place elegant enough to fritter away my fortune, the sleet started in again, harder than before.

Weighted in the balance, the sleet was more of a threat to my general wellbeing than whatever the cops might do about a violated deadline. I knew that State Street was in the middle of the forbidden territory; I also knew that it had lots of doorways and stores and somewhere the elevated railway crossed it. One way or the other, State Street meant shelter. So I screwed up my courage, breached the LaSalle Street deadline and headed south.

Traffic was heavy. I ducked in and out of doorways dodging early Christmas shoppers and cops and eventually found the intersection with the El. Unfortunately, it was no help. Even though it covered the street from sidewalk to sidewalk, as I had remembered, it was too high to break the wind and about the only thing it did was change the sleet to ice water.

Wet and disgusted I straggled along another block or two and saw how the neighborhood had mutated from expensive department stores and exclusive boutiques to pawn shops, greasy spoons and penny arcades.

Finally I ducked into a recess in a yellow painted brick storefront. A sign spelled out "Amusement Devices" in flashing incandescent light bulbs above the door. Behind the door glass in silver glitter letters on a blue card was "Ladies Invited--You Must be 21 to Enter." The last time I had seen a glitter lettered blue card was on the wall of a West Virginia coal miner's living room. It proclaimed “Jesus Saves.”

The thing that really caught my attention was a "Help Wanted" notice penciled on shirt cardboard and taped to the doorframe. I grabbed the cardboard off the door, and hustled inside. The only visible person was a three hundred-fifty-pound blob perched on a kitchen stool, chewing a toothpick and sweating as he read the pictures in a *Sunshine and Health Magazine*.

"I'm looking for work. Whom do I talk to?" I asked, as I looked around the room. Two pinball machines, one with "Out of Order" grease penciled on its scoreboard, a popcorn warmer, a gadget to seal drivers licenses in plastic and three double rows of stag movie machines were the only other occupants of the dimly lighted room.

The red-faced hulk tore his close set eyes away from the page and focused on me. "Can you read and can you make change?” he asked in an unexpectedly high pitched, rasping voice.

"I can and I can."

"Know anything about movie projectors?" He looked doubtful about my prospects.

"Yes."

"What do you know about them?"

"I used to know a guy that owned one."

Unexpectedly, that seemed to satisfy him.

"Pay's forty-five a week. Hours are noon till midnight. Any objections?"

"None, what do I have to do?"

"Make change. Every frigging thing in here takes dimes. When the film breaks or jams, you fix it. I'll show you how. Keep the friggin' perverts and the J.D.'s out. At midnight you sweep up. If you need a place to sleep, there's a cot in the storeroom. We're open every day. You want it? Yes or no?" The recitation sounded so well rehearsed he must have hired a new man every other week.

"I want it. When do I start?"

"Wait a minute. You ain't through listening to me, boy. Now I don't pay no friggin' communist social security. You take your pay in cash. I don't take out for no friggin' income tax neither. If you want to pay the friggin' government, you pay it yourself. Well, what about it? You want the job?

I said, "Yes." It was slightly better than no job at all, but his limited range of adjectives and the idea of showing dirty movies for a living stuck hard in my West Virginia craw.

"Then get behind this friggin' counter so I can get out of this friggin' place and make some friggin' money."

Such as it was, I had found a home.

For the next three weeks, I spent twelve hours every day watching sheep-faced middle age men invest ten cents a minute to stare at out-of-focus I6 mm. movies featuring females in and out of their skivvies. During that entire time, not one soul asked for change to play pinball, eat popcorn or seal drivers licenses.

Clearly, in the Second City the love of cinematic art transcended all other worldly pleasures.

Chapter Three

I soon learned that the fat man's legal name was Romeo Lillard, but he was called "Grease Ball" by all the bagmen, who used the place as a drop. That was one part of the fat man's business I left strictly alone. It was bad enough to sit all day in his stinking place handing out dimes to sweaty palmed visiting yokels. I sure as hell didn't want to spend time in jail on a trumped-up numbers racket charge.

On the first day of December 1958, Grease Ball removed the perpetual toothpick from his fat mouth and announced that naturally we would stay open on Christmas Day. I was in a foul mood anyway, and this bulletin was one too much. Generally, I don't mind people getting their kicks however and whenever they want, but on Christmas Day they ought not be in some sleazy joint looking at dirty movies.

"I quit," I told him. "I'm not showing skin flicks on Christmas Day."

"You can't quit." He scratched his crotch while he thought about it, and then he grinned. "She-it boy, ain't I treated you just like a son?" That was some big deal. Any son of his would be glad to trade places with a bastard orphan and pay boot for the privilege.

"You've treated me O.K., Mr. Lillard, but I have another offer and I'm going to take it." I didn't add that the offer was nothing but a vague hope of drawing unemployment insurance until I could find a decent job in a decent place. The grin was still on his face but there was no humor in his eyes. "Listen to me, hillbilly. I said you can't quit me and that friggin' well means you can't quit! Besides, I know all about what you've been doing when I'm not around."

I blew my stack. "What the hell do you mean 'what I've been doing'?" I shouted. "The only thing I've been doing is running your damn dirty movies."

His phony grin faded. "That's enough of that crap! I've told you a thousand times these here are not dirty movies. They are friggin' art film, -ART films. As to what you've been doing, you've been screwing me out of half the friggin' policy money that comes through the friggin' door. Boy, you've been dippin your sticky fingers into my private candy jar!" A little dribble of spit replaced the absent toothpick in the corner of his mouth.

I angrily denied it, since there wasn't a word of truth in it, and then I told old Grease Ball he was a horse's rear end. I also suggested a few more things, mostly about his ancestry, and all of it shouted at the top of my voice.

And then, because I was too worked up to think straight, I made the worst mistake of my life. Instead of just turning and walking out of the place like I had good sense, I decided to throw a goodbye punch at the old devil. I suppose I figured he was too fat and too slow and too stupid to do much about it. Well, I swung. Grease Ball leaped aside like a Russian ballet dancer grabbed a big glass ashtray off the counter and pole-axed me. He probably put the boots to me too, but I was out cold and didn't feel it. Apparently, after he got tired of working me over, he called the cops to clean up the mess.

They must have done the job for him, because when my next completely conscious moment came, I was standing on wobbly legs in the reception room of a Chicago jailhouse rubbing my very sore head and hearing some bored sounding turnkey clerk ask if I was hurt bad.

"Naw. He's O.K. He just got his feathers roughed up a little when he tried to assault and rob one of our honest businessmen," replied the bald-headed cop holding me by my arm.

"Real hot-blooded, American outlaw huh? What's your name, bandit?" he snarled.

I started to tell him, and then, for some obscure reason, decided to lie.

"My name is Smith," I mumbled.

"What's your first name and middle initial, Smith?"

He believed me! Well, why not? I had no identification on me. My wallet was still on a shelf back at Lillard' s blue movie heaven. He wouldn't put a name to me because of fingerprints either. The only time I had been printed was in the service and the odds were good they wouldn't take the trouble to get at those.

It's Okey, Okey P." Where the hell had I gotten that name? Wherever it came from I was stuck with it.

"Stop muttering and speak up! What's your address, Okey?" At least he wasn't calling me "Bandit" any more.

"I lived at Lillard's Joint on State Street, in the back room. I guess I won't be welcome there again, so just put me down for wherever you want."

"No known permanent address. O.K., Smith, Okey P, park it over there while we check you through the wanteds." He waved his pencil toward a steel bench under a bulletin board covered with F.B.I. record cards.

I sat on the bench and nursed an unbelievable headache. It was a stupid choice I had made. Instead of spending Christmas Day watching middle-aged perverts ogle pornographic movies, I was going to spend it with a collection of real certified criminals behind the walls of a Chicago jailhouse. God rest ye merry, gentlemen. They finally charged me with "aggravated assault with a non-deadly weapon." Supposedly I had attacked Grease Ball with the glass ashtray in an effort to rob him. They weren't the least bit interested in my story about how he laid me out with that "non-deadly" weapon.

Chapter Four

It took four long hours to run me through the ritual of setting a bond I could never make. Then they traded my clothes for a jail uniform, and herded me into a place called B-Block where I found out that my all-expense-paid vacation was to be spent in the immediate company of another good citizen. He was sacked out when they escorted me into the cell.

For the first few moments after the cell door slammed, I just stood there, looking around and taking inventory of my latest home away from home. It was about ten feet long, six feet wide and maybe eight feet high. It was decorated in early American institutional--two steel bunks covered with dirty mattresses and suspended from the wall, one over the other. My new friend was on the bottom one. We had a head, without tank, lid, or cover and a basin with one faucet--the cold one. Our walls were bilious green concrete and U. S. Steel did our window and door. The air was carbolic disinfectant fresh and the temperature hovered around eighty-five degrees. Yes sir, there's no place like home.

Having taken in all the sights, I swung myself up into the top rack. That was one thing I remembered how to do correctly from my navy days. On the ceiling someone had candled "The Dragon was here" in smudgy black letters. Scratched and smeared into the concrete walls were a hundred other epithets or maybe epitaphs.

Since my cellmate hadn't spoken yet, I hung over the edge of the bunk and looked at him. He was still flaked out on his back sound asleep, but his mouth opened and closed regularly like a politician making promises. His shoulder length hair was straight and snow white. Deep creases spider-webbed across his wizened face, and his eyes, closed as they were, looked Oriental. A thin white scar cut vertically across the left side of his lips. He was the color of a worn fox pelt. He looked thirty centuries old.

"Hey, old man, wake up and meet your new cell mate. "

He woke up, but he hadn't understood me. He lay there staring at the ceiling with his mouth still moving. There's something wrong with him, I thought. He's probably working his way off a drunk. Gradually his gaze floated away from the ceiling and onto me.

I tried again, slower and louder. "I'm Okey Smith. What do they call you buddy?"

For a moment I thought he was going to speak. Then his eyes drifted again. His mouth and jaw continued to work like a nibbling mouse. I was still hanging upside down looking at him, when I felt someone's eyeballs on the back of my neck. "Put you in with old Koo-cheese, did they," wheezed an asthmatic voice at the cell door. "Well, don't worry, he won't bother you none. He's crazy as a football-bat, but he don't do nothing but eat and sleep. I don't even believe he takes a crap. He's a real honest-to-God full blooded American Indian, they tell me."

I sat up in my bunk and saw that the voice at the door belonged to another dried up little guy dressed in a faded blue denim jail uniform like mine. His almost transparent skin hadn't seen the sun for a long time. Back home we called that color poolroom pallor.

"Who the hell are you?" He didn't look like a regular jailer.

"I'm your lifeline, friend. You be good, and don't cause me no more trouble than old Koo-cheese there does, and I'll be good to you."

"For example?"

"For example, you got any smokes?"

That was the first I had thought about cigarettes. I reached in my breast pocket and discovered it was empty.

"I knew you didn't have none," he giggled. "The screws took them away from you."

"So you knew it, so what?" My headache was back in full force.

"So listen up. Here's the deal. If you want to smoke tailor mades, you get them from a Square John or you get them from me. Otherwise, you smoke state dust--provided you have matches. Know any Square Johns?"

"I don't know what a Square John is." The tittering clown had worked his way onto my hate list in less than one minute. That was probably a new record.

"This your first fall? Hot damn, I've got a fresh fish on my row. Square John is what you was before today, but what you ain't never going to be again, fish."

"O.K., wit. I hear you."

A surprised look crossed his face. "How'd you know my name, fish? Did old Koo-cheese talk to you?"

"I don't know your name. What do you mean, how did I know your name?"

"Witt. You said it. Witt. How'd you know what my name is? How'd you know my name is Witt? I didn't tell you, did I?"

"The boys told me." I said, trying to sound like a movie gangster. He didn't seem impressed.

"Besides, I don't need them," I added.

"You don't need what?"

“I don't need butts, I don't need Square Johns, and I especially don't need you standing there cutting off my view.” I said with more force than I felt.

"Suit yourself, fish," he said and shuffled away.

Well, I was almost alone again. I figured I hadn't exactly scored any points with that twerp at the door, ‘Witt’--his friends probably called him Half.

And, since I was thinking about half-wits, what about that mumbling half-wit Indian on the bunk below me? I wondered what his name really was. I was willing to bet it wasn't Koo-Cheese. Maybe it was Rain-in-the-Face, or Squanto, or something like that. That would be my project for the day--to get the old man to tell me his name. Boy, that cell was hot! It felt like our stinky old seaplane tender did when it was parked in Guantanamo Bay.

I leaned over the hunk again.

"Hey, old timer," I tried to sound friendly, "did you see that little guy at the door? Is he as important as he thinks he is?"

That time he didn't even look at me. He just laid there, his eyes staring at the ceiling and his mouth moving slowly.

"Well, if you don't feel like talking to me, then just tell me to shut up." That was neat. He would have to talk to get me to stop talking. It didn't work. I lay back on my bunk, and started wondering how long I'd be there.

Chapter Five

At suppertime they brought around the food in trays stacked on a rubber tired steel cart. Two metal trays and two tin cups were slid through the slot in the bars of our cell door. They'd fill the tin cup with coffee if you held it up close to the bars. The only tool they gave us to eat with was a plastic spoon.

Old Co-Cheese got up for supper. At least he sat up in his bunk and put his feet on the floor.

I handed his tray to him. He took it without a word. I handed him a cup of coffee. He placed it on his tray and then just sat there and looked at the concrete floor.

"Sometimes he don't eat nothing," said one of the food cart handlers.

"He ain't et nothing for damn near a week now, " said the other one. "It wouldn't surprise me none if the stubborn bastard died on us." That crack went right against my grain. They shouldn't have talked like that in front of him.

"I'll take care of the old man," I growled. "You guys go peddle your slop. Me and my buddy here don't need running comments with our supper."

"Sure thing, fish. You be his nursemaid and you'll go to Indian heaven - you and all the other do-good, Bible toting tub-thumpers.

They rolled on down the corridor.

"Come on, pal," I tried. "This is going to be a mighty lonesome time unless you and me talk a little. How about it? Eat up and talk to me. What's your name? Tell me what your real name is. I know damn well it isn't 'Koo-Cheese'."

Not a word.

"Well, you don't know what you're missing," I said. "Spooned up collard greens, white beans, corn bread and sugar cookie tastes damn fine to me."

After a few days of this semi-solitary confinement I would hold all kinds of two-way conversations with myself. I decided to name my roommate Charlie, after Charlie McCarthy. I told him he could call me Mr. Bergen. He cooperated beautifully. He lay there on his bunk and flapped his mouth while I supplied the words. If I could have gotten him to move his head as well as he moved his mouth we could have gone on the vaudeville stage.

"Hello, Charlie," I'd say.

"Hello, Mr. Bergen," I'd say for him.

"What's new, Charlie?"

"I'm going to speak all by myself today, Mr. Bergen."

"That's great, Charlie. What are you going to talk about?"

The absurd monologue would go on for hours. He never seemed to hear it, but I figured it kept me from going crazy like him.

Every now and then when they brought the supper trays around I would fill his spoon with food and try to get him to eat something, like you do with a baby, but most of the time he wouldn't let me poke anything into his mouth. He'd just sit there for a half an hour while I ate and then sink back onto his bunk and back into his silent song. At breakfast and lunch, he seldom even got up. Before long, if he didn't change his ways, he was bound to starve to death.

Chapter Six

It may sound strange to say, but with all those people in it, and with all the noise and stink they make, a jailhouse is still a lonely place. Aside from the food cart pushers and an occasional guard wandering by, the only visitor Charlie and I ever had was Half-Witt. He was allowed out of his cell as an unofficial trusty, mostly to help the guards cool down newly arrested drunks, He also sweep the corridor and delivered the piddling little dribble of mail that some of the other prisoners received.

I found out that Witt wasn't kidding about the cigarettes. If you wanted to smoke factory rolled, you had to get them from him. If you didn't have your own free world source, your only other choice was to try to roll them out of the dust dry tobacco the state handed out once a week. The trouble was that the state didn't supply matches. Half-Witt had that exclusive concession and he sold them. Two pads of paper matches for one pack of cigarettes or ten cents for one pad of matches was his price. If you had the money, you smoked. I never could manage to roll my own and since I was stone-broke, I gave up smoking as a penance for my past and present sinful thoughts.

In addition to being our neighborhood capitalist, Half-Witt was also the source of all our news. He claimed he had a direct pipeline to the outside world. The claim was probably true. For example, I hadn't been in long before he found out everything about my charge. Naturally, he hurried around to show off his newfound knowledge.

"I hear you're building time because you hit Romeo Lillard," he wheezed. "That wasn't very bright. He's real heavy out on the bricks. Didn't you know he's the juice man on South State?"

"You know Grease Ball?

"You can bet-ya-sweet-ass I do. I been in on some sweet deals with him."

Half-Witt was obviously proud of his association with old foul mouth Lillard. They probably hung around alleys and rolled drunks together.

"Half-Witt, if you're so damn smart, why don't you tell me what's Charlie's real name is and what he did he do to get tucked away with all us desperate criminals?"

For a change he didn't know. He said Charlie had been in the joint when he came and that because he never got mail, Witt hadn't seen his name written anywhere. He promised he would ask one of the flunkies around the Operations Office for me, but, since there was no money in it for him, he promptly forgot.

It would have been useless to ask the guards to tell me Charlie's name. When the screws called us anything, they called us by the numbers stenciled on our pants or else by some nickname they invented. Half-Witt didn't need to tell me it was the screws that named Charlie "Koo-cheese."

Twenty-five dreary days passed and Christmas finally arrived. On Christmas Day, the absolute worst day of the year in a jailhouse, a covey of sour looking Holy Rollers came and sang hymns at us as we tried to eat half raw turkey buried in lumpy sage dressing. Instead of the usual bag of dust, the State lavished upon us a little cardboard pack of cigarettes like the airlines used to give away. Half Witt had a banner day trading matches for cigarettes. I traded him three cigarettes for one wooden kitchen match. Then, to test my self-control, I decided to hang on to my one cigarette and one match for six more days in order to celebrate New Year's Eve with a smoke.

I hid the match between the concrete wall and the steel side rail of my bunk. Then I laid the cigarette on the basin while I took a leak and the damn thing rolled in the sink and the paper dissolved. It didn't matter. I just left it there. I could take smoking or leave it alone.

The way it worked out, though, it was a lucky accident.

Chapter Seven

Another week passed. Old Charlie had become so thin you could see all his bones. He was real shaky, too. One day he shook so hard that I asked the screws to get him a doctor, but they didn't want to go to all that trouble for a common drunk. They said he was only being stubborn and that if and when he got hungry enough he'd eat.

February arrived.

It was a Friday night. The lights had been turned out and the late cell count had been made. I was lying on the bunk holding my usual one-sided conversation with Charlie.

"Did you spend lots of money on the old sauce, Charlie? I'll bet you did. They tell me you Indians really go for the firewater in a big way. I've heard you can't drink even a tiny drop of white man's booze without getting bombed out of your skulls. One little bitty drink and then you can't stop. Is that right, Charlie?"

"Anglo," came a voice from the bottom bunk.

There were so many different noises around that jailhouse at night that I thought my ears were playing tricks on me.

"Anglo," he called again.

I leaned over the bunk.

"Is that you, Charlie? Are you calling me?"

"Anglo, I want to smoke."

I piled down off my rack and squatted beside him. "Sorry, old timer, I don't have any smokes or any matches either."

"I have tobacco," he said, "and you have one match. "

I started to tell him I had no matches and then I remembered that Christmas match hidden behind the bunk rail.

"You're right, I do. How the hell did you know?"

"Do not make me waste words." His voice sounded like those WWII short wave broadcasts from London-full of static, fading and then growing stronger.

I found the match and climbed back down beside him.

He eased his legs over the edge of the bunk and assumed his fetal dinner position. Then he reached into the pocket of his wrinkled blue shirt and came out with a small wad of tobacco.

"Where'd you get that?" I whispered.

He didn't answer, but I would have bet a dollar to a doughnut that he had salvaged my wet cigarette out of the sink at Christmas time.

What he did next, I still don't believe even though I saw it with my own eyes. He wadded the tobacco and some mattress stuffing into a tight little ball the size of a walnut. Then he made his left hand into a fist and stuffed the wad down into the hole between his forefinger and his thumb. He held his clenched fist up against his face with the bottom of it level with his mouth. He took the match from me and struck it on his bed rail. And then, heaven help me, he held the fire to the mixture and started to smoke his own fist like a stemless pipe.

"What the hell are you doing" You'll burn your hand off!" I shouted.

"Quiet down in there," yelled some screw.

Charlie ignored the commotion and continued to puff on his fist without showing any sign of pain.

I smelled his flesh starting to burn.

"Come on, man, you're going to burn yourself bad and get us both in trouble." I was whispering again but I wanted to scream at him.

He must have sat there for three minutes, slowly puffing and then deliberately blowing the vile smoke toward the ceiling of the cell. His fingers and his thumb popped up in big wet blisters, sizzled and then burned to the bone. Pieces of black, half roasted flesh hung from what was left of his fist. He paid not the slightest attention to it or me.

I squatted there beside him during the whole appalling performance. I wanted to stop him but I didn't. I mean, I was mesmerized and I just sat on my haunches and stared at him.

He finally finished and lowered his burned hand to the mattress beside him. Greasy foul smoke hung in the air.

"Get some water on that hand and I'll call a guard to get a doctor," I hissed. I was sure one of us was completely insane.

"I have called my fathers," he said. "I have told them it is time to make the journey through the next lake and into a brighter place."

He fastened his gaze on me.

"You, boy, you must do a thing for me. You are good at heart in your own way."

"Yeah, sure. Anything. What do you want?" He had become Mr. Bergen and I was Charlie the dummy.

"You must go to my home in the city. There you will find my wife. She is very old, like me, and she can no longer do what I am asking you to do. You are to tell her what I have done. You are to tell her what you have seen. Tell her every part of it. Do you understand?"

"Yes." How could I forget what I had just seen?

"Then you are to tell her to get the 'key.' Only when she has heard all of this will she show it to you. When she gets the 'key,' you must help her deliver it to my son. He will know what to do with it and he will reward you. I will speak for you in the brighter world. But remember this well, Anglo, only my son is to have the 'key.' "

With that said, he lay back on his bunk. His body stopped trembling and for the first time his lips were still.

"Wait a minute, Charlie. I don't understand. What the hell are you talking about?" I shouted and shook his shoulder.

"If you people don't knock it off in there, I'm going to hose you down," yelled the guard.

"Charlie! Charlie! What did you mean?" I continued to shout. "What city? Where do you live? What kind of key are you talking about? I don't even know what your name is!"

It was wasted breath. Charlie was dead.

The screws came with truncheons ready to make us be quiet. When they saw Charlie, they had him hauled off in a rubber body bag. Later on that night I heard from Half-Witt that Charlie's wife came to the jail morgue and claimed his body.

Chapter Eight

The next day they gave me a new cellmate. This one wasn't crazy like Charlie, but he nearly drove me up the wall with all his talking.

From that time on Half-Witt came by the cell a dozen times every day and always maneuvered the conversation around to the same question." What the hell did you and old Koo-cheese do in here that night he died?"

"We played checkers and roasted peanuts. And stop calling him Koo-cheese. Have a little respect for the dead. "

"No crap, Smith, I heard you guys talking in here. What did he say to you?"

"Half-Witt, you've been such a good friend to me, I'm going to tell you the truth. He told me about a secret buried treasure. When I get out of this place, I'm going to buy a boat and sail off to a secret island and dig it all up. I'll be filthy rich for the rest of my life."

"No shit? You wouldn't be kidding me, would you?'"

"Come on, Half-Witt, you're too smart for me to pull your leg."

"Jesus! Buried money! I figured it was something like that you two was talking about. Jesus, you really are on to something big."

A week later my trial date finally came up and, would you believe it, Romeo Lillard, the fat jerk who owned the Amusement Devices arcade and who had me arrested, didn't show up in court to testify. Since he was the prosecution's only witness, they had no choice but to turn me loose.

Three lousy months in a lousy Chicago jail with a crazy damn Indian, and it was all for doing nothing. It's one weird world.

When the so-called trial was over, there was no need to go back to the cell to pick up my gear; I didn't have any. They took me straight to the property room to get my street clothes. While I was waiting for the clerk to locate my stuff, I thumbed through the picture magazine he had been reading. A photograph of a burned child made me start thinking about old Charlie.

The turnkey came back with my clothes in a big wad.

"Check this stuff out against the inventory. Make sure it's all here and that it's all yours, and sign this form. You can also put down my damn magazine," he said, as he dumped the clothes on the counter between us.

"It's all there," I replied, without looking. "Can you tell me something?"

"Strip, and give us our uniform. You can do it over there." He pointed to a folding screen across the room.

I carried my wadded up clothes behind the screen. I could look over the screen and watch him lick his finger and hunt for his place in the magazine while I changed.

"Hey, Buddy", I shouted over the screen. "How about telling me something?" I asked as I pulled off my jail blue coverall.

"What is it? What could I ever tell a smart guy like you?"

"You remember Charlie--the one they all called Koo-cheese? He was that old Indian they had celling with me, the one who died about a week ago?"

"Yeah. I remember him. So what?"

"Do you know what his real name was?"

"Are you kidding? We get a thousand guys in here every week and you expect me to remember all their damn names? You gotta be out of your mind."

"Well, don't you have records or something that would show what his name and address was?"

"Sure. We got records, and do you know what they'd show?" He continued on without wanting my answer. "They'd show his name was Smith. Just like you. Is your name really Smith? Hell no. You are no more Smith than I am. But our records say you are and, brother, that's good enough for me. "

"Could you just look, to see what he said his name was?" I buttoned my shirt.

"Our records are for official use only, Mr. 'Smith'. And, Mr. 'Smith,' as of today you ain't no official nothing." I tossed the jail clothes on his counter and walked out the door and into Chicago's winter.

Chapter Nine

If I didn't freeze my rear end off or catch pneumonia or die of hypothermia, it would be a major miracle. It was one o'clock in the afternoon, it was early March, it was about to snow, and there I was out on the streets again with no money, no place to sleep, and especially no desire to go back to jail.

I thought about going to Lillard's stag movie joint to get my suitcase and my back pay. I didn't think about it long. If I showed my face there, that fat hood would figure out some new way to send me to the pen. Knowing him, he'd hocked my gear anyway.

So I decided to find a mission. The cage joints charged fifty cents a night and that was exactly fifty pennies more than I had to my name. I knew if I could pray long and loud enough one of the missions would give me supper. Then, if I were sufficiently sanctimonious, they might spring for a dry sack until dawn. They might even come across with a warm coat or a job. Wow! My stretch in the joint had made me as crazy as old Charlie. The day those holy rolling psalm singers handed out warm coats and jobs would be the day hell got as cold as Chicago.

Then I remembered something. Old Charlie had said he wanted me to find his wife. If she were in Chicago and I could find her, she might give me a handout.

She might get generous if I told her I was Charlie's friend.

Charlie's friend? Some friend. I didn't even know his name. I could just see it happening:

"How do you do, madam, I'm Charlie's friend."

"Who's Charlie?"

"Why, he was your husband, madam, I'm the nice man that helped him burn his hand off before he died."

"Well then, please come in, any friend of Charlie's is a friend of mine."

That little scene appealed to me so much that I embroidered on it as I walked.

The door opens and there stands an Indian doll that looks like Keely Smith.

"Good afternoon, doll. My name is Smith and I'm Charlie's best friend."

"Thank heaven you've come. Quick! Inside! I need a great big handsome man like you!"

I played it over four or five more times, and each time it got more ridiculous until it was no longer fun, even as a daydream.

I stopped and looked around me. Hell, I must have walked half way to Milwaukee. As I stood there trying to figure out where I was, the man at the weather bureau pushed a button and started the snow again, right on schedule. I gave up, wiped my runny nose, turned left, and headed down one more street. A piece of newsprint blew by with the snow on its trail. Maybe, I could find enough old newspapers to build a fire in a dumpster to keep from freezing to death. I might even start a second great Chicago fire. Mrs. O'Leary's cow and I would both have a place in the history books.

My maudlin thoughts were interrupted by another wad of trash swirling around my feet. It blew on past me and hung again on the base of a No Parking sign. I shivered and watched, as it broke loose and tumbled aimlessly down the street. Just like me. That's all I had done for months, drift and hang. At this rate, I'll wind up dying in some God-forsaken Chicago jail cell just like old Indian Charlie. Oh, well, they say the only good Indian is a . . . Wait a minute, that isn't funny. Charlie is really dead. I wondered if anybody, even me, gave a damn whether he was alive or dead. And then I had an idea. In this day and age, dead Indians in Chicago might be rare enough to make good newspaper stories on a slow day. Especially if there aren't too many of them and there isn't anything else to write about. Maybe, just maybe, one of the local newspapers had written something about old Charlie's death. If they had, then I could learn his real name, find his wife, keep my promise, and hit her up for a few bucks as my reward.

The more I thought about it, the better I liked the idea. I replayed it a while longer and finally decided that the only way to get hold of a week old newspaper was to find a library.

Well, I finally found a library, but I had to walk forty frozen miles of city streets to get to it. It was DeJohn University's downtown library. How about that? Here I was out of jail and back into college all in the same day. This really is a land of opportunity.

Inside, the building was warm and I got sleepy half way up the first flight of steps.

The librarian at the front desk, a nasty looking piece of work, was distinctly under-joyed to see me.

"Do you want something?" was her warm greeting.

"Yes. I want to look at last week's newspapers. "

"Last week's newspapers from where?"

"Last week's newspapers from Chicago. I want to check on the death of a buddy of mine and..."

"So sorry," she cut me off mechanically and turned to a young woman shuffling through a huge stack of filing cards.

"Miss Lamb, help this man, please."

The card shuffler named 'Miss Lamb' pushed open the swinging gate and came around to the front of the counter with me. She had long red hair and enough freckles on her pug nose to win a Norman Rockwell poster model contest.

“Yes sir, what can I do for you?” She looked me over carefully and, apparently decided that I was a certified member of the human race.

“A friend of mine passed away last week. Here in Chicago," I added quickly. "So I thought maybe the newspapers might--- "

"I'll look up the obituaries for you. Tell me the date of your friend's death."

"Friday, a week ago. "

"And his name?"

That was the jackpot question. "Well, you're going to find this strange, but I don't know his name."

She surveyed me over again carefully and then said, "Wait here. I'll be gone for a few minutes." Then she disappeared behind the counter and into the stacks.

I looked around the cavernous reading room. What had I gotten myself into? That female Tom Sawyer probably went to call a cop. Well, it was too damn cold to go back outside voluntarily, so I decided to sit down and enjoy the warm room while I waited for them to cart me off to jail again. At least the jailhouse was dry and they fed me two times a day.

I must have dozed off, because the next thing I knew Librarian Lamb was standing beside me shaking my arm.

"Wake up, sir. I have your newspapers."

"I thought you’d gone for the cops." The words were out of my mouth before I could stop them.

Her expression did not change. "Should I have called the police?" she asked calmly.

"Not unless being broke and being in your library at the same time is a crime." I tried a puny smile.

"The combination is not unknown to us. We are here to help anyone with a legitimate need for our services." Again she scrutinized me carefully but not with the hostility for all mankind that some librarians seem to radiate. Finally, she shifted her gaze away from my face and became very business like.

"If you don't know your friend's name, how do you propose to find out about him in these newspapers?" she asked, pointing to a stack of newspapers on the table in front of us. Evidently she had piled them there while I was asleep.

"Well, I have a little information that might help. He was an Indian, an American Indian. I called him 'Charlie,' but that was just a name I made up. He was very old. He died in jail and I was in there with him when he died." She hadn't changed her expression, so I continued on. "The night he died he told me he had a wife in the city. I'm guessing he meant this city, Chicago. As he was dying, Charlie gave me a message for his wife. I want to locate her and give her the message, that's all there is to it. That's the whole story."

"That's different enough to mean it's probably true," she flashed her first quick smile. "Now here is what I think we should do. We'll both search through the obituaries. If either one of us finds a name that sounds sort of 'Indian,' we'll read it out loud and try to decide if it could be your friend. Does that suit you?"

"It suits me," I agreed. I was amazed at the change in her attitude. I wondered if it was because of the 'Indian' angle to the story.

We started to hunt through the stack of papers. To my great surprise, it didn't take long. I was the one who found it. There wasn't much, so I read the whole thing out loud to her.

"TAAIYALOTE, Alowish. 1878 (?) -1958, American Indian. Valenci pueblo. Survived by wife, Liawu (sp?). Patterson & Marshall Funeral Home. Arrangements incomplete."

That was all there was. For some reason or another I had expected more. I'm pretty sure this is it," I said, and handed the paper to her.

"Are you certain?" she asked after she had read it through again for herself.

"No. Of course I'm not certain, but it sounds right."

"Then I suggest the logical thing is for you to call the funeral home and find out if it was your friend. While you're doing that I'll look through the rest of these papers just to see if there are other Indian names." She turned back to the stack of newspapers.

"Well, I've got another little problem--no money for the phone. "

She didn't look up. "Use the telephone in my office. Go through that door and then all the way down to the end of the corridor. Turn right and you'll see my name on the door. It's unlocked and in case you've forgotten, my name is Lamb. "

"Aren't you a little worried about me being in there alone? "

This time she looked up from the newspapers. "I would be," she said evenly, "but there are four other women in the same office that will keep an eye on you."

"Thanks."

"You're welcome." She turned back to the papers with an exasperated snort.

Chapter Ten

I decided to place the call in a hurry. If she got too steamed at me, she might change her mind and call the cops after all.

I found her office, and sure enough, four pairs of curious female eyes followed me the whole time I was there.

"It was Charlie." I reported back to her. I didn't tell her that the funeral parlor man knew it was the person I asked about because he remembered the burn on Charlie's hand.

"Did you find out where his wife lives?"

"Yes."

"Where is it?"

"The man said it was on Western Avenue, somewhere around 79th."

"That's much too far out of my way. I thought if it weren't very far I'd volunteer to run you by there on my way home, but Western's in the opposite direction and a long way besides." She sounded apologetic. Hell, I hadn't asked her to take me anywhere.

"I'll figure out a way to get there. But thanks for the thought."

"How will you 'figure' to get there?"

"I can hitch a ride, or something," I added lamely.

"When was the last time you had something to eat?"

Where did she get that? Who was talking about food? She might be pretty, in a 'girl-next-door' way but she was much too bossy and nosey.

"I'm on a diet. Thanks for all your help." I got up to leave.

"All right, Mister High-and-Mighty, I will take you to see your friend's wife. But first I'm going to take you home and feed you before you bite somebody else's head off. Now just sit back down while I finish what I was doing when you interrupted me. Then I'll get my hat and coat and we'll go." She stood up straight as a ramrod and marched through the door toward her office.

More lights were turned on in the library. I glanced at the clock over the front desk. It was ten minutes after five. I was, in fact, very hungry and I hadn't even started to hunt for a place to sleep. It looked bitter cold outside the windows and the sleet was still falling.

"Well, Miss Red Head Lamb," I thought, "maybe you'll change my luck. At least you're the first fairy godmother I've found today."

I must have dozed off because there she was shaking me again. "Wake up. Sleeping is not allowed in the Reading Room, and besides, I am now ready to depart."

"I don't hear any trumpets. Where is your swan boat?"

She didn't seem to appreciate my attempt at humor. I didn't care much for it either, but I'd bet even Bob Hope isn't funny when somebody wakes him from a nap.

As we left the library, it was dark outside and colder than a Siberian ice mine.

At the far end of the parking lot, Her Majesty's royal coach turned out to be a very old Jeep station wagon. She must have brought it second hand because some sort of lettering showed through the $29.95 Earl Schibe paint job on its side. She caught the look on my face. "Well, it may not be the limousine you are accustomed to, but it's going to get us home through this snow storm. That's more than you can say for most of them," she added, looking at the other snow-covered cars in the parking lot.

"I've got no complaints. How long have you worked at the library?"

"Just over two years. The girl who had the job before me married a law student at the University of Chicago and moved back East somewhere. What do you do for a living--when you're not in jail? By the way, you didn't say why you were in jail.

I slammed the door on the passenger side. "How soon can you get the heater going in this Sherman tank? I'm about to freeze."

"It takes a while to warm up. Quit trying to change the subject. Answer my question. What do you do for a living?"

She certainly was persistent. She reminded me of someone from a long time ago--someone special who had liked me. Probably someone in my imagination.

The jeep carved a trail through the snow. Out of the parking lot, traffic was heavy and the blowing, freezing sleet and snow made seeing nearly impossible.

She must have been navigating by the taillights on the cars in front of us. The heater showed no signs of life and the windshield had frosted over from our breath.

"You'd better get that defroster going," I said, "unless you have some kind of radar in here."

"Thank you for the advice. Now, for the final time, please answer my question."

"O.K., Perry Mason. Most recently I made my living showing dirty movies to dirty old men. I got put in jail because they claimed I assaulted one of those dirty old men with a non-deadly weapon. Now that you have heard my revolting crime story, you can let me out anywhere along here."

"You're certainly rude, but I suppose there is some more complete explanation. You're not ignorant enough to be a real criminal."

I declined to comment. We drove on through the snow.

"One more question--what was it your Indian friend asked you to tell his wife?"

"Only that he loved her and that he would see her in the happy hunting ground." I didn't feel like telling her the story of Charlie's last hours. I figured that Charlie wanted privacy in his death just as he had in his life.

"You really don't expect me to believe that kind of nonsense, do you?"

"Why not? You believed everything else I told you."

She didn't respond.

We turned onto a street lined with apartment buildings.

"Now you answer a question. Why are you doing this for me?" I asked. I thought I already knew the answer. She was one of those compulsive do-good Samaritans who take in stray dogs and patch broken bird wings.

"You look like you could use some help, and you look like a decent person- 'no matter what you say'". The last part of that speech was made with elevated nose and stiffened lips.

"And do you help out every vagrant who comes in the library?"

"Every single one! There's certainly nothing special about you!"

Chapter Eleven

The snow came down harder than ever but at long last the heater had started to work. I broke the strained silence. "What was printed on the side of this ark before you had it re-painted?"

She got a big happy smile on her face for the first time.

"Believe it or not, it's a hand down from the Salvation Army. I'm one of the few people in the world who has a car so worn out that the Salvation Army doesn't even want to keep it."

"Now you're pulling my leg."

"No, I'm not. It's the honest truth. They offered it for sale because it had been in a wreck, and it would be too expensive to repair. A man who comes to the library runs a garage. He's a friend of my father. He told me about it and said I could get it really cheap and that if I did, he would fix it up for me. He would only charge me for parts. It was because he likes my dad."

"And obviously you got it."

"I certainly did. Absolutely free and the repair parts only cost me one hundred and seventy-five dollars, cash on the line. "

"Some people have all the luck."

"Some people make their own luck." She wiped off the smile and put on her reformer look again.

We slowed and turned into a narrow alleyway between two brick houses. She stopped the car. The motor was still running, and the headlights were shining on an ancient wood garage door.

"Open the garage door, please. I don't want the Jeep to get snowbound."

I stepped out into freezing cold. The snow had slowed but the wind had grown stronger. She parked the Jeep in the garage. Together we pushed the doors closed and started for the back porch. At the top of the steps, she stopped short. I nearly ran into her.

"For Heaven's sake! I just realized that I don't know your name. Who are you?"

"Smith, Okey P. Smith. I wondered if you were ever going to ask me." I would have to think up a better name. That one was a real nothing.

"Well, Okey P. Smith, welcome to my home."

She opened the door and we walked into a kitchen that would have been considered old fashioned in the 1930s.

"What's for supper?" were the only polite words that came out as I looked at the ancient appliances.

"Let me put up my hat and coat and then I'll see. I'll be right back. There's probably a bottle of milk in the refrigerator if you'd care to look." She disappeared into another room.

I opened the icebox and looked. There were four half-filled jars of pickles, some unidentifiable greenish-yellow glop in bowls, several unopened packages of grayish looking lunch meat, a carton of eggs and two bottles, orange pop and grape juice. I took the orange pop. Grape juice always gives me the trots.

"Where is the bottle opener?" I yelled at the open doorway.

"There's no need to shout," said a strange male voice behind me.

I turned and there before my eyes stood Santa Claus. The only thing missing was the fuzzy red suit. But unlike Santa Claus, this fat man was swinging a vicious looking big black cane.

"Who the hell are you?" I blurted.

"I believe you had best tell me the same thing or shall I assume you are a burglar?"

I stood there, orange pop in hand, mouth wide open, and watched that big black cane start to agitate the air near my head.

"Speak up! Who are you? What do you want? What are you doing in my kitchen?"

The old buzzard with the club in his hand weighed close to two hundred and fifty pounds. On his squatty frame most of it had found a home around his middle section. His face was a full circle bisected by a great shaggy white walrus moustache. He was trying very hard to scowl but it came off more like a bad case of indigestion.

Nevertheless, that baseball bat size cane he was poking at me was getting uncomfortably close to my scalp.

"The lady said..." I ducked away from a close swing.

"She said . . .," I ducked again.

"At the library . . ." This time when I ducked I hit my face on the open icebox door. Blood spurted from my nose.

"Damn it, you crazy old coot. You've made me break my nose." I mumbled through my cupped hands. It probably wasn't broken but it hurt like hell.

He immediately dropped the cane and hurried to my side clucking like a mother hen.

"Oh my goodness! Oh dear me! I didn't mean to injure you. Sit down. Sit down, sir. You look pale. May I get you a glass of water? Should I call our physician?"

"No, thanks. Just let me sit here for a minute till my nose stops bleeding and then I'll get out. You ought to be careful. You could kill someone with that club. "

He soaked a dishtowel in the kitchen sink, and started mopping at my face.

"Where did Miss Lamb go?" I asked.

"What's that? What did you say? You're mumbling through the towel."

I laid aside the towel. "Where is Miss Lamb?" This time I enunciated each word carefully.

"Aha! So that's your game. That's what you're doing here?" He thundered. "You're here to molest my daughter! Well, we'll just see about that!" He started for the cane again.

"Father!" came Miss Lamb's voice from the kitchen door. "This is Mr. Smith. He's a friend of mine from the library. What happened to your nose?" The question was directed to me.

"I accidentally hit my nose on the ice box door. "

"That certainly was clumsy," she said primly. "And besides, it's not an 'ice box', it a Kelvenator."

"I must apologize to you, Mr. Smith," he said. "It seems I've made somewhat of a fool of myself. "

"No apology is needed, sir," I tried to sound very southern. "You should be commended for your vigorous defense of the household." I figured that ought to hold him for a while.

I turned to Miss Lamb. "As I was saying, before my clumsy accident, what's for supper?"

"For someone who isn't hungry you certainly are interested in food. "

During dinner I learned that Miss Lamb's first name was Dorothy, and that she could not cook anywhere near as well as the trustys in the Chicago jail. Her father's name was Roscoe Lamb. He was a Professor Emeritus, of Anthropology at Colonial University in Macon, Georgia. She and her father had moved north to Chicago when he reached the mandatory retirement age. When they came, they must have brought every book in the State of Georgia with them, because the house was stuffed to the rafters with books. The book- cases were full from floor to ceiling and each table, chair and shelf was burdened with piles of books of all descriptions. Even the floor was partially covered with books. There appeared to be no order to it at all. It was total chaos. Detective stories were jammed together with reports from the Smithsonian Institution. Books on Indian Art were piled on ten-year-old magazines.

After dinner, while we washed the dishes I told them most of the story about Charlie. The Professor was immediately interested in the fact that the newspaper obituary had said Charlie was a Valenci Pueblo Indian.

"Do you know what that means?" he asked me.

"No sir, I don't. Before we read that obituary I had never heard of a Valenci Pueblo Indian. Anyway, the truth is that old Charlie was the only Indian of any kind that I've ever known."

"The newspaper story left out a great deal of important information, as usual," he said. "The Valenci Pueblo, apparently your friend was a member of that tribe, is the modern survivor, along with the Zuni, of the prehistoric-to-historic Basketmaker-Pueblo cultural continuum known as the Anasazi. They occupied the high plateau country in the area where New Mexico, Colorado, Utah, and Arizona join. Now according to. . ."

"Father!"

"Yes, my dear?"

"Father, Mr. Smith does not require a lecture. His interest in Indians is only a temporary one. "

"Yes. Yes, of course you're right, my dear. Nevertheless that is a fascinating part of the world, especially northwestern New Mexico. I was there at the time of the Peabody Museum dig in the early 1930s. We worked a number of sites in Zuni and a few in Valenci too, but I never felt we had developed them completely. I wanted to go back, but then I got interested in the Olmec Civilization . . . I've got a book here, someplace," he said waving his hand vaguely around the room, "about our dig, you'll have to find it for Mr. Smith, Dorothy."

"I'll try." She smiled at him.

"Professor Lamb, Miss Lamb, this has been mighty nice, but I'd better get along," I said. "It's late and I've still got to find somewhere to spend the night."

"I'm not going outside again. There is entirely too much snow," Dorothy said. "So, unless you want to walk, you'll just have to spend the night with us. We can look for your friend's wife tomorrow."

"Yes. Yes, certainly. By all means. We have plenty of room. Dorothy, make up the studio couch in the library for Mr. Smith," the Professor directed.

I mumbled a demurrer without conviction, but all three of us knew I wanted to stay. I stayed.

Chapter Twelve

We couldn't find the address on Western Avenue. All we could find were used car lots. She of the freckles and red hair had rousted me out of the sofa bed in time to eat. Her idea of a big breakfast was boiled eggs, graham crackers and fried lunchmeat. Then we spent a freezing twenty minutes shoveling snow away from the garage door. Miss Lamb called the library and told them she was 'indisposed,' and we were off on the hunt. Unfortunately when we got to Western Avenue, we couldn't find the address.

"Okey, are you certain that's the address the funeral home gave you?" she asked, for the third time.

"Yes, I'm sure. I wrote it down and then had them repeat it."

"Well, it's obvious there is no such number on Western," said the Professor. Maybe it's on 79th."

We drove the Jeep up and down 79th but there was no address even remotely like the house number I had written down on the slip of paper.

"What do we do now?" asked Miss Lamb.

"We could go to the funeral home and find out if they can tell us anything more," I suggested.

Fifteen minutes later we were ushered into the Director's Office at Patterson and Marshall. I had expected something out of a Charles Addams cartoon, but it was a very ordinary office and a very ordinary middle-aged man who said his name was Everett Fogglesong greeted us.

Yes, we prepared Mr. Ta--Ta--, I'm sorry. I don't remember how to pronounce his name. He was an elderly Indian gentleman. We prepared his remains, but, let me make this clear, we did not conduct his funeral services."

"May we see him?" As soon as I asked it, I realized how stupid the question was. Charlie had been dead for over a week.

"Ah, well, he's no longer here."

"No, of course not, but where did you bury him?"

"As I told you, we only prepared the remains. "

"That's not what I mean. What I want to know is where is he now?"

"I see. Yes. Well, frankly speaking, it is somewhat unusual." He sat down in his desk chair and rocked it from side to side. "You see, the family was quite poor, or so they said, and they wished to handle the services themselves. Technically we're not supposed to allow that, but under the circumstances . . . I mean he was an Indian."

"Look, Mr. Fogglesong, we're not here to cause you trouble. All we want to know is what happened to Charlie's body and where we can find his wife. "

"He might also explain to us what he meant by 'they said' and 'they wanted.' Obviously, there must have been someone other than the deceased's wife present," injected the Professor.

"Yes. That is correct. There was a large Indian gentleman with the widow. I don't recall the name." Fogglesong started picking at a potted fern beside his desk.

"So, what happened to Charlie?" I felt like a broken record.

"The other gentleman and I placed your friend's remains in--now, you must understand," he began to squirm violently. "You must understand that under normal circumstances . . ."

I cut him off. "Just tell us what you did with Charlie."

"All right. All right. Since you insist, we placed your friend's remains in the back of a pick-up truck."

"A pick-up truck?"

"Yes, a pick-up truck. The widow and her large friend paid us fifty dollars for the preparation and then they wrapped the remains in a large woolen rug. The man and I loaded it in the back of their truck and they drove off. That's all I know." He looked as drained as one of his clients, once he had told us his secret.

"That doesn't surprise me in the least," said the Professor calmly.

"It doesn't?" asked the funeral director with a note of hope in his voice. “You mean you've heard of such things before?"

“Oh, yes. It’s quite common, quite common. Many tribal groups insist on immediate possession of the corpse of their tribesman."

"Why would they do that?" I asked.

"So that they may return the dead to their rightful place in their own sacred soil, of course," said the Professor. "Does that surprise you? It shouldn’t. Doesn't our own tribal government make a big effort after each war to bring home the bodies of the boys they have sacrificed in their foreign enterprises? Why does it seem so strange to you when a smaller tribe does the same thing for its citizens?"

"When you put it that way, it doesn't," I agreed.

"Very likely they are already in New Mexico with the body,” he added.

The funeral director breathed a visible sigh of relief. New Mexico was a long way from Chicago, and he could stop worrying about the body showing up in a Chicago alley and being traced back to him.

"I don't suppose they left any address?" I asked, without hope.

"No, no, they didn't. Now, if you people will excuse me..."

"Just one more question," I interposed. "Why did you give me that phony address for the widow?"

"I didn't have the correct address. And frankly, I thought you might not care enough to press the matter. I'm sorry for the little deception, but I really must go now."

There was nothing more to say. We let him go.

"Now what?" I grumbled as we walked back to the car.

"I believe it's time for you to forget the whole episode and start worrying about yourself for a change," said Miss Lamb.

"I guess you're right."

"Of course, you could go to Valenci and keep your promise," said the Professor.

We were silent as we wove through the noon traffic toward the center of the city. I couldn't get the Professor's suggestion out of my mind, but I couldn't see any realistic reason for doing it. Why chase all over the West after people I didn't know only to tell them something I didn't understand? The reward his son would give me for the key, whatever that might be, couldn't amount to a hill of beans, because they were bound to be dirt poor. As for old Charlie speaking for me in the brighter place, well, I could use all the help I could get, I acknowledged, but that wasn't much of an incentive. No, the whole thing was foolish. I made up my mind to forget about it.

Chapter Thirteen

"I certainly want to thank both of you folks for being so nice to me and for the meals and for the help and for the place to sleep, but I'd better get busy finding me a job and a place to live. So if you'll just let me out when we cross Madison Street . . ."

"Oh? Yes, yes of course. We'll be happy to." The Professor's voice had a tone of disappointment in it.

"Let us hear from you sometime, Mr. Smith." She sounded disappointed, too.

We mumbled strained goodbyes as I climbed out of the car near Madison Street. They had been kind to me and I was sorry to see them drive away. I stood and watched until they were completely out of sight. Finally, I looked around at my world, picked a direction out of an imaginary hat and started to walk.

"Dishwasher Wanted," the printed sign in the window read. "Inquire within." The "within" was a standard skid row greasy spoon. The pay was twenty-three dollars a week with meals. The hours were 4 p.m. until midnight except Sundays. Sunday was a day off, unless one of the other menials didn't show. If you missed a shift you were fired, no questions asked or answered. If you showed up too drunk to work, you were fired. If you broke too many dishes, you were fired. The list of how to get fired was a long one, and the owner, one Vladimir Borrilli, recited all of it with great solemnity. After I hired on, I asked the boss if he knew someplace I could stay. He raised his arms and his eyes toward the ceiling and assured me the world was filled with rooms for rent.

"Yes, but all of the joints around here make you pay by the night, cash in advance. You said I get paid by the week, at the end of the week. Now you know you need me to wash all those dishes back there and, I need the job, but unless we resolve my little housing problem we won't be able to help each other very much, will we?" I tried very hard to sound reasonable, but all the way through my monologue he shook his head as if I were speaking Chinese.

"You're crazy. You don't get paid nothing, not one damn cent till you work. You don't like that, then get the hell out of here. You bindle stiffs are all alike. You think I'm a sucker, a fool? Go on; get your ass out of here!"

"Hang on there, Mr. Borrilli, just look at how those greasy dishes are stacking up on you."

He looked through the serving slot into the cluttered kitchen, and it was easy to tell he didn't like what he saw. He grimaced and turned back to me.

"Look, Mister Drifter," he said, "you do the job, you start right now, right this very minute, and I pay you at the end of this day. You stick around and come back tomorrow and do the job, then I pay you tomorrow. I do that one whole week. Then we talk. This way you get pay for a room and I get the dishes washed. We got a deal?"

"Sure we do." I was back in the real world again.

Precisely at midnight, Borrilli's straw boss handed over my first day's wages, $3.33 for the hours from 4 to midnight and 82 cents for the time from when I started to work until 4 P.M., making a grand total of $4.15.

"Hey, dishwasher! What'll I tell the boss? Will you be here tomorrow?" he asked.

"I'll be here." I would, that is, if my broken back straightened up, or, if I didn't get jungle rot from the accumulated sweat and grease under those long sleeve rubber gloves I had used to scrub a million dirty dishes.

It was too late at night to hunt for an open mission so I took a room in the first cage joint I came to.

A Chicago cage joint is exactly what the name implies. Some pseudo-humanitarian with money to invest rents a big empty loft and partitions it into little cubicles with cheap plywood walls. Then he had chicken wire stretched over the top of the whole kennel to keep the paying guests from crawling over their wall and into someone else's cage. The prospective overnight guest buys admission at the front door from a ticket seller behind a steel grill like the one in front of a movie theatre. When the clerk gets his money, he punches a buzzer and lets the customer into the big room with the cages. Each cage has an old war surplus double-decked bunk in it. If you want a cage to yourself, you pay double. If you want one with a screen door, and a bolt lock you pay treble. Grand total for the best room in the house is $1.50 cash in advance. A side room houses two leaky showerheads, a row of crappers and five washbasins. Showers cost a quarter, rental razors cost fifteen cents, towels cost a dime, and you can take a crap for free. Oh, yes, one more thing. Admission entitles you to go past the buzzer gate only one time. If you go outside the buzzer door, you pay to get in again. No rain checks are welcomed.

I paid fifty cents for an open double and ten cents for a towel. I put the remaining money in my sock and then put my sock and shoe back on again. Not that I didn't trust the other prosperous gentlemen in the room with me, I just like the feel of money against my instep.

Only a person who has slept in a Chicago flophouse has heard snoring. There will never be words adequate to describe the huffing, hacking, rattle and whistle that a hundred exhausted men can cram into one night's sleep. But on that particular evening I was too worn out to marvel at it. I just joined the chorus.

Reveille comes early in a cage joint. At 6 A.M. the guests vacate the place, and that means all the way out onto the street. No matter how sick they might be or how drunk, or what sad stories they dream up to sneak another hour in the rack, they get out. All of us were well trained. Most of the crowd was gone before the ten-minute whistle blew. Even I managed to wash my face and leave before the hired hands started the cage by cage roust.

The streets at that hour in the morning were engulfed in icy dead-still air. Each breath produced a great white cloud of steam. Before long the cold had cut through my shabby clothes and deep into my hide. As the icy dark chill gradually gave way to weak, grey, winter light and the morning traffic started to build, I came alive for a time. There was nothing to do but walk. If you lingered in a doorway, the cops were on you. If you panhandled, the cops were on you. If you walked into a store, the owner and the cops were on you. So, I walked. As the hours crept by, my legs wearily protested every additional step. My head hung down on my chest and my eyes saw onIy the crazed, filthy sidewalk at my feet. Those were the hours when every thought was deep, heartfelt, maudlin self-pity. Each second was a minute, every minute was an hour and the damn clock ran backward.

Chapter Fourteen

On the afternoon of the third day of this exciting new life, Vladimir burst into the kitchen and walked purposefully toward my sink.

"Hey you, drifter . . . Smith!" he yelled.

I slopped the soap off of my rubber gloves and wiped them down the front of my apron.

"Yes, sir, boss. What's up?"

His normally florid face was fire engine red. "You're fired. That's what's up. Get your stuff and get the hell out of here. Right now," he added.

"What for? I've been doing the job. What am I fired for?" I didn't believe he was serious. Maybe this was his idea of a practical joke.

"I don't want nobody working here when I find out the cops are after him. Get your crooked ass out on the street, hoodlum, where they can find you. Move!" he shouted.

"Up yours!" I shouted back at him as I tore off the apron and gloves. "I'll leave, you old bastard, but not until you pay me what you owe me." I was really burned.

"Here." He jammed his hand into his pocket and yanked out a handful of change, some of which fell on the floor. "Here's your money, Mr. Criminal Hooligan. You've already stuffed your gut with stolen food. Now hit the bricks."

I almost made the same mistake with him that I had made with Grease Ball Lillard at the end of my last job. Almost, but not quite, This time I swallowed my pride took the money and walked quietly out the door.

Out in the cold again, the sun was gone and the streetlights had already been turned on. Dirty snow was piled high in the gutters. I stood in the middle of the sidewalk and tried to blow the stink of hamburger grease out of my nose.

Then I counted my money; nine dollars and eighty-three cents. At this rate it would take me at least another week to become a power player in the stock market. Well, what the hell, nine dollars and eighty-three cents was better than nothing. I wondered where Borrilli got the idea the cops were after me? I hadn't done anything except walk the streets, wash his filthy dishes, and sleep in that fifty-cent zoo. Maybe I ought to go back inside and try to reason with him. Oh, shit, let him hose down his own grungy dishes.

With no goal in mind I started walking toward the Loop, sorry for myself one minute, and happy to be out of Vladimir's Ptomaine Domain the next.

Before I had covered a full block, I heard the clatter of footsteps behind me, and then a hesitant voice over my shoulder called, "Wait, Okey, Mr. Smith! Wait please!"

"Dorothy Lamb! What are you doing here?"

"That's what I want to talk to you about." She had a most peculiar look on her face.

"Well, then let me buy you a cup of coffee and we'll talk about it." Buy her a cup of coffee? Listen; when I have $9.83 burning a hole in my pocket I'm just another Diamond Jim Brady.

We walked into a drugstore, ordered coffee, black, and carried the mugs to a booth in the rear near the prescription counter.

"I'm mighty glad to see you, Miss Lamb, but why…."

"Look, Mr. Smith, Okey" she interrupted, "sometimes people do things with the very best of motives and then . . . well, and then they realize they had no business . . . what I mean is . . ." she faltered.

I had a sudden insight. "You're the one who told that old bastard Borrilli that the police were after me!"

"Yes." Her freckled face blazed like a neon sign in a beer joint window.

"Why in the world did you do that? How did you even know where to find me?"

"I've been hunting for you for several days now. About an hour ago, I saw you through that restaurant window and that's when I got the idea." Her embarrassment was painful to behold.

"And then what did you do, Miss Nosey Librarian Lamb?" I wasn't as mad as I tried to sound. I hadn't liked the damn dishwashing job, but she wasn't going to get off the hook until I found out what she was up to.

"I went inside and asked to speak with the proprietor. When he came, I told him you were a criminal on the run and that the police were hunting all over the city for you and that when they found you there would probably be a terrible gun battle."

"Good God Agnes! No wonder he fired me! I'm damn lucky he didn't come in the kitchen and shoot me. You're a nut. You know that, Miss Lamb? You're a total nut."

"I know, and I'm really sorry. I shouldn't meddle in your affairs."

I was sorry, too, but for a different reason. I was sorry because I was making a very pretty girl feel awfully bad over something that really was unimportant.

"Tell me one more thing," I growled.

"All right," she sniffled. "I'll try."

"I want to know why you did it."

"Well, because . . . well, just because."

"What the hell kind of an answer is 'just because'? Educated librarians don' t say 'Just because.'"

"I did it because father and I talked it over, and we decided you needed to quit frittering away your life. We thought you seemed like a good man and if you just had a little fire lit under you, you might amount to something. Father says you should go find Charlie's widow and tell her whatever it was you wouldn't tell us about. And I think . . . well, never mind what I think. Obviously we were both wrong! "

During the first part of that speech her head had hung, and she sounded as if she were trying to apologize. Then about half way through she got mad and her eyes shot fire at me. By damn! Old freckle face was really quite a woman.

"You know something else, Miss Lamb?" I asked.

"No. I mean, yes. I mean, what else?"

"You're a real sweet doll!"

Chapter Fifteen

Professor Roscoe Lamb was in his bathrobe in the kitchen, waiting for us. "I knew full well that Dorothy would find some way to get you here tonight," he said with a sly grin on his face. "I taught her how to catch fish when she was just a little girl."

"Well, I'm a 'fish' in more ways than one. Wait till you hear how she caught me."

We struggled through another one of her boiled goat dinners and then Dorothy, the Professor, and I sank down in misery in the living room for a talk.

"If you will, Okey, tell me more about your Indian friend."

"That's what I would like to do. I didn't tell you much before because I had, in fact I still have, a notion that things I saw and heard were very private."

"Of course, you don't have to tell us anything, but if you do, we will treat what you say with the utmost discretion."

"I think maybe I'd better tell it all to you. I honestly don't know what to do about it, and I could certainly use some good advice."

So, I told him the whole story. He interrupted only once to make me repeat the part about the 'key.'

"Are you sure he said 'key'? Could it have been some other word that sounded like 'key'?"

"I'm certain. I remember it exactly. He said, "then you are to tell her to get the 'key.' And a little bit later he said 'When she gets the 'key,' you are to help her find a way to deliver it to my son."

"Did he say anything more about this 'key'?"

"No. Nothing. Absolutely nothing. I've told you the whole thing. So what do you think he was talking about?"

“We certainly seem to have a conundrum here,” he mused, "I am unaware of anything in the Pueblo culture which relates to a key. Of course, modern Valenci Indians use keys and locks just like everyone else, but I have the feeling this has some significance other than a key to a modern lock. Do you agree?”

"Professor, I have no basis for agreeing or disagreeing. As I told you the other night, until I read that obituary I had never heard the word ‘Valenci.’"

"Another mystifying thing, is this business of cremation,” he continued. “ I presume that when your friend burned his hand so terribly, he was performing a symbolic act of cremation. Historically the Anasazi practiced interment as far as we know. In any event, in light of all you've told me this evening, I must renew my suggestion."

"What suggestion?" I thought I already knew the answer to that question.

"I feel you have a clear duty to seek out his wife and tell her everything your friend said and did," he said firmly. "If she gets or gives you the mysterious key, whatever it might prove to be, then, it seems to me, you will have the further duty to help her find their son and deliver it to him. Do you agree?"

"I guess I do. Yes, well, I think I do." I wasn't sure whether the Professor had conned me or whether I had accidentally conned myself.

"We knew you'd do it,” said Dorothy. “Now, when will you start?"

“I suppose right now. Sure. Why not. I’ll start right now.”

"You mean tomorrow morning?"

"No, I mean right now." As long as I was going to get involved, I might as well go whole hog. "Will you take me back to Madison Street tonight?"

"Madison Street? I thought you would be going to New Mexico. Now why would you be going back to that horrible street? Are you going to start washing dishes again? I thought we were finished with that most unfortunate episode of Okey P. Smith."

Chapter Sixteen

"Miss Lamb, -Dorothy, you and the Professor aren't the only ones who have been thinking. I've been pondering about poor old Charlie for several days now. After all, you have to think about something other than greasy soapsuds while you're washing dishes. I believe I might have figured out a part of what happened to him. For instance- I'm dead certain the police found him on skid row. They bring lots of old men like Charlie into the jail. While I was there, ninety-nine per cent of them came from skid row. Almost all of them were revolving door drunks. After a few hours they sobered up and were dumped back on the street. But some of them, the really sick ones, stayed in jail. And some of those really sick ones stayed there for a long time. No one at the jail was in any hurry to make them leave. The decent turnkeys seemed to know that, if they sent those pitiful, sick and forgotten old men back onto the streets, they would soon be dead. So they just pretended they were not there. They fed them and let them stay. I believe that the way they acted about Charlie meant they just looked on him as another one of those derelicts who was too old and too near death to bring to trial or to turn back on the streets."

"Is that lawful?" Dorothy asked. "Can the police just keep a man in jail until he dies without giving him a trial? That's just terrible."

"I don't know," I said. "I'm no lawyer, but it probably isn't legal. Legal or not, though, in cases like that it seems to me like the right thing to do. Those poor old guys needed a dry sack and decent food much worse than they needed a lecture on constitutional law. They were too far-gone to take care of themselves. If they had families, they had lost track of them. There just wasn't anyplace left in this world for them to go. What I'm trying to get across is that those old worn out men were being given the privilege of spending their last few weeks of life under a roof, like a human being. The police weren't going to force them back out in the streets to die in an alley like some poor old stray dog."

"And you are convinced that's what they were doing for Charlie?"

"I think that's what they thought they were doing. But what if it happened this way. Suppose old Charlie got drunk or got sick or maybe even got poisoned some way or another. The cops find him passed out on the street in skid row and haul him into jail. But then he doesn't dry out overnight. Some jailhouse medic takes a look at him and says there's nothing wrong except he's an old drunk with advanced D.T.'s or something, And in addition to that, he is terminal. So the screws just leave him there in the jail until somebody claims him, or until he gets well or, more likely, until he dies. "

"I guess it could happen that way," she said, "but you haven't answered my question. I still don't understand why you want to go back to Madison Street."

I tried to think my way through it and talk at the same time.

"Look, Charlie said he had a wife in the city, right?"

"Correct, " she responded.

"Well, what would you do if you had a husband and he didn't' come home?"

"Obviously I would try to find him."

"And one of the ways you would try to find him, if everything else had failed, would be to go to the police, wouldn't it?"

"If he had been gone for a long while, I might. "

"Well, look at what happened here. During all those months Charlie's wife never found him, even though he was right there in the same town and in jail and very much alive.

And yet almost the very minute he died, she shows up with some guy and claims his body. Doesn’t that sound more than a little odd to you?"

"I didn't think of that. It does sound peculiar."

"If you assume she was interested in finding him, it sounds peculiar, alright. Well, I think she was interested, and I've got an idea of how such a thing could have happened."

“OK, how?”

"Suppose Charlie's wife is as old as he and too crippled up or too feeble or maybe too sick to take care of herself. She might not even speak English. That's possible isn't it, Professor?"

"It's quite common among older Indians."

"In that case, what if she had some person on whom she thought she could depend, some person who was an Indian but who spoke English? She would likely use that person to help her find her husband, wouldn't she?"

"Yes, that certainly makes sense," agreed Miss Lamb.

"Well, what if that person, the one who was supposed to be helping her, didn't want Charlie found, at least not for a long time?"

"If he didn’t want him found, he could just have knocked Charlie in the head or killed him or something couldn't he?"

"Of course he could, but why take a chance like that if he could trick the police into doing the job for him?"

"You'll have to explain what you mean."

"Charlie had some kind of a thing he called a 'key.' It might be something really valuable. Assume it is. Now what if there is a man, perhaps another Indian, who wants to get that ‘key’? For some reason he knows that Charlie would never give it to him voluntarily so he decides to steal it. But the deal is not quite that simple because the man doesn't know where the 'key' is. Maybe he doesn't even know exactly what the 'key' looks like. So he works up a plan to get Charlie out of the way for as long as necessary by having him kept in jail like a common drunk. He gets Charlie all tanked up, or maybe even poisons him and puts him out on the street for the cops to sweep up. As long as Charlie is kept in jail this guy can work on Charlie's wife, play on her sympathy or something like that, and all the time he's trying to get his hands on the 'key.' If Charlie were out of his way, then he didn't care whether Charlie was dead or alive. All that time he's pretending to help Charlie's wife to find Charlie. When he learns that Charlie had actually died, that gave him an even greater opportunity to take advantage of the widow's predicament to get the 'key.' "

"If he did all that, then he must already have the 'key,' " said Miss Lamb.

"He probably does," I agreed. "But there is still a possibility that Charlie's widow is too sharp for him. Maybe Charlie told her never to turn it over to anyone unless she was sure that person was the one who was supposed to have it."

"You think she might still have it then?"

"Well, that's a sixty-four dollar question. At least there's an outside chance she has it. But there is an even better chance that he has her. I can't believe he would allow her to go back to her real home in Valenci until he got the 'key' from her. That's why I think it might be a waste of time to go to Valenci until we are reasonably certain she isn't right here in Chicago."

"Then it's important to locate her as soon as possible."

"That's what I think."

"But I'm still not sure I understand why you want to go back to skid row. What does that have to do with finding the widow?"

"That's one of the very few places where a trick like that could be pulled on the police with any hope of success. So he must have known the skid row area pretty well. If he spent much time there, he talked with people there. Maybe he talked enough for me to find someone who knows who he is, or where he is or where he has gone. At least, that's what I'm hoping," I said.

"I don't think your plan makes any sense at all," said Miss Lamb.

"I probably agree with you, but it's the only plan I have. There's no use trying to get the police to help us. As far as we know, no crime has been committed. The cops aren't going to spend their time and the taxpayers' money hunting for some old Indian woman just because I have a message for her from her deceased jailbird husband. I know damn well they won't buy my line about her being in danger. So where does that leave us? Besides, I can't search the whole City of Chicago. "

"I agree. I think you might have an outside chance to find out something about them on skid-row," said the Professor. "It's a very long shot, but it does make some sense to me. "

"Sure it's a long shot, but like the man said, ' it may be crooked but it's the only wheel in town'."

Chapter Seventeen

An hour later I was back on Madison Street. This time, though, I was not drifting. I was hunting. It was going to be a lot longer hunt than I had bargained for.

"What can I do for you, brother?" asked the night clerk as he painfully forced his way out of a folding aluminum lawn chair and shuffled behind the counter of the Brighter Day Mission. He looked like he had never 'done' anything for anyone, ever.

"I'm broke and I need a place to sleep." It was no lie. I had been back on the row for four days without finding a single trace of Charlie's wife or her "friend." Not only that, but I was down to my last few dollars.

"Fill out this card," he said pushing a white file card and a badly chewed yellow pencil across the counter in front of me.

I read the card. There was a series of letters -- "W N O AI Other," on it.

"What does all that mean?" I asked.

"That don't need concern you. All you have to do is put down your name and your Social Security number and your occupation, if you got one."

"I don't sign anything unless I know what it means. "

"All right, but you're mighty touchy brother. What that there letters is, is something for me to mark when I give you permission to come in to sleep here. "

He pulled a pair of steel rimmed glasses from his pocket, slowly unfolded them and carefully hooked them over his ears. It was the high point of his day. He was on the lecture platform and he had an audience of one.

"Now this here 'W' you see here, that means 'white', like you," he said. "Once you get inside, I'll take this pencil and draw a little circle around the 'W'. I do that for all the Hebes and the Spicks and the Greaser's too. Now this next one means nigger. If you was to be a coon, I would put a circle on this 'N'. The 'O' stands for your Japs and Chinks and the like. Any of them slant eyed yeller boys come in here we mark the 'O'."

I don't believe I had ever heard such racist crap even from the screws in the jailhouse. I wondered if he were the product of any known race or nation. Maybe he came in a pod from outer space.

"What's the next one for?"

"I don't know. I never used it."

"It says 'AI;' could that mean American Indian?"

"I never thought of that. It might well, brother, it might well."

"Do you ever get any American Indians here?"

"Hell mister, we get every kind of foreign trash in here. I reckon some of them is a redskin."

"You got any 'foreign' American Indians here now?"

His face hardened. I had pressed too hard.

"You're a cop, aren't you? How come you think you can come in here and ask a bunch of questions and not tell me you are a stinking cop?"

"Come on, buddy, do I look like a cop?"

"Hell! How should I know? Do you want a bed or not? Make up your mind."

It was late and I was sleepy. "I want in, brother. Believe me, I want in."

"Hold on a minute," he said, "I seen you before. You're the dishwasher at Borrilli's, ain't you?"

"That's me. The king of the greasy pans."

"You ain't no cop then?" His face opened up again.

"I ain't no cop. Now what about that bed?"

"What was it you wanted to know about them Greasers?" he asked.

"I wanted to know about Indians. All I asked was do you ever have any Indians staying here?"

"Yeah. We had one for a while, not too long ago neither. He was a great big sonofabitch, a hell of a lot bigger than you, and mean as a snake."

"Is he still here?"

"Naw. He pulled out close to a week ago."

"What was his name?"

"He called hisself Bentura, or something like that. I caint exactly remember."

The name meant nothing to me.

"Were there others besides him?"

"He's the only one I remember. But, I'll say this, he was a mighty queer one,"

"Why do you say that?"

"Because he was nosey as hell, just like you. He kept asking me if I ever seen any Indians. Every evening he would come in here and ask me the same thing--had I seen any old, gray haired Indian man? Said he wanted to be sure to know it when his friend got out."

"Got out of what?"

"Hell, I don't know."

I was elated. The first link in the chain had been forged.

"You say 'he pulled out' about a week ago, Do you happen to know where he went?" I couldn't hide the eagerness in my voice.

“Well hell no. Why should I know that?”

"What about other friends. Did this Bentura have any other friends?"

"As I recall, he hung around with old Shulsey Dan some. They’d do a little bottle hunting together, but that don't mean they was friends."

I had another thought. "Did Bentura sign one of those white cards?"

"Not while I was here, he didn't. But he might of signed one for the day man."

"Could we find out?" I asked, and eyeballed the card index file on the desk.

That blew it. "I knew it! You're a god-dammed cop. Well, mister dishwasher-cop, we're fresh out of beds. We're full up tonight." He slammed back down in his folding chair and turned away from me.

Chapter Eighteen

I spent the night in a cage joint. My resources were almost shot. I had three dollars and twenty cents left. Something more substantial was going to have to come my way and it was going to have to happen soon or this hunt was over.

The next morning at 6 A.M., I left the cage joint and, as usual, stood with the crowd of other former tenants rubbing my hands and gazing at the sidewalk.

"Hey, Okey. Look over here. Okey, it's me," whined a voice from the corner of the building.

"Well, I'll be damned, it's old Half-Witt. How are you? When did they let you out of the slammer?" Half-Witt looked in bad shape. He was obviously on the bitter end of a Bay Rum and Sterno bender.

"Listen, to me, Okey. You and me was buddies once wasn't we?"

"We still are."

"Well, Buddy, I need a drink real bad. Could you lend me enough to get just one pint. I swear to God I'll pay you back. You know I'm good for it don't you?"

"I know you are good for it but I'm tapped out too, pal."

"Oh Jesus--God Okey don't tell me that. You ain't the kind to forget your poor sick friends," he was shaking all over.

In the alley behind Witt I saw another figure slumped against a row of trash barrels.

"Who's your friend, Witt?" I asked trying to change the subject.

"Hell, that ain't a friend You don't need worry none about him, we ain't together, honest. That's just old Shulsey Dan. I ain't with him. I don't even know him. Now come on Okey, how about that bottle?"

This might be the break I had hoped for. "Half-Witt you've got yourself a bottle if you can sober up Shulsey Dan long enough for me to talk with him."

"Shulsey, you old piss-ant, come out here, we've found our angel," yelled Half-Witt.

Shulsey Dan climbed uncertainly to his feet and fumbled on shaky legs out of the alley. He was in worse shape than Half-Witt if that were possible, but at least he could walk.

"Talk to him, Shulsey. Talk to the man," prodded Half-Witt.

"About what?" he muttered.

"Shulsey," I asked, "do you remember a guy you hung around with who was an Indian named Bentura?"

"No. Yeah. What if I did? So what?" He mopped his face with his dirty sleeve and shook his head uncertainly. Spittle oozed down through the two week old grey stubble on his chin.

"Damn it, be nice to the man, Shulsey, he's gonna get us some store bought," hissed Half-Witt.

"What happened to Bentura, Shulsey? Where did he go?"

Shulsey squirmed around and tried hard to remember, but too much of his energy was being spent in trying to stand up. His brain refused to function.

"Maybe a little drink would help us remember," volunteered Half-Witt. "Give me the money Okey and I'll go get us a bottle."

"Half-Witt, it's not that I don't trust you buddy, but if a bottle is to be got, I'll do the getting."

"Well, it sure would help us to think," he urged.

"Keep Shulsey here and keep him awake. I'll go get some squeeze," I said.

Bottle stores open early on skid row. I found one within half a block and spent ninety-seven cents on a pint of vintage Dago Red.

The pair eyed me eagerly as I returned to the alley. I unwrapped the bottle and broke the seal.

"O.K., Shulsey. As soon as you remember where Bentura said he was going, you get a drink."

"What about me?" squeaked Half-Witt.

‘You get one too, but not until Shulsey talks. "

Sweat rolled down Shulsey's forehead.

"I'm trying. Honest to God, Mister, I'm doing my best."

"Wait a minute. I remember! I remember!" His face broke into a toothless smile.

"Gimme my drink," yelled Half-Witt.

"He was going off to bury somebody. That's what it was. Somebody died and he was going off to bury him,"

Shulsey was jumping up and down all over the alley. I had to keep him on the subject while he could still think.

"Where, Shulsey? Where was he going to bury somebody? Who was he going to bury?"

"He said he was going to bury somebody and then he and his old lady was going to get something and then they was going on a world class toot."

"But where? What were they going to get?" I pressed him.

"All I remember is he said he was going to be a rich man. He said he was going to get rich and then he was going to drink dry every bar in Albuquerque. "

"Where did Bentura live, Shulsey," I waved the bottle under his nose, "where did he stay?"

"Tell him Shulsey, Damn you, I need that bottle." Half-Witt grabbed Shulsey by the arm and started tugging at him.

"Make him let me be," Shulsey pleaded.

"Let him go, Half-Witt," I said separating them. "Now calm down Shulsey, all I want to know is where Bentura lived. Tell me just that one little thing and we'll both let you go."

"Hell, that's easy. He lived over top the Elite Pool Room, the one on Clark, I think. I went up there with him once. He was a mean son of a bitch, he was. You better not mess with him. Now give me my drink. Please!"

They got the bottle.

Chapter Nineteen

If North Clark Street were chopped into sections and laid out neatly on a prairie somewhere, the result would be a complete city without further addition. Slum apartments, wealthy mansions, garages, movie houses, bars, dry cleaners, all imaginable kinds of enterprises, legitimate and otherwise, found a place on North Clark Street.

The only one I was interested in stood in front of me. 'Elite Billiards' read the broken neon letters on a rusty, black metal sign. The building was brick, three stories high with what appeared to be apartments on the top two floors. A stairwell without a door opened on the south side and led to the apartments above. Inside the doorway was a collection of bent and paint-chipped mailboxes, all without names. The rubber runner on the stairs had been torn loose and shredded beyond repair. The smell of stale beer, unwashed diapers and mildew hung like a fog in the hallway. My only choice was to knock on every apartment door until I found Bentura.

No one answered the first door. The second door was opened the width of its chain latch by a sour looking little girl.

"Does Mr. Bentura live here?"

The child looked at me but said nothing.

"Is your mamma or daddy home?"

No response.

"What about someone else? Is there an adult here?"

The child turned and yelled back into the apartment, "Hey, Maw, there's some ol' man at the door. "

"What's he want?" came an answering voice.

"I don't know."

"Tell him to go away, I'm busy," came the voice again from the back room.

"My maw says for you to go away. She's busy now," she started closing the door.

I quickly leaned against the door to keep it cracked open and yelled through the narrow opening. "I've got a nice little surprise for you, ma'am. I found that money you lost."

The voice from the back room materialized at the crack in the door in the form of a dumpy woman in an unbuttoned maroon sweater.

"What fuckin' money?" she asked suspiciously.

"This dollar bill," I said fumbling hurriedly into my pocket and hauling out one of my two remaining dollars.

"What's this all about, Mister? I didn't lose no damn dollar. What are you trying to pull here anyhow?" Her mouth said 'no' but her eyes were fixed on the dollar bill.

"I just want some information," I said. "Answer one little question and you get the money.

"What question?"

"Where does a man named "Bentura" live in this building?"

"Is that all I have to answer?"

"That's it."

"You'll give me a dollar and all I have to do is tell you where some guy named Ben-whatsit lives?"

"Yes."

"I don't believe you. First give me the dollar and then I'll tell you."

I decided to gamble on her honesty and hand over the money before I got my answer.

"I ain't ever heard of him!" She snatched away the dollar bill, slammed the door and threw the bolt.

I stood there staring at the wooden door listening to the cackling laughter on the other side and feeling very foolish. Finally, I recaptured some small sense of ego and climbed up the remaining flight of steps. The third floor appeared to be completely deserted. Dust hung in the air. I heard a baby crying from the floor below. A pile of sucked dry wine bottles and empty beer cans lay in the middle of the hallway. A broken toy car and some particularly salacious graffiti spray painted on the walls completed the decor.

I stepped over the piled up trash, walked to the end of the hall and knocked on the only door.

There was no answer.

I knocked again and then tried turning the knob. The door swung open easily.

"Mr. Bentura?" I called.

I called again, opened the door all the way and stepped into the room. The shades were pulled and the room was dark. I tried the light switch. Nothing happened. The power was disconnected or all the lights were burned out. "Hey, Bentura."

Then I saw her. She was lying on her back crosswise on a bare mattress on the floor. Her arms were flat against her sides. She was partially covered with an old woven blanket. I hurried to her side and almost fell over a piece of torn linoleum. There was no need to hurry. She was very dead.

I stood for a moment and looked down at the body. It was an Indian woman, probably Liawu. The woman had been very old, almost as old as Charlie, but in death she was hard looking, with none of Charlie's great dignity. I wondered why such an unlikely pair had become husband and wife. Maybe the Valencia Tribe had some sort of planned marriage tradition. She was a large woman, dressed in severe black like a thousand other old ladies. Around her neck was a heavy necklace set with dozens of small pieces of turquoise. Without that necklace she could have passed for the Wicked Witch of the West from the Wizard of Oz movie. Clutched in her left hand was a wad of feathers. White powder, the consistency of corn meal, was spilled all around her on the floor. The whole scene was alive with big roaches. I finally tore my eyes away from her pitiful corpse and gazed around the room. The furnishings were few and shabby. It was just another slum apartment.

Quickly, I shooed away additional armies of roaches and searched through every drawer and both closets. Then I went through the kitchen cabinets. There was nothing in the whole apartment, which offered me a clue as to what had killed her, how she got there, or how long she had been dead. As I concluded the empty search, a disturbing thought crept into my mind. What if Bentura had murdered her? She didn't look murdered, but what if she had been. If I called the cops, I would certainly wind up as their number one suspect. It would take the police a long time to clear me and in that time Bentura would be able to accomplish whatever he had in mind to do with the 'key.' On the other hand, if he hadn't gotten the ‘key’ away from her, then my detention by the police would give him a clear field to keep looking for it. All in all, I was in a very vulnerable spot. What if that old bat downstairs got suspicious and called the cops? They might be on their way that very minute. My imagination picked up tempo. I'd better get out of here, and fast, I thought. Action quickly followed the thought. I hurried down the steps and out onto the street. No police were in sight, but I had convinced myself they would be there any second. Where could I go? They would expect me to head for skid row so that was out. The university that was it! I would head for DeJohn and the Lambs. I hailed a taxi cruising north on Clark. The police wouldn't think to look for me in a taxi.

"How much to take me to DeJohn University?" I asked as I jumped into the back seat.

"Which campus?"

"Huh?"

"Which campus, uptown or downtown? What's the matter? You drunk or deaf?" He leaned over the back of his seat to look at me.

I was on the inside edge of panic. "Take me a dollar's worth toward the uptown campus. "

"A whole dollar's worth? You're a real sport aren't you, buddy?"

"Forget it. I'll get there myself." I fumbled to open the cab door.

"Oh hell, sport, stay put. I'll drive you there for a buck if you forget to notice that I forget to turn on the meter. Deal?"

"Yes, sure, but hurry, please!" I thrust my last dollar bill at him as he pulled into the stream of traffic.

Chapter Twenty

As soon as Miss Lamb saw me signal to her from the library door, she got her coat and hurried out to the parking lot. I waited for her hunched down beside her Jeep.

"Let's get out of here, quick!" I said. "The cab driver was suspicious and may be going to tell the police he brought me here."

"What on earth is the matter with you, Okey? You act as if you had seen a ghost."

"No talk now, please. The police may be after me. Take me someplace. Take me to your house." I was so nervous it came out sounding like pure gibberish.

She wasn't about to hurry. "Okey Smith, have you done something wrong?" she asked, posed with her fists parked on her hipbone.

"Uh, no. No. Nothing. Please, Dorothy, let's get in the car. We've got to hurry!"

"Very well, I'll get in, but I certainly hope you haven't done something to be ashamed of."

We drove in complete silence. Apparently she intended to hear my story only one time, and she wanted her father to hear it at that same time with her. By the time we had arrived at the Lamb house I had collected my wits enough to tell the story of the hunt and the unexpected find with only a slight tremor in my voice and body. When they had heard the story from beginning to end, they both agreed that it was possible I might be in a jam. They also agreed that the cops might be looking for me.

“Why don’t I just call the police and ask if they found the body of the old woman?” Dorothy asked.

"And just how would you explain knowing enough about what happened to ask the question?" responded the Professor.

"Point well made!" she cheerfully conceded in a 1930s tennis match voice.

The balance of the day was spent in desultory discussion about what I should do. The professor was adamant that I should leave Chicago as soon as possible and go to Valenci. Miss Lamb felt I should not even leave their house until there was no longer any danger from Bentura or the police and then I should go directly to Valenci. Despite their feelings, I wanted to make one final effort to locate Liawu's actual residence on the long-shot gamble that before Bentura lured her away to his place he had failed to find the 'key.'

At last, more because of exhaustion than faith in my idea, both Lambs agreed

I could spend two more days with their help looking for Charlie's wife's former residence and, in turn, I agreed at the end of those two days to leave Chicago and head for Pueblo country.

"But we're not going hunting until tomorrow morning," Dorothy said with a determined look on her face.

"I'm too pooped to argue with you about that," I agreed. I was physically and emotionally worn out.

At breakfast the following morning we worked out the plan we would use to try to find out where Liawu had lived. Dorothy was to go to her library office, and from there call the public welfare agencies. The Professor was to remain at home and call as many of the organized Indian societies and social clubs as he could discover in the city directories. I was to go to the funeral parlor, being careful to avoid any policemen, and try to pump more information out of Fogglesong, the mortician.

We were ready to leave the house when I had a thought, which made me feel slightly foolish. "We've overlooked the obvious," I said.

"What might that be?" asked Dorothy.

"I thought we were more than thorough in our preparations," demurred the Professor.

"We haven't looked in the telephone book. Maybe Charlie had a telephone."

"If they were as poor as you seem to think, then they wouldn't have a telephone, but I'll look in the book just to make sure," said Dorothy striding back into the house.

In a few moments she returned. "Sorry, no such name. Let's get on with the job."

Chapter Twenty-One

Mr. Fogglesong at the funeral parlor was less than happy to see me. He insisted he had given me all the information he had the first time I had paid him a visit. He made it more than clear he expected this to be my last free consultation.

"Here, Mr. Smith," he said. "Here is our entire file on that man. As you can see, I told you everything."

He handed me a single sheet of paper. It was very short printed form.

"Who filled in the name of the deceased and who signed it?" I asked. "And who said he was from Valenci?"

"The large and very unpleasant Indian gentleman who accompanied the widow. He did it on her behalf and in her name. All the information in that form came from him."

I read the sheet again. It was just a standard release form and required nothing more than name, birth date, and race of the deceased, and the signature of a relative or close friend. The signature was undecipherable.

"Are you finished now, Mr. Smith? I really have a great deal of work to do."

I thanked the man and walked out of the funeral parlor. Damn it all to hell, there had to be someway we could locate Liawu's apartment. Fogglesong had played it straight with us on everything except Liawu's address. What was it he said to excuse that misinformation? Something about it was only an Indian and he didn't think I would care.

For ten minutes, I sat in the Jeep trying to collect and organize my thoughts. A red flag was flying somewhere in the back of my mind, but I didn't know why. Then, I had an idea.

Fogglesong was openly hostile when I barged into his office again.

"Now, look here Smith, I've given you all the time you're going to get. Please get out of here and leave me alone!"

"Let me see that release form just one more time, Mr. Fogglesong."

"Here. Read it and then get out."

I read it again and there it was. Both Fogglesong and I could have made the same mistake. The reason he had given me a phony address might have been because he had the wrong name and couldn't find the correct address himself. The printed form called for the deceased's name, last name first. The penciled name was Taaiyalote Alowish. Both of us had assumed that the person who wrote the name followed the printed instructions. Neither of us was familiar with the surname or the given name of a Valenci Indian so we had no reason to suspect a mistake. There was at least a chance the person who filled out the form had not followed instructions. "Taaiyalote" might be Charlie's first name and "Alowish" his last name.

"Do you have the, alphabetized City Directory, Mr. Fogglesong?" I asked in my most diplomatic voice.

"Oh, my Lord! What next? Yes, over there. No, not there, there! How arc you fixed for socks, Mr. Smith? Could I buy you a box of candy?" His sarcasm fell on deaf ears.

It took only a few seconds for me to find it--Alowish, T., 2449 Conqueror Ave., Apt. 24C. I was off and running again.

"Mr. Fogglesong, if I ever die, I promise that you can bury me, socks candy and all," I said cheerfully as I hurried out the door.

"I would like that very much, Mr. Smith," he shouted after me, "very much indeed!"

Chapter Twenty-Two

The address on Conqueror Avenue proved to be another shabby walk-up apartment building in worse condition, if possible, than the one that housed the Elite Poolroom and the deceased Indian woman. The apartment- manager stood in the doorway surveying an overturned garbage can as I walked up the front steps. I knew he must be the apartment manager because of his hospitable welcoming address.

"We're full. Try down the street."

"Which apartment belongs to Alowish?"

"What business is it of yours?" He gave me a hard eye.

"I'm from the Bureau of Indian Affairs," I extemporized. "We are required to inspect all housing supplied to American Indians who live off the reservation."

“Oh, Jesus! Not another bureaucrat.” He may not have believed me but he probably wouldn’t want to take a chance that I was telling the truth.

"She ain't paid her rent for two months," he groused. "I'm getting ready to move her out. The old bat ain't been here for a while though, so I figured I'd do her a favor and not throw her stuff out until till she gets back."

"I don't need to see her. All I'm interested in is the condition of the premises. Now, we have quite a few forms to fill in. So, if you…."

"Oh for crap sake, do I have to mess with another bunch of government forms?" He kicked at the garbage can.

"Well, my instructions don't actually say you have to be present, but we usually want the manager to accompany us. "

He took the hint and 'persuaded' me to inspect the apartment without his help.

I got the door key from him and climbed to the Alowish apartment on the sixth floor. Liawu’s apartment was wrecked.

Someone, probably Bentura, had been there before me hunting for the 'key.' All the drawers were pulled out and the contents spilled onto the floor. The closet door was open and every piece of clothing had been ripped from the hangers. The mattress had been cut open and eviscerated. Cotton wadding covered the floor. I walked into the tiny kitchen. The refrigerator door hung wide open and the plastic ice trays were scattered and empty in the kitchen sink. In the bathroom, even the lid on the toilet tank had been removed and was lying broken in the tub. Whoever had done this job seemed to me to know his business. The search had been thorough. I sat down on the side of an overturned slat bottom chair and stared gloomily around the devastated living room. Could he have missed anything? Did he find the 'key'? What the hell was the damn 'key' anyway?

"Great God almighty! Why did you make this mess?"

It was the manager. He must have had second thoughts about turning me loose with a key in the building he was supposed to protect.

"You know damn well I haven't been here long enough to make this much trouble," I growled.

He walked in, kicked at a smashed end table and sat down with his head in his hands.

"When the old lady gets back and sees this mess she's gonna kill me," he moaned.

"Well, I've got good news and bad news for you. The good news is that you can worry about something else. I don't think she will be coming back. The bad news is that it wouldn't surprise me if the police showed up. As a matter of fact, you ought to call the cops yourself."

He looked even more dejected.

I picked up a Bible with the cover half torn off and looked around the room. He had a snake's nest on his hands all right. Bentura hadn't missed a thing. Even the pictures had been torn off the wall. One of them, a modern art disaster with a cow and the sun had fallen into the mattress stuffing, and was the only picture without a broken frame. The room looked like the aftermath of a bombing raid. I tossed the torn Bible on the floor in disgust.

After a decent period of mutual commiseration, we closed and locked the apartment. The manager said he would call the police and I told him that if the police wanted to talk with me my name was Romeo Lillard, and that in my spare time I ran an Amusement Devices establishment on South State Street.

He said that was an odd thing for a government man, but, he would tell them.

The gathering at the Professor's house that evening was far from cheerful.

"Will you still try to go to New Mexico, or are you ready to abandon the project?" asked the Professor.

"I don't know, Professor. Every time I think I'm getting somewhere, fate throws another roadblock on my path. But I guess I'll stick with it. Not because I care, but mostly because I don't have anything better to do."

"We understand, Okey. But you really shouldn't be so ashamed of the fact that you are genuinely concerned," Dorothy said in a surprisingly warm voice.

We discussed other possible alternatives to going to New Mexico but each time we worked our way back around to the position that I ought to make the trip.

When I got there, I should find Charlie and Liawu's son, tell him about his mother and daddy and help him find the 'key'.

"I've come-a-cropper in Chicago, but you never can tell, I might just go to New Mexico and do something useful."

"Well now, that's the spirit," said the Professor. He reached across the table and squeezed my arm.

Dorothy rooted around in her pocketbook and came up with an envelope in her hand.

"Okey, Father and I want you to have this," she said.

I opened it. Inside was a bus ticket to Gallup, New Mexico, and a twenty-dollar bill.

"I wish we could afford to do more," the Professor said, "but my retirement pay …"

Chapter Twenty-Three

At 10 p.m. the snow was three inches deep and still falling. The train, designated Way Freight 137-B, had been delayed over two hours in the South Chicago yards by a series of frozen track switches. The bored crew sat in the locomotive cab waiting for a clear track. The big diesel engine throbbed in the compartment behind them The panel lights glowed softly.

“Did you hear that we're getting them new Fairbanks-Morse units before the end of the year?"

"I’ve heard that crap before and I doubt it. We'll probably ride this worn out stinkpot for the rest of our natural lives. Remember the old days when we took steam on this run?"

"Hell yes, man. I sure do. That old gal could really pick 'em up and lay 'em down. She was one high strutting mama!”

“I’ll tell you something else too. Did you hear they're gonna tear down them ugly old tenements over there?"

"That's what I heard. Ain' t they miserable sons-a-bitches?”

"Well, if the city condemned them, they'll be coming down before long. "

Twenty-nine cars back of the locomotive was an empty Missouri-Pacific fifty-ton PS-1 boxcar scheduled to be deadheaded to Hastings, Nebraska, to pick up a load of machine parts for Sioux Falls. Some careless person had left the eight-foot loading door standing half open.

One hundred yards from the train, inside the walls of a city-condemned tenement was a very large man and a very old woman.

She could not see him. Her eyes had swollen shut. Her lips were torn. Fresh blood pooled in her mouth, and dripped onto her withered breasts. Her left arm was broken. Three ribs were shattered and her left lung was punctured.

"Tell me where it is!" the man shouted.

She thought of how warm her real home would be. It was so much nicer than the one in the city. The man seized her hair and jerked her head upright.

"Talk to me!" he commanded. "Talk to me you old bitch."

She wondered what had happened to her nice blue coat. It had a fur collar. It had felt so good that first winter in the city.

"Damn you. I'll rip your puny arm off and beat you with it. Talk to me! What the hell is it and where did you hide it?"

The big man put his hand under her chin and slammed her head back against the cinderblock wall.

It would soon be time to climb the mountain and gather peaches. The children always loved to get the peaches. What were those boy's names? Oh yes, John and Larry. They were not very nice children. Too bad they had such an evil mother. She deliberately made them mean.

"Maybe this will help you remember." A kick from the man's steel toe work shoe opened a long bloody gash in her side.

Spring was the best time. There were so many different flowers in the desert--much too many to count. They were such tiny flowers too. If you didn't look carefully, you would miss them.

Under the cover of the snowstorm, the man carried her limp and broken body from the tenement and threw it into the open door of an empty boxcar standing in the South Chicago yards. The boxcar was Missouri-Pacific Line's 50-ton PS-1 boxcar attached to Way Freight 137-B.

The woman would be found in several days.

Chapter Twenty-Four

The sun was at the top of a giant blue sky when the bus arrived in Gallup, New Mexico. The bus station was small and, to my surprise, so was Gallup. Outside the temperature was only a few degrees warmer than it had been two days ago in Chicago, but, for some reason, it didn't feel nearly so cold. A few men in quilted jackets, blue jeans and outsize cowboy hats lazed against the station wall watching the handful of passengers exit the bus. A dark-skinned woman with a heavy woven blanket wrapped around her shoulders stood talking with the men. I caught a glimpse of a blue stone-encrusted necklace like the one I had seen on the woman's body in Chicago. That quickly served to remind me of why I had come to Gallup.

Inside the bus station was a tourist information booth attended by a horse faced woman wearing a straw cowboy hat and reading *True Movie Stars Magazine*. She had a huge wad of chewing gum, which she chomped on each time she turned a page.

I stood in front of the booth and watched her. She finally looked up and seemed to remember that she had been hired to do something other than snap gum and read Hollywood gossip.

"Howdy! Can I help you? Welcome to Gallup," Snap-snap-snap went the gum.

"What can you tell me about a place called Valenci?"

"It's an Indian pueblo about sixty miles south of here. There's not much to see there. If you want to buy Valenci jewelry, several stores here in town sell it. Zuni jewelry is very nice too. " She showed her teeth and shifted the gum to the other side of her mouth.

"Thanks. I'm not interested in jewelry. How do you get to Valenci?"

"I don't know," Snap, Snap, Snap. "Unless you have a car."

"There's no bus?"

"Nope. You have to drive. Unless you want to take a long hike,'" she added disinterestedly moving the mountain of gum to the other cheek.

"Which road do I take?"

Snap went the gum. "Straight out that street," she pointed, "for about thirty miles. When the paved road ends you turn west. It's another thirty miles beyond there to the pueblo. I'll tell you though, if you're going out there to buy Valenci pottery, they don't sell it anymore. " Snap, snap went the gum. "A lot of the stores here in town sell Acoma pottery. Is pottery what you want?"

"No, I'm not here for pottery."

"Well, what do you want?" The huge wad of gum fell partway out of her mouth before she shoved it back with her fingers.

"A ride to Valenci."

"You're not likely to get it," she said, and snapped the ball of gum before going back to her adult comic book.

That was a great introduction to the Wild West. I walked to the corner and looked south along the street that began the road to Valenci. Curio shops, furniture stores, restaurants, camera stores, souvenir stores and western clothing stores--it looked like a thousand other tourist trap towns.

I walked on. The paved sidewalk gave way to gravel road berm. I followed it up a slope and past a lumberyard, a filling station and an Indian trading post. At the top of a long hill outside of town I stopped. My breath made steam in the cold dry air. From there I could look ahead and see the road running over sandstone hills toward the south and Valenci. I ought to back into Gallup, hop a Santa Fe freight to the west coast, and forget this whole stupid mess. My shoes were covered with fine tan dust. Despite the cold temperature, the skin on my forehead felt dry and hot. My arms were beet red. For the first time I understood why cowboys wear big hats. For the first time I wished I had one too.

There was nothing to be seen. There were no shade trees. Away from town, on the far hills I could see what looked like patches of snow but here with me was nothing except sand, saltbush and sagebrush. I sat on a post at the edge of the highway and looked north back over the town. Not a car in sight coming my way and not a cloud in the sky to block the sun. How could the temperature be just above freezing when I'm sweating like a pig at election day? I reached into my pocket and retrieved the paperback novel the Lambs had given me for the bus trip. I tried to read until a car came by, but, it was much too bright out and the pages dazzled my eyes. I tossed the book into the weeds next to the road.

After what seemed like hours, I heard a car motor. An old rusty and battered pickup truck came toward me from Gallup. I jumped to my feet and stuck out my thumb. It's exhaust made a blue and white plume of vapor into the cold air. When it got close enough, I could see that it was crowded with people. To my amazement, it creaked to an uncertain halt almost directly in front of me. A young Indian boy jumped out of the cab and climbed into the bed of the truck. The driver, an Indian man, leaned over to look at me.

"Get in," he commanded.

"Thanks, buddy." I climbed into the cab beside a woman. She was dressed like the one at the station, a blanket like coat, and a long black skirt. She too had on jewelry covered with bright blue stones.

"Where are you folks headed?" I asked as they squeezed over to let me into the truck.

"Home." He ground up ten pounds of ancient transmission gears and we groaned back onto the road to continue our way south.

Through the rear window I could see into the bed of the truck. Five youngsters, half a dozen bags of groceries, two worn tires and an old woman seated in a ladder back wooden rocking chair made up the load. They were all expressionless.

"Listen," I said, "why don't you let me ride in the back and let that old woman ride up here?"

"Why?"

"Because she's an old lady and it's cold and windy out there in the open."

"That's why she gets to sit in the chair. If you were old, we might let you sit in the chair. But you aren't. You're young. You sit up here."

While I let that soak in, we rattled on at a flashy 20 miles per hour. The road, completely snow free, climbed up the edge of a line of stubby hills. Then it ran straight for a time and then suddenly tumbled down a heavily eroded bank, and across a dry streambed. The monotonous cycle of hill and dry creek bed repeated again and again.

"Where's home?" I finally asked. "Where do you folks live?"

I was hoping he was going to say Valenci, or at least that he lived somewhere close to Valenci.

"Chichilligato."

"What was that?" I asked.

"Chichilligato.

"That's what I thought you said. Are you a Zuni Indian?"

"No."

More hills rolled by. A few juniper trees, low and scraggly, freckled the hillsides. The whole countryside was bone dry. Out this far into the desert the dried up sage and saltbush looked as if they had been dead for generations.

"Are you going through Valenci to get to that place?"

"Nope."

"How close to Valenci are you going?"

"Right here," he slowed the truck and then turned onto a barely visible dirt track. He stopped the truck.

"You get out here. Valenci's that way." He pointed to the south along the main road.

"Thanks," I said as they drove away on the dirt track in a great cloud of fine tan dust and bright blue exhaust smoke.

Chapter Twenty-Five

Now I had really messed up. I was at least thirty miles out of Gallup and right in the middle of a god-forsaken desert. I hadn't seen a house since they picked me up. Half a dozen pinion pine trees created a small patch of shade at the edge of the road. I sat down in the shade to wait for death, or my next ride, whichever came first. A dry wind started to blow and dust devils formed on the roadside. No cars were in sight. Twenty minutes passed and still no cars came. I was miserable and starting to get very cold and I was thirsty as hell. I was going to throw a major pity-party before long.

I could see for miles in every direction and every direction looked the same. The sandstone hills were bare of visible vegetation. The bottom half of the hills was a dull brick red and the top part was tan. They were flat topped and deeply eroded, probably by wind because there sure wasn't any sign of water. It would have struck me as very beautiful if I hadn't been so wrapped up in my own self-pity.

I must have dozed off because I came back to consciousness to the sound of an approaching motor, but then I realized it came from the wrong direction. Disappointed, I sat back down in the shade. It was another pick-up truck, but this time it was a shiny new Chevy. Like the first truck, it was crowded with Indians. I was surprised when it stopped.

"Want a ride?" asked the driver.

"Thanks, but I'm headed in the opposite direction, towards Valenci."

"If you're still here when we come back, we'll give you a lift. He waved and drove on toward Gallup.

"If I'm still here? Good grief, am I going to be here forever?" Then it struck me. Two cars have passed me and both stopped. If I had been back East, I wouldn't have been able to get two cars to stop if three hundred had gone by.

Five minutes later car number three came from the direction of Gallup. I jumped to my feet and stuck out my thumb. He sped past and disappeared over the next rise. Oh well, I thought, two out of three is still a great average. A minute or two later he came back over the hill from the south. When he spotted me he slowed and stopped.

"I thought I saw someone. Need a ride, or would you rather freeze?"

"I sure do want a ride," I said and got in.

"Three out of three, unbelievable," I mumbled to myself.

"What was that?" he asked.

"Excuse me. I was just talking to myself. Do you know that since I started hitch hiking only three cars including yours, have gone by and each one offered me a ride? Isn't that something?"

"We don't pass up anyone out here if we can help it. This is no place to get into trouble. It's a long way between water holes in this part of the world." He was a large, suntanned man, dressed in a long overcoat and a western cut business suit. Most of the hair was gone from the top of his head, but he sported a generous sized, iron-grey handle bar moustache.

"Where are you headed, son?" he asked.

"I'm going to Valenci."

"Well now isn't that interesting, I'm going to Lava. I'll run you on over. Why Valenci? You got friends there?"

"It's a long story. Where's Lava?"

"Only a couple of miles this side of Valenci. You've never been here before?"

"No, sir. This is my first time."

"I thought so. You look like you're from back East someplace, and you sound like you're from the South. Am I right?" He looked me over carefully.

"Yes sir. I'm a genuine Hillbilly. I was born in West Virginia and I just got off a bus from Chicago."

"I've been in Chicago but I've never been to West Virginia. What's it like?" The tone of his voice made the question sound like a casual inquiry. Much later I realized that it had been the opening gun in a skillful cross-examination.

I told him some hillbilly stories. He laughed at all the right places, and that made me want to like him. I even started to like the miserable dry countryside after he talked about it for a while.

"What's your name, son?" he finally asked.

"Smith. "

"Is that right? Smith, what?"

"Okey P. Smith." I had done it again. I had hooked that stupid name to myself.

"Well, Mr. Smith, let me introduce myself. My name is Parks, Howard Parks. I'm the Law and Order man for the BIA. at Valenci."

A cop! I didn't know how I managed to do it, but there I was two thousand miles from home and already a cop had latched on to me.

"Is that some kind of policeman?" I tried to sound casual.

'"Oh yes, Mr. Okey P. Smith, you know damn well it's some kind of policeman."

We topped a hill and suddenly the country changed. Instead of seeing scrubby wastelands we were looking down into a wide valley ringed by bright red and. white-banded sandstone mesas. The sun was halfway down in the western sky. Purple and pink clouds wafted up from the horizon. It was still dry, but compared to the country we had just passed through it was an oasis. We drove past a redwood sign with an Indian design announcing "Welcome to Valenci, Land of the Giant Sky" in brightly painted red, white and yellow letters.

"You're in the Valenci nation, Mr. Smith. This is my jurisdiction. Perhaps I can be of some help to you. First you tell me who, or what it is you're looking for, and while we're having this little chat, suppose you tell me where you intend to stay while you' re here. "

He was a cop all right. Well, I had a choice to make. I could play it straight and hope he would mean what he said about helping me or I could make up a big lie and hope it was good enough for him to swallow.

"While you're trying to decide whether to tell me the truth or not, Mr. Smith, let me give you a little information. There is no motel or hotel or boarding house in Valenci, although you don't exactly look like you could afford it if they did have one.

The fact is, Mr. Smith, there are only two places for you to spend tonight. One is the jail in the Pueblo. I'm sure you have seen the inside of a jail before. We can let you stay there for free. The other place, Mr. Smith, is my home in Lava. If you would like, we'll see if you can't be our guest for the night."

He turned toward me. He had spoken in a quiet and very matter of fact way. There were no implied threats, he was quite explicit. For no logical reason I trusted him. Maybe it was because my brain had stopped working in the cold dry air or maybe it was because he had a highly developed skill for inspiring confidence. Most probably it was a fortuitous combination of both coupled with the fact that I was in real need of some help.

"Which one will it be, Mr. Smith?" His eyes were on the road and his voice was very soft. We slowed down. The paved road ended and we turned right, toward the north, and drove along a dirt road across the floor of the valley. The massive red and white mountains towered above us.

"Mr. Parks, if I told you the truth, you'd think it was a lie."

"Perhaps, but try me." He still wasn't looking at me.

We slowed, turned right again, passed beside a half frozen, reed clogged shallow lake and drove into a cluster of small buildings and houses.

I made one last effort to change the subject. "Is this Valenci?"

"No. It's Lava. Now what's it going to be, Mr. Smith? Are you going to tell that story?"

We were parked in front of a small clapboard covered white frame house. There was a single scraggly fruit tree of some sort in the dusty yard. There was much more dust and dirt than grass inside the fenced enclosure.

At first I meant to tell him only enough to get me off the hook and enlist his aid to help me find Charlie's boy. Then I got started talking and the first thing I knew I was running off at the mouth like a spring flood. He just sat there and frowned a little, or raised his eyebrows or grunted, but he never interrupted me a single time to ask a question. Almost an hour later, when I finally ran down, I realized I had told him the whole story--all about Charlie, Miss Lamb and the Professor and even about the dead woman over the poolroom. I had told him how we got Charlie's name, Taaiyalote Alowish mixed up and finally unraveled. I spilled all the beans.

At the end of my unexpected catharsis, he sat quietly for several moments. Finally, he looked up and said, "Let's go in the house and see what's for supper, Mr. Smith. After supper, I'm going to take you for a little walk.

"Not to the jailhouse, I hope."
"No," he said, "not the jailhouse."

Chapter Twenty-Six

Betty Parks was as far above the average cook as Dorothy Lamb was below.

"Are you sure you won't have just a little more, Mr. Smith?" she asked.

"Miss Betty, if I had room for more I'd eat it. But I'm full. This is the first really good meal I've had in months." It was no lie and she seemed to know it.

"If you're finished then, let's take that walk, Okey."

We walked across his yard and onto the dirt street. A hundred yards away from the house he stopped.

"Look over there and you'll know why this place is called Lava."

I looked and saw that the whole little community was built on the flat top of a huge ancient lava flow. The rock was as black as West Virginia coal.

"Must have been one hell of a big volcano," I commented.

"Yes, but that was a mighty long time ago even in geologic time."

"They do any mining around here, Mr. Parks?" The black rock made me think of the coal mining at my home in West Virginia.

"They've run samples on every square foot of the reservation, and there's absolutely nothing worth mining. Believe me, if prospectors had found oil or gold or anything else they could dig up and sell, then Valenci wouldn't be here today. As it is, there isn't one damn thing in or on this whole reservation that the white man wants, so he's left the Valencis alone. It isn't even on a direct route to anywhere so there are no paved roads and no railroads. It's the ultimate boondock. I firmly believe that is the greatest blessing they have, to have nothing."

We walked further out the dirt road and into a field of silver-brown grass clumps and sagebrush.

"Have a look over that way, Okey. "

I looked toward the Southwest and saw a mountain standing dead center in the great valley, yet towering a thousand feet above the valley floor. It was red and white banded, but the colors were even more vivid than those in the surrounding hills. Two tall rock columns stood freed from its deeply eroded side. A thick flat layer of brown sandstone capped the top of the mountain. Half a hundred gnarled black trees clung to its almost vertical sides.

"I've lived here for years and that mesa looks different every time I see it," he said.

"It's magnificent," I agreed. "I've never seen anything to match it."

"Those dried up little black bushes you see along the side there are peach trees. Believe it or not, Coronado's men planted them over four centuries ago, and they're still alive. Every year the Valencis still get peaches from them."

We stood for a while and watched the mountain change color and gradually fade from view as the twilight turned into darkness. The moment the light disappeared the cold began to ease into my bones.

"Does that mesa have a name?" I asked, as we started back to his house.

"On some maps: it's called Father Mountain. And I've heard it called Thunder Mountain. But that's not what the Valencis call it. To them, that mountain is sacred. They have their own name for it."

"What is it?" I was beginning to shiver.

He hesitated for a moment then stopped walking and looked directly at me.

"It's called 'Taaiyalote.'" Now Okey, before you start to ask me a lot of questions, I've a few more things to tell you. The first one is that I know every man, woman and child in Valenci, and there never has been a family here with the last name Alowish. The second thing is that 'Liawu' is an exotic name all right, and it sounds Indian. But Okey, Valenci women have names like Daisy and Evangeline and Celestina. I've never known or heard of a woman with the name Liawu. The third thing you need to know is that I have never known or heard of a Valenci man named Bentura. I've been the Law and Order man on this reservation for over twenty years and, if there were people here with names like those, I would know them."

"You mean all this time, somebody's been feeding me a line of pure baloney?" I was thunderstruck by his information. It was as if the last few months of my life had suddenly disappeared down a rat hole.

"It looks that way to me, It sure does."

We walked back to his house in silence. Now I was not only cold, but I felt empty inside as well. It was a long time before I could get to sleep that night. A thousand gloomy thoughts crossed and re-crossed my mind like water sloshing back and forth in the bilge of a tramp steamer. When I finally gave up and went to sleep, it was almost dawn.

Chapter Twenty-Seven

Howard Parks was an early riser. "Come on out of there," he yelled through my bedroom door. "All decent people have been up for hours!"

"You're worse than the rouser in a Chicago cage joint," I growled.

"You can explain what that remark means at the breakfast table," he laughed.

"Okey, since it seems like you have made a trip all the way out here for nothing," he said as we ate out breakfast, "Betty and I don't want you to go back to Chicago without something good to tell your friends about. We talked it over this morning, and we want you to spend a couple of days with us. You can meet some of the Valencis and when I get a little time I'll take you out to look over the reservation. Hell, we might even climb old Taaiyalote. How about it? Will you take us up on our offer?"

Nothing could have suited me better. I wanted a chance to clear my mind and his good intentioned proposition was made to order.

"That's wonderful! I accept, but, are you sure you can stand me for a few more days."

"Well, we'll try. Now the first thing we're going to do is get you some decent looking clothes," said Betty Parks. "Howard, you and Okey are about the same size. Give him something to wear so he won't look so much like some Eastern dude."

Twenty minutes later I was a genuine New Mexico cowboy, complete with ten-gallon hat, flap pocket corduroy jacket with tapered pockets, and a pair of wobbly high heel boots.

"You look almost civilized," Betty said with some doubt in her voice.

"I'm going to the pueblo in a few minutes," said Howard. "Why don't you ride over to the Tribal Council Hall with me, and while I'm earning a living, you can look around the town."

"If I can learn to walk straight in these fancy high heel shoes, I'll be ready to go with you."

The Council Hall, a rectangular, one story, pink stucco building, stood alone in the center of a dirt parking area on the north edge of the village. When Howard (I was no longer calling him Mister Parks) went into the building, I walked away on streets that were unpaved and deeply rutted. Dogs, chickens, and even a speckled pinto pony wandered unrestrained and unnoticed through the streets. A pair of scrawny turkeys, with their tail feathers missing, gobbled and quarreled in an empty lot. When a little Valenci boy tested his aim by throwing rocks at them, they ducked under a shed. One of his stones bounced off the door of a pick-up truck moving by in a cloud of red dust. The driver yelled at the boy and the boy ran away to hide with the turkeys. Red dust covered everything in sight.

It was apparent that most of the Valencis lived in houses clustered together on a low hill on the south side of the main road. The houses were box shaped and constructed with yellow ochre colored adobe bricks or purple sandstone blocks or both. A few daring souls had built ordinary cinderblock additions to their homes. Stubby, broken rock, and mud-daubed walls wound around the houses. Piles of kindling wood were stacked everywhere. Each household seemed to have at least one outdoor oven. Quite a few had more than one. The ovens were all beehive shaped and made with adobe bricks.

At one of the houses I saw a man chopping great piles of cedar wood. A woman was tending a roaring hot fire in an oven. I stood and watched. After the fire burned down to a mound of smoldering white ashes, the wife swept out the oven with a broom made of pinyon pine boughs. Then, using a long handle wooden paddle, she placed rolls of raw dough inside the heated oven and closed off the narrow opening with a flat stone. Later, I saw another woman using the same kind of wood paddle to remove hot baked loaves of bread from an oven. One woman I saw used a tattered and blackened old army overcoat for her oven door. Over the whole town, the fragrance of burning cedar wood and baking bread mingled with the stink of horse droppings and open sewers.

At the very top of a little hill, the houses were all flat roofed and stacked on top of each other like a disorderly pile of Lego bricks. The few that stood apart had roofs of every shape and style. Common to all the houses was the great number of wooden frame, glass paned windows in each wall. Almost all the window frames were painted white. Through open doors and windows I caught an occasional glimpse of linoleum floor rugs and overstuffed furniture. The pueblo swarmed with people. Old men and young men gathered in small groups to gossip. Women and children baked bread and hung out newly washed clothes on rooftop clotheslines. With one exception, there was nothing to distinguish the clothing the Valencis wore from that seen in any other American small town. The exception was the silk headband which most of the older men affected. Few of the people paid any attention to me as I squeezed between their houses, strolled through their courtyards and clambered over their roofs. The few who did, only smiled and nodded good morning.

I stood .in the very center of the pueblo and gazed at ten-foot thick walls that had once been part of an old mission church. The roof had long ago collapsed onto the floor of the nave. In front of the old ruin was a small cemetery. Its plain dirt surface was dotted with dirt coated artificial flower wreathes. Two very small stores, like old-fashioned grocery stores adjoined the pueblo structure. One proudly displayed a single gas pump and an empty rack for oil cans. The two made up the entire business district of Valenci. To the south of the village, a tiny, sluggish stream meandered, its course marked by patches of ice, faded green marsh grass, and an accumulation of garbage and empty beer cans. A crowd of small children played on the dirt banks and splashed through the icy water.

There was no question that Valenci was a city planner's nightmares come to life; on the other hand, it possessed a strange charm unlike any small town I had ever before visited. I had a sudden premonition that Valencia was going to become a very important part of my life.

Chapter Twenty-Eight

The sun blazed down. My feet made the decision long before my brain did that it was time to start hobbling my cowboy boots back to Howard Park's office in the Council Hall.

The shortest way appeared to lie between two sets of adobe houses and then up the hill through the center of the village. As I emerged from the narrow passageway, I found myself in a small closed in courtyard. The exit I had expected to see wasn't there. Inadvertently, I had wandered into a dead end. Irritated at myself, I turned to backtrack and found the only exit completely blocked by a large Indian man.

A flabby beer-belly hung over the strained waistband of his dirty blue overall pants. Muscles bulged through the sleeves of a too small T-shirt as he placed his hands on his hips and gave me a hard look. His head seemed to grow directly out of his torso without any intervening neck.

"Hey asshole, you lost or something?" he asked. His face was expressionless.

"I guess I took a wrong turn." He looked like more trouble than I could handle.

He shuffled closer to me.

"You God damn Anglos take a lot of wrong turns. Don't you? What's the matter with you? Are you all stupid, or something?"

It was very clear that he wanted trouble but I didn't.

"Look, if I've trespassed in your courtyard, I'm sorry."

He moved toward me again, this time forcing me to step backwards. The smell of whiskey surrounded him like a foul cloud.

" They tell me that all you white boys have chicken guts. What about you? Do you have chicken guts? Huh?" He bumped his fat belly against me.

I tried to walk around him. Without warning, his ham size fist lashed out and smashed against the side of my head. I staggered back and fell on the dirt floor. My eyes went out of focus and the whole world turned neon blue.

"You're a real smart ass, Anglo. You're a smart ass, and I don't like smart asses. I specially don't like you. Now, I've got a message for you, smart-ass. Go back where you come from. We don't want you messing around out here. Leave us alone or something a hell of a lot worse is going to happen to you."

With that he turned and swaggered out of the courtyard. Slowly and painfully I raised myself out of the dust, rolled over onto my knees and retched.

"Holy catfish, you look awful. What the hell happened to you?" exclaimed Howard as I dragged myself into his small office.

"I just got a message," I said and described to him what had happened.

"That sounds like something Luke Ring would do. He gets a load of liquor in him and then he gets nasty. We have to cool him off every week or so. File a complaint and I'll gladly jack up the jail and put him under it."

"Nah, to hell with him. It's not worth the effort. What I really want is to know what you make of that 'get out of town' message."

"I don't make anything of it. He was just drunk and spouting off. Cindy!" he yelled through the open door. "Cindy, get Chester and Rob to come in here."

"Yes sir, Mr. Parks. They both just came in the door," replied the Valenci girl in the outer office.

Chester was short, fat, and forty years of age. He was dressed in a crisply pressed brown police uniform complete with Sam Browne belt and an oversize silver and gold badge. The other deputy, Rob, wore an open neck blue shirt and blue uniform pants. He was half the age of Chester. His dark round face and inky black hair set off a physique that could have been used in a health club advertisement. Both tribal policemen had pistols strapped to their hips.

"Luke Ring is drunk and acting up again," Howard said to them. "Keep your eyes on him. I don't want him bothering Mr. Smith here or anybody else. Got it?"

"Got it, Boss. You don't need to worry about that jerk anymore," Rob said to Howard but looked at me.

"Chester, have you ever heard of a Valenci named Bentura?" Howard asked.

The older man screwed up his face to give the appearance of thought.

"Rob, have you?" Howard turned to the younger man.

"No, sir," said Rob.

"I haven't either," Chester joined in.

"What about a man named Alowish?"

"No, I haven't," said Rob. "Is he supposed to live around here?"

"No. I haven't either," added Chester.

"Do you know a woman named Liawu?"

"Named what?" asked Rob. "Would you repeat that, sir?"

"Liawu. "

Both Indian policemen exchanged puzzled looks.

"You know, I think maybe I have heard that name," said Rob.

"Where?" I interrupted eagerly. "Who is she?"

"Well, I've never heard of her. She doesn't live around here," Chester chimed in. "You must be mistaken," he said looking fixedly at Rob.

"No, I'm not. I've read about her. She's someone in a book."

"Someone in a book? Rob, you're full of it," said Chester.

"Sorry, guys, but you asked if I had ever heard the name and that's where I heard of her. I read about her in a book somewhere."

"I told you there is no one around here like that, " Chester added, with a bit more heat than the occasion seemed to call for.

"O.K., guys. Thank you both. Don't forget Luke Ring."

When they had gone, he turned back to me "Do you feel like going on a tour this afternoon, or would you rather put it off? How do you feel?"

"I feel fine. I hardly hurt at all. Let's do it."

We drove back to the Parks home. I soaked my sore head in the kitchen sink while he got his gear together.

We drove East through the valley and passed the intersection of the Gallup Road. Howard shifted into his role of unofficial guide.

" About 30 miles north east of here is a big rock named El Morro. It's a cliff with a water hole at the bottom of it. The early settlers carved graffiti all over the cliff. Not too long ago Congress made it a national monument. If you keep on going East, down the road past El Morro, you come to the town of Grants. A lot of uranium mines are located near Grants, so it's been a real modern day boomtown. You ought to see it and El Morro as well while you're out here."

"If Luke Ring has his way, I won't last that long," I whined.

"Are you still on about him? I told you he's nothing but a blow hard drunk. He has people buffaloed just because he's big and he's loud. Don't judge the Valencis by the likes of him. Most of them don't like him any better than you do. Give the folks here a chance. When you get to know them you'll discover the Valencis are the finest, most friendly people you'll ever meet. And as far as Luke Ring is concerned, if you want me to, I'll get Rob and we'll thrash the owls off his clock."

"Nah, forget it. My pride was hurt a lot worse than my head. I was just feeling sorry for myself."

"Don't let it get to you." he smiled. "I've lost track of the number of times I've been knocked on my ass."

Try as I might, I couldn't imagine anyone knocking Howard Parks on his behind. He just wasn't the type.

Chapter Twenty-Nine

We turned off the main road and wound our way up into the mountains on a steep and narrow dirt road. Patches of snow lay in the deep shady pockets in the mountainside.

"There are quite a few old ruins up in the mountains here," he said as he parked the car in the middle of the path we were following.

"Don't look at me like that. It's perfectly OK to park here. Ours is the first car that's been up here in months so we aren't exactly creating a road hazard."

"I thought you might like to get a look at one or two of them."

"One or two of the cars that haven't been up here for months?"

"Ha, ha. Very funny. Do you want to see these ruins or would you rather tap dance your way back home?"

Sometimes my sense of humor gets weird. We got out and walked a dozen yards across the hillside to the remains of a low stonewall. Snow still clung to the shady side of the wall.

"This one was once a Kiva."

"What' s a Kiva?"

"I thought you would never ask," he grinned at me. But, since you have, the best way I can describe it is to call it a combination church and lodge hall. The Valencis have a number of secret societies. Both male and female are initiated into them when they're very young. The place where they meet is called a Kiva. You may see some of the Kivas dance while you're in Valenci."

"Dance? Is more of your 'tap-dance' humor?"

"No, I'm quite serious. The word 'dance' is as good a description as any. It's a tribal religious observance. The members of the Kiva get all dressed up in traditional costumes and shuffle around in the pueblo for hours. It's their way to pray to their Gods for rain or crops and the like. It works too."

I let his last statement go by without comment. He couldn't have been serious about dancing for rain and getting it. So, it must be another joke. We walked for a while up the side of the mountain, stopping occasionally to look at the crumbling ruins of some ancient Indian structure. It was impossible for me to know what they had once been but it was obvious they were very old. Howard knew the history of some of them. We were getting higher on the mountain all the time. I suddenly realized that I was out of breath.

"How high have we climbed?"

"Valenci Pueblo is about 7000 feet above sea level. I guess we're a little over eighty five hundred feet along here. What's the matter? Is the thin air getting to you?"

"No. I feel fine." I lied. I was puffing like a worn-out steam locomotive.

I stopped to catch my breath and spotted a smooth, colored piece of clay on the ground. I picked it up and saw that it had an irregular design apparently molded into it.

"That's a potsherd," said Howard. "They're all over the place. It's a piece of a clay bowl or pitcher, of some kind that was dropped and broken by an Indian many years ago."

"How old is it?"

"It could be as much as a thousand years old," he said. "The Valenci have been around here since before 1100 A.D. and up here was one of their earlier villages. 'Broken-House,' the ruin I showed you back down at the intersection of the paved road is supposed to be the oldest, but I've always figured these up here were much older."

"Why? They all look the same to me."

"Well, the Valenci migrated here from Chaco Canyon, that's about one hundred and twenty miles north of here. And this place is closer to Chaco than 'Broken-House' is. But the thing that really makes me think it's older, is the fact that the Kiva ruins here are round and the ones closer to Valenci are rectangular."

"I don't get it."

"Chaco Canyon Kivas are round," he said. "So if they came from Chaco they probably continued for a few years anyway to do things the way they did them in Chaco. Later they might have changed. Does that make any sense to you?"

"I guess so. You're the expert."

He continued," The professors might not agree with me though. There's always some university professor poking around the ruins, they follow the Valencis around with tape recorders and cameras. They ask them more damn fool questions than you would believe possible. In the summertime they are as thick as mosquitoes."

"What do the Indians think about all those professors?"

"Some of them enjoy spinning lies for the anthropologists. Then when the professors are gone they sit around and laugh about the line of bullshit they palmed off. The Valencis are damn sharp. They have to be or they wouldn't have survived all these years."

We climbed the side of a very steep slope. Two hundred feet up we stopped. My legs felt like rubber bands.

"Look over there," he said pointing to the face of a cliff.

All I could see was brown sandstone, then suddenly I saw that carved into the sandstone cliff were dozens of weird little figures. Some looked like animals and some like dancing men. Some were spirals and some were wavy lines.

"What are those?" I asked.

"They're petroglyphs. No one knows for sure how old they are and no one knows, for sure, what they mean. Even the all-wise professors don't claim to understand what they were for. I get a big kick out of coming up here just to look at them. "

For more than an hour we moved slowly along the face of the cliff. The further up we climbed, the steeper the cliff and the trail became. As we got higher and higher the number of little dancing figures increased tenfold. Each figure had been pecked about an eighth of an inch deep into solid rock. Some were a foot high and some were as small as my hand. Some looked like strange little fat men playing musical instruments. Some were animals or insects and others were just designs. All of them appeared to be centuries old.

"Hey, Okey. Come over here," yelled Howard

"Where are you?" I couldn't see him.

"In here," he shouted. "Look what I've found."

I edged along the narrow cliff face and found that he had climbed a short way down into a opening in the side of the mountain.

"What is it, the mouth of a cave?" I asked leaning over his shoulder to take a look.

"It's not much of a cave. It only goes back about fifteen feet," he said. "We don't have big caves in this part of the state. Look what I found. Isn't that a beauty?"

He pointed to a large petroglyph carved into the rock wall at the back of the shallow cave.

"What is it? I can't see it good from here."

"Here, let me squeeze back by you, so you can get in and see it better."

Very carefully I moved around him and into the narrow hole.

"It looks like a sun and a cow and a bunch of guys drilling a hole," I laughed. "Maybe some unknown ancestor of Picasso drew it on a bad day."

"Let me see it again," he said.

I climbed out of the cave and sat down on the narrow path. From my perch I could see a long way up a U-shaped valley speckled with sagebrush. The blue sky out here in New Mexico seems a thousand times larger than it does in the East. Off in the distant valley a flock of sheep moved slowly across the valley floor. Heat waves shimmered off the sun-warmed rocks. A crow circled lazily high over his domain. I felt peaceful for the first time in many months.

After a while, Howard sat down beside me and lit a cigarette.

"Yes sir," he said," these petroglyphs are real mysteries. No one knows what they mean."

A faint bell rang in the back of my mind. I tried to summon up the thought for a few seconds but I couldn't'.

"Why are you looking so sober?" he asked.

"Oh, I thought of something just now but it slipped by before I could grab it."

"I do that sometimes too. Then I worry all day trying to remember what it was. The older I get the worse it is." He climbed slowly to his feet.

"Are you ready to go back?" I asked.

"Might as well. By the time we get to the car, it will be getting cold and dark. We'd better shake-a-leg too, because I didn't bring a flashlight. This mountain is no place to be in the dark."

Thousands of stars decorated the dark sky by the time we reached the car.

At the supper table I found myself again lost in a brown study.

"What's the matter with him?" Betty Parks asked.

Howard laughed. "Either he's gone over the edge or he's still trying to remember something he forgot. "

"Maybe Luke Ring hurt him worse than you think. "

"I'm sorry. There's nothing wrong with me. I was just day-dreaming."

As tired as I was, I still lay awake for a long time that night reviewing the events of the day and trying to recapture that elusive memory.

Chapter Thirty

When I got up the next morning, I found that Betty Parks had tacked a note to my door saying that breakfast-lunch was in the oven, and that she and Howard had driven to Gallup. It also said for me to make myself at home.

I ate and then sat listening to a radio station in Gallup. The president of Ireland was visiting in Washington, and Russia had signed a new loan agreement with somebody or another. I decided to walk into Valenci and let the world solve its own problems.

From Lava two parallel roads lead into Valenci. One, the main road, is a quarter of a mile south of the other. The other, lesser used, road follows the course of the Valenci river. That was the one I decided to follow. As soon as the road leaves Lava it descends a steep hill and then flattens out. It passes through dry fields where corn has been grown but only the stubble remains in this season. Betty had told me about the local corn planting. In the spring, the farmers plow up the ground and then into each mound of dirt they plant three kernels of corn. One kernel is for the Gods, one is for the crows and one is to grow. She told me that the Valenci planted Zuni corn. The Zunis had developed a dry land corn that required almost no rainwater to grow. Their special corn seed was valued highly amongst the Pueblo people and, in fact, the U.S. Department of Agriculture sent representatives to Zuni to learn the secrets of the Zuni corn.

As I walked, I saw two Valenci boys playing near a brush pile fence that surrounded one of the barren cornfields. They watched me coming toward them on the road. When I was close enough to be talked to, each boy raised his right arm and, with palm toward me, said, "Ugh." Then they dissolved in gales of laughter at the expression on my face. Only in Saturday afternoon cowboy movies do Indians say, “Ugh.”

I grinned at their joke, waved, and continued on down the road.

The post office in Valenci is housed in one of the small grocery stores across the road from the main pueblo structure. As I passed the open screened doorway, someone called my name.

“Mister Smith. Mister Smith. I have something for you," came a voice from the interior of the building.

“Who’s that? Did you say you had something for me?"

A smiling Indian lady dressed in a flowered dress came out of the building. "Yes. It's a registered letter or I would have delivered it to Mr. Park’s house on my regular route. I couldn’t do that because the Post Office rules say the addressee has to sign for it personally."

"How do you know who I am? And how did you know I’m staying with Mr. Parks?”

"Oh, everybody knows you, Mr. Smith," she smiled. “Now come in and sign for your letter.”

Small towns are the same the world over, I thought as I walked into the post office. Everyone knows everything about everybody. But, I couldn't deny I was sort of pleased to think that the Valencis knew who I was.

"Thank you for keeping it for me," I said and signed the receipt.

It was a fat brown envelope addressed to Okey P. Smith in care of General Delivery, Valenci, New Mexico. "Please Hold for Arrival" was hand lettered beside the typed address.

I tore open the envelope and removed a sheaf of legal size yellow tablet paper.

Attached to the top page was a square of notepaper with tight Spenserian handwriting on it.

"Dear Okey," it read. "I just wanted to append a note to father's letter. Take care of yourself and please come back to Chicago as soon as you're through with your business so we can hear all about it. Best wishes, Dorothy."

I wondered if I would ever go back to Chicago. Probably not, still it would be nice to see Dorothy again. Someday she might want to see me too. I walked outside and sat on a bench in front of the post office to read my letter.

"Dear Okey:

"After you departed on the bus, I returned to my library and decided to try to put together a few bits and pieces of information for you on some of the lesser known history of the Valenci people. By now you may have learned most of this yourself, since you seem to have an inquisitive mind, but I'm going to send it on anyway.

"At the present time it is believed that the Valenci is an amalgam of two earlier tribal groups, one group migrating from north of the present site of the Valenci Pueblo and the other coming from the south. How long ago this occurred we cannot be certain but it appears to have been about a thousand years ago. These two groups did not make war on each other but seem to have blended together and formed a new society. From the ruins throughout the valleys we conclude that this new group was scattered about the countryside in small family units. Perhaps, because of the hostile tribes to the west and south, they began settlements and gathered together to promote the common defense. This transition gradually occurred in the years from 1100 AD to 1300 AD. These dates are, of course, rough approximations that were secured from tree ring dating and from examination of potsherds. It seems clear that the newer, larger communities were highly organized not only along economic lines but also in ritualistic matters. The Anasazi or "the ancient ones," as they are known, buried their dead and many of these early burial sites have yielded valuable historical information. There is evidence too that cremation was performed by some groups in Valenci. The experts now think that cremations were a derivative from the southern band and the burials from the northern group.

"I'm sure when you were in school you read of Coronado's dismal exploits in that part of the world so I won't go into all that.

"By the way, I think you should be informed of a strange rumor. For years there has been a persistent story that a white man came to Valenci long before the days of Coronado. As far as I know, there has never been the slightest shred of proof that this ever happened. This mysterious man supposedly came from somewhere in the East, which makes it sound even more implausible, and, so the story goes, he remained in Valenci, eventually becoming some sort of tribal official. I mention this to you only so that if you should hear such a fabrication, you will know that there is no truth to it.

"Finally, I have some bad news for you. The name Taaiyalote is not likely to be correct. I did not realize when I heard you pronounce it, or should I say mispronounce it, but when correctly spelled and pronounced it is simply the name of the large plateau or mountain in the middle of the valley right where you are. This means that the name Alowish is also likely to be false.

"We both wish you luck in your quest. Dorothy speaks of you quite often.

"With kindest regards, Roscoe Lamb.

"P.S. We have watched the papers carefully and have found nothing about that supposed murder you discovered on Clark Street. I still do not think it wise to inquire. The police might be waiting for just such a mistake. --R. L. "

Chapter Thirty-One

I walked back to the Tribal Council building. Howard had not yet returned, so I sat in the outer office, thinking about the letter. Finally, tired of waiting, I wandered outside again and ambled around to the backside of the building.

"Hey, Anglo," came a whispered voice.

I looked behind me and saw a dark face in a small window recessed in the stone wall. Iron bars covered the window.

"Hey, Anglo, come here a minute. "

"What do you want?" The man calling me was in a cell in the jail in back of the tribal building. It must be the jail Howard had offered as an alternative to me on that first afternoon. I was glad I had chosen as I did.

"Anglo, they haven' t fed me. I'm starving to death. You're such a big shot, make them give me something to eat."

I moved closer to the window and then I could see his face. He was an Indian and appeared to be forty-five or fifty years old. His eyes were sunken in deep, dark ringed sockets and looked unnaturally large in his pinched face. His voice was an unpleasant whine.

"I'll go and ask," I said, and walked back into the Council building.

Once inside, I found the white steel door, which was the entrance to the jail wing. Alongside the door was a string of FBI wanted posters and a notice about V.D. prevention. An orange plastic forest fire fighter's helmet hung on a rack on the wall.

I walked into the adjoining room. A deputy I hadn't seen before sat behind a desk, slowly typing.

"Pardon me," I said. "My name's Okey Smith, and.. ."

"Hey, Mr. Smith. I know who you are. I'm John Perez. I'm the office deputy. What can I do for you?"

"I was standing outside, back of the building, just now, and some guy in one of your cells yelled at me and said he was starving. Do you think you ought to see about him?"

John Perez looked at me with a puzzled expression, then sat down and ran his fingers over a set of file cards in a holder on his desk.

"Mr. Smith," confusion clearly demonstrated by the tone of his voice, "we have no one in the jail today."

"Maybe they forgot to make out a card for him. Maybe he came in late, or drunk or something." I fished for an explanation.

"Well, tell you what, I'll look in there and see," he said cheerfully. He grabbed up a ring of large keys and walked into the room behind the white steel door. I heard him insert the key and slide open the door. A minute later I heard him closing the door and returning.

"Mr. Smith, there's no one in there. I looked in every single cell and as far as I'm concerned, they're empty."

"I guess it was just my imagination." I didn't know what Perez was trying to pull, but I resolved to wait and ask Howard about it when he returned.

"How long are you going to be with us, Mr. Smith?" he asked as he sat back down at his desk.

"Not long. I came here looking for some people, and no one seems to have heard of them. I guess I'll be moving on pretty soon now."

"Mr. Parks mentioned those names to me," he said, "and I've never heard of any of them before."

"Rob said he read about one of them in a book somewhere, but he couldn't remember what book he had read it in."

"Rob is a good man," said Perez seriously. "His grandfather was an important person here in Valenci before he left to go to the city. Did you know that Rob's parents were both killed in an automobile accident last month?"

"No. What happened? "

"They were on their way to Gallup and some drunk driver ran into them. The drunk was killed and both of them were killed, too."

"I'm sorry. That's really terrible."

"It was hard on Rob. His only brother died in Korea, so he's pretty much alone now."

"Is Rob a full time policeman?"

"He sure is. He's the best we have. He might go to college someday. He isn't afraid of anything. Some of the deputies don't like to go out on patrol alone, but he doesn't mind. He isn't afraid of witches either."

"Witches?"

"Some, mostly the old people, still believe in witches. Like that guy Luke Ring who bothered you yesterday--he claims to have an in-law that's a witch. He doesn't, but he has some people really scared. Not Rob, though. Rob says this witch business is a load of crap."

"Well," I laughed, "I hope Rob is right. I'd hate to run into a real live witch out here."

"I see you and John are hard at work wasting Uncle Sam's tax money," came Howard's voice from the door.

"When did you get back, Mr. Parks?" asked John.

"Just now. Okey, come on into my office."

"Howard," I said after he closed the door, "something very strange happened a few minutes ago."

"Good. I was afraid a whole day would pass without something strange happening to you. What happened this time?"

I repeated the story of the face at the jail window and Deputy Perez claiming not to find anyone in the cell.

Howard smiled. "I can explain that. You saw someone all right. I put him in there myself. It's a worthless character named Larry Denti. He got drunk and started raising hell late last night; long after you went to bed. They called me, so I came down and locked him up. I'll probably turn him loose after while."

"Well, why--"

"Why didn't Perez admit he saw him?" he finished my question. "John didn't see him because, to John, he doesn't exist."

"Doesn't exist? What do you mean?"

"Larry Denti and his good-for-nothing brother, I believe his name is John, used to be Valencis. In any event, they got into some sort of a scrape with the tribe. The version I heard was that they stole a lot of tribal relics and sold them to an Indian trader in Colorado. Well, whatever they did," he paused to light his cigarette, "was bad medicine. The Cacique and the other religious leaders got together and the next thing the Dentis knew they were banished from the tribe. At least that's the story I'm told."

"You mean they had to get out of Valenci?"

"No. That's the funny part of it. I'm told they didn't have to leave. They just became non-people. They can stay in Valenci, but no one will have anything to do with them. What I'm trying to say is that as far as the Valencis are concerned, the Dentis no longer exist."

"That sounds pretty rough."

"I've thought about it-occasionally, and, in my opinion, it's just about the worst thing that could happen to anyone--to be completely ignored by everyone around him."

"So," he continued, "if what I've told you is true, John Perez wasn't deliberately lying to you. John is a dedicated member of one of the Valenci religious orders. Very probably he really did not see Denti."

"That's a little hard to believe," I said. "Self-induced blindness to only one thing in a room full of things? I can't buy that."

"You'll see and hear a lot of things in Valenci that wouldn't be believable if they happened anywhere else in the world. I may as well admit to you that I have seen things happen out here that would be called miracles in a white society. Someday, if you stay here long enough, you may see one of them for yourself."

"Are you recruiting for the tribe or just acting as a tourist agent," I asked jokingly.

"Afraid not. They don't sell tribal membership like some of your moth-eaten animal lodges back in the East," he replied with a wry smile.

"By the way, what happened to the other Denti brother?"

"You mean John Denti? I don't really know what happened to John. He hung around for a while and tried to suck up to some of the B.I.A. people without any luck. Then he got to drinking pretty heavy and finally he just left. He was a great big son-of-a-bitch and mean as hell. I haven't seen John Denti for a long time. "

We sat silent for a few moments.

"Oh, I just thought of one more thing about the Dentis that might interest you," he said.

"What's that?"

"Luke Ring, the guy who gave you such a bad time--he's their brother-in-law. He married the Denti's sister. I don't remember what her name was. She died several years ago. In any event, it's the Denti's mother, Mora, who everybody says is a witch. She's Luke Ring's mother-in-law."

"I've heard her mentioned so often, I'd like to see her sometime," I said.

"She's been gone from here for almost a year now. I'll tell you this; if you ever did see her, you wouldn't forget her. She was a great big horse of a woman who always dressed in black. She really looked like a damn witch. Now go and stick your nose in one of those magazines and let me get some work done before we go home for supper. O.K.?"

"O.K.," I agreed.

Chapter Thirty-Two

I picked up a pencil and a yellow tablet and absentmindedly started to doodle while I thought about what Howard had told me about the Dentis and Mora, their strange mother. My thoughts drifted back further. Charlie kept flashing in and out of my mind. Then I started to worry about Bentura again.

Hey, Okey, you've just drawn the Allolowishkeh," said a voice over my shoulder. I snapped out of my daydream, looked up and saw Rob standing behind me.

"A what?"

"Allolowishkeh," he said with a grin. "Don't tell me you don't know what that is?"

"Well, I've always suspected that I could be a great artist, but this thing is just a spiral doodle. To be honest, I was so wrapped up in my thoughts that I wasn't paying any attention to what I was doing. What did you call my beautiful picture?"

"Allolowishkeh," he repeated. "My grandfather said the Allolowishkeh represents the story of the ancient ones who traveled around and around the whole universe in search of the very center so that they might settle down and build their permanent home."

"Were the 'ancient ones' the Valencis, by any chance?" I asked.

"No. They were the ancient ones. Only after they settled down here at the base of Taaiyalote did they become Valenci."

"Pronounce the word, once more, please," I asked.

"It's like All-Low-Low-Wish-Ca", he enunciated each syllable.

"Al--low-wish. . .", I started.

"You Anglos are all alike, " he laughed. "You can't speak right. You have the accent all wrong, and you forgot half the syllables. When you say it, it sounds like Alowish. It's Al-low-low-wish-ca, not Al-low-wish.

Howard and I looked at each other. Rob had just pronounced us the other half of Charlie's name--Alowish. Taaiyalote Alowish. Then Rob realized what he had said.

“Wow, somebody sure has been giving you some weird stuff," he said shaking his head.

"Well, whoever that somebody was, he knew an awful lot about Valenci," said Howard.

"He sure did," I agreed.

Chapter Thirty-Three

"Did I tell you about our gold mine?" asked Howard as we sat around the table after dinner.

"You've certainly never told me about it," said Betty. " As a matter of fact, Okey, the only time he tells anything is when we have company. I look forward to company just to find out what's going on in the world." Her tone showed she didn't mean her comment to be taken seriously.

"No, you haven't told me about it. Either," I added maliciously.

"Well, it isn't worth all this production," he growled. "Anyway, an old Valenci man named Hassigo, claims he has a secret gold mine. He's sort of a full time crackpot. He spends most of his days fishing up at the lake. Normally no one would pay any attention to him, but once a year he vanishes for a few days, and when he comes back he has just enough gold to keep him in food and fishing gear for another year."

"That's a lot of gold," I said.

"By your standards it might be, but old Hassigo is pretty much of a hermit, I'd guess his needs are few. It wouldn't take much gold to keep him happy. "

"Where does he get the gold?" I asked.

"I've already told you, from a secret gold mine. He won't tell anybody where it is. Occasionally someone tries to follow him on his annual pilgrimage, but he's too sharp for them. Before long, they discover they' re following their own tracks, and old Hassigo has disappeared into the mountains."

"I thought you said geologists tested the whole reservation and found nothing worth mining. "

"That's right, they did, but they couldn't cover every square inch. Occasionally, in this region, you will find a little bit of gold. But the vein is always thin and it takes a hell of a lot of time and work to get it out. "

"But you said," I persisted, "that he would only be gone a few days."

Howard laughed out loud. "Boy," he said, "nothing gets by you this evening. Well, try this on for size, Perry Mason. The gold he gets is not dust and its not nuggets."

"Well, what is it then?" asked Betty.

"It's plate. Hammered plate. Little paper thin pieces of beaten gold, and every one of them have a small round hole."

"I don't believe a word of that," said Betty. "You don't find hammered plate gold in a gold mine. He probably steals it some place.

Before Howard could answer her, the telephone rang in the kitchen. Howard answered it and, from the tone of his voice it was apparent that he didn't like what he was being told.

"What is it, Howard?" asked Betty when he returned to the room.

"I'm sorry, but we've got to break up this party. I've got to go to the office."

"Is there anything I can do?" I asked.

"Yes, maybe there is. All three of my deputies are over in Ramah tonight helping out the Navajo Police on a rape case. I might need a little help with this one, so, since you volunteered..."

All of a sudden I wished that I had kept my big mouth shut, at least until I knew what I was 'volunteering' for.

"Howard, don't you get hurt and don't you let Okey get hurt either."

"No problem. It's just a routine drunk-on-a-rampage case. We should be back before midnight, but don't wait up."

Ten minutes later, we were leaving the Valenci Tribal Police office. On the way to the car I noticed that distant heat lightning flickered on the horizon.

"Looks like rain," I said casually in an effort to cover up the nervous feeling that had begun to creep over me. "So, where are we going, and why?"

"We're headed up in the general area of that mountain where we took our hike the other day. We're going up there to try and catch a guy who got all tanked up in one of those bars outside the reservation. He left the bar and went to this lady's house and broke in. He stole her husband's 30-30 rifle and told her and the kids that he was going to kill a damn lawman. Then he said if they told anyone he would kill them too. Finally, before he left, he said something about killing himself. The lady said she did not recognize him. She told one of her neighbors, and it was the neighbor who called me. We're going to stop by their house and see if there is any more information before we go see if we can find him."

Chapter Thirty-Four

The soft glow from the dashboard lights illuminated our faces. The night seemed to grow darker. The heat lightning continued to flicker on the horizon. Our headlights picked up the flashing white tail of a deer running across the highway.

We drove steadily on for another half an hour.

Howard broke the silence. "The lady who called said they would meet us at her house. That ought to be just up ahead here.

"Are they going with us?" I asked hopefully.

"Nope. It's just you and me."

"Oh?" I experienced a sudden queasy sensation in the pit of my stomach. The car headlights swept across a small group of people standing on the road beside a pickup truck.

"That's them," he said. He parked our car just behind the pickup.

As we opened the doors to get out, two men, a woman, and three small boys rushed to gather around Howard. They spoke and gestured so excitedly that I could not understand a word they were saying. After a time, Howard walked around the front of his car and looked into my window.

"Well, it's like we thought. He's got a gun and some shells. It's an automatic rifle and he took a whole box of shells in addition to whatever was in the gun. He ran off up that ridge. We'd better get on up there after him before he hurts himself or somebody else."

He opened the car door and removed a flashlight from the glove compartment.

"I have only the one light," he said. "I forgot to bring another one."

"That's O.K. I don't intend to get very far away from you," I chattered nervously.

"Let's move 'em out then.

We climbed over a low brush fence and started up a narrow ridge. Except for the circle of light from his flashlight, we were submerged in the inky black night.

"Be careful. Don't fall into one of those little ditches. The ground is pretty well broken up around here, so be careful."

"I'm with you, Chief"

We walked on for another twenty minutes. Our boots made crunching sounds in the sandy soil. Occasionally, we stopped and listened to the soft noises of the night.

"How do you know we're going the right way?" I asked during one stop.

"Well, I think I'm tracking him. See there?" He shined his flashlight onto the ground a yard ahead of us. "See that heel mark? That's the trail I'm following."

I looked and saw the clear imprint of a boot heel in the dusty soil.

"How do you know it's his?"

"I don't know for sure, but I saw several of those prints down where we parked. See that notch in the heel print? Well, the tracks are fresh and they aren't yours and they aren't mine, and as far as I know, we're the only three people up here tonight. So they must belong to our man, right?"

"I'm still with you."

We walked on, climbing over quick rises and sliding on our heels down deep draws filled with sagebrush and sharp pointed prickly pears.

"Watch out for rattlers. "

"Sure!" Now I had something more to worry about. I wished he hadn't warned me.

The night gathered still closer around us like a pall. Except for an occasional screech owl, our feet made the only sound as we stumbled across rocks and crackled through the dry scrub brush.

"Where do you suppose he is?" I needed another break to catch my breath.

"Well, you never can tell. He might even be dead. A guy like that is unpredictable. He could have hanged himself on one of those pine trees along the ridgeline there. I ran across a man once who hanged himself on a fence post. When a man is set on killing himself, he's usually successful. If that's what he was out to do, we'll come across his body before long. "

We started uphill again, but this time Howard switched off the flashlight.

"No use giving him too good a target," he said. "I've got a feeling we're getting pretty close."

“Do you think he knows we're here?"

"If he isn't dead, he's sitting somewhere up in those rocks watching us with that rifle in his hot little hands."

A rancid ball of fear formed in my throat and slid down to lodge in my stomach.

"Howard, I hope you know where we are because I sure don't. We've circled around so many different ways, that I'm completely lost."

"I have a pretty good idea of where we are. See that glow in the sky over there?"

I looked and couldn't see any difference in the sky. It all looked black.

He chuckled softly. "Well, I see it anyway," he said. "It's a reflection from the city lights in Grants. Oh sure, that’s a long way from here, but it helps keep you on the track even this far away. You easterners must think the nights are mighty dark out here on the desert."

"They are."

We crossed a barbed wire fence line and scrambled on our hands and knees up a steep crumbling bank.

"Along that ridge over there, to the northeast," he pointed off into the blackness, "is where we took our hike the other day."

"I liked that hike a hell of a lot better than this one."

Suddenly he stopped. "Listen!" he whispered, and put his hand across my lips.

I listened but I heard nothing except my own labored breathing.

"What is it?" I whispered.

"He's up on that hill. I'm sure I heard him." Howard spoke softly but rapidly. "I hate to do this to you, but now is when I need your help. I want you to stay low along the edge of the hill here and walk slowly in that direction. Keep moving until you come to the end of the hill. Don't go too fast. Take this light with you and keep it close to the ground. Don't swing it around. I'm going to the top of the hill, and try to flush him out."

"What will I do if he comes out on me?"

"Same as I'm going to do--figure it out when the time comes. Keep in mind, though, that he'll be a lot more frightened than you are."

I knew that was a lie. No one could be more frightened than I was.

"Listen," I said, "since you're going up where he's likely to be, you take the flashlight."

"Quiet!" he commanded in a whisper.

From the top of the hill came a sound straight from the bottom pit of hell. It was a long, wavering, gut-tearing moan. Goose pimples formed all over my body.

"Let's get going," said Howard. He vanished up the hillside as silently as fog moving across a lake.

I snapped the light on and began to stumble around the base of the hill. From time to time, I turned the flashlight off and stood quietly as I tried to pick up any sound from Howard or the man we sought. Nothing. No sound. Not even a cricket. The air was heavy. It felt like it does before a rainstorm. I stumbled on.

Ten minutes later, I reached the extreme limits of the base of the hill and nothing had happened. I sure hope Howard knows where I am, I thought. I turned off the light, and leaned against a rock. Sweat rolled down the inside of my shirt. It was actually cold out. I wasn't that hot. Most of the sweat came from raw fear. Somewhere off to my right a twig snapped.

"Howard? Is that you?" I whispered.

There was no answer. If it weren't Howard, then it had to be the guy with the gun. If it's him, then he heard me, and knows where I'm standing. I'd better move. I didn't dare turn the flashlight on for fear I would be seen.

Then I heard another sound- a footstep. It was even closer. My knees felt weak. I moved slowly and awkwardly to the left. It was no more than ten paces before I tripped and smashed my cheek against a sharp rock. Blood drained down my face and gathered on my jaw. The flashlight rolled down the slope and came to rest with the beam shining on the sky. I slowly pulled myself up and rubbed at the blood. I must be too close to the bottom of the hill. Maybe he wanted me to climb up higher. I scrambled up the incline. Loose rocks, dislodged by my hands and feet, clattered down the hillside. I sounded like the Russian Army trying to sneak through a nursery. Howard didn't say to climb; he said to stay at the base of the hill. I wanted to go hack down again and get the flashlight, but if I went down that guy might be waiting for me. Indecision locked me into position.

"Anglo, you were told to leave Valenci! Now it's too late for that."

In a panic I jerked around, but before I could cry out, I felt a sharp blow on the side of my head. My last hazy memory before total unconsciousness was trying to yell to warn Howard. I tumbled down the side of the hill.

It may have been a few seconds or it may have been hours before I became vaguely aware of the world around me. I was lying on my face in a rock-strewn pit. My head was about to explode. My ears rang. It was so very dark. I rolled to my back and tried to sit up. A tide of nausea swept over me and I again lost consciousness.

Chapter Thirty- Five

"How badly is he injured, Doctor?" The voice through the haze sounded like Howard Parks.

"He's had a moderately severe concussion, and he's covered with deep lacerations and abrasions. It looks like somebody, or some thing, decided to pound on him with something."

"Yeah, with my good flashlight," said Howard.

"Well, I've sewed up his head, and the other deep cuts. He should regain consciousness soon, but he must remain in bed for a day or so. He can stay here in the hospital. We're not overcrowded. "

I opened my eyes and the world swam into focus.

"Here he comes now," said Howard. "Okey, are you with us again, boy? Can you hear me?"

I was in a hospital room. Howard and a doctor stood beside the bed and stared down at me. A nurse moved across the end of the room.

"I'm O.K.," I mumbled, looking at all the bandages.

"Sure you are," he said. "You're just fine. But what happened to you? Did you just fall, or did something else happen?"

"Somebody hit me. "

"I'm sure he's right," said the doctor. "His wounds have all the appearance of blows from a dull instrument. It could easily have been your flashlight."

"Who hit you?" Howard asked.

"I don't know. I guess it was that guy we tracked. Did you get him?"

"I got what was left of him."

"What do you mean?"

"When I finally got to him, he was dead. He had taken a piece of barbed wire, made a noose and hanged himself from a juniper snag stuck out over the edge of a cliff."

"I'm sorry. I guess it wasn't he who hit me."

"You're sure somebody hit you. You didn't just fall?"

I repeated, as best I could remember, what had happened after we separated. "OK, you get some rest, buddy. They'll take good care of you here at P.H.S. I'll see you later on. Watch out for him, nurse," he grinned. "He has a bad habit of pinching pretty girls."

The nurse frowned and stuck her nose in the air. She had heard this line too many times before.

I remained in the Public Health Service Hospital two full days. During that time I was treated like visiting royalty. Howard and Betty, John Perez, Rob, Cindy, and a dozen others came by to see how I was getting along. No one mentioned my claim that I had been the victim of an assault and battery.

Shortly after lunch on the second day, a surprise visitor added his unwelcome name to my guest list. Luke Ring came unannounced into the room. The corridor outside was empty. I felt well enough to climb out of the bed and run, if I had to. Surprisingly, Luke didn't have that hostile look on his face he had used on me in the Pueblo courtyard.

"I hear you got hurt, Mr. Smith. Are you hurt real bad?" he almost smiled.

"What's on your mind, Ring? Are you here to give me a hard time again?"

"Aw, listen, Mr. Smith, that don't mean nothin'. I wasn't really trying to hurt you. I just got a little drunk, that's all. I didn't mean to push you around none. I was out of my head. You know how it is."

"Are you the sonofabitch who hit me on the head up on the mountain?" I didn't really expect him to tell me the truth but I did want to rattle his chain.

"No sir. Honest to God that wasn't me. That's what I come to tell you. Mr. Parks and his deputies worked me over pretty good yesterday. He said he figured I was the one that put you in the hospital, but that ain't true. That's why I'm here. I want you to tell him it wasn't me. I wouldn't do nothing like that. Hell, I wasn't nowhere near you that night, and I can prove it."

"Is that the reason for this visit, to tell me you're innocent?"

"No. I want to make up to you for what I did when I was drunk and couldn't help myself."

"Get to the point."

"I want to tell you something."

"What?"

"I want to tell you who it was that told me to push you around the other day. He's probably the man who put you in the hospital this time."

I sat up excitedly. "Who? Who is it?"

"It's Rob Gaiule. "

"Who?"

"Rob Gaiule, the cop. You know, the one that works for Law and Order under Parks. He's the one. He told me to scare you and he probably hit you on the head."

I laid back down on the bed again. "Luke Ring," I said.

"Yes?"

"You're as full of shit as a Christmas turkey. "

He glared at me in an oafish way for a moment and then turned and stormed out of the room.

Chapter Thirty-Six

I pushed open the door to Howard's office. He and Rob Gaiule were engaged in conversation.

"I can't understand it, Mr. Parks." Rob was leaning across Howard's desk,

"Well, what exactly are they doing?"

"It's hard to describe, but they aren't treating me like a policeman any more."

"You mean they're giving you a hard time?"

"No, that's not it, they..."

"Excuse me, gentlemen," I said.

"Well, look who's here! Welcome back, Okey! When did you get out?" Howard stood smiling and reached out to shake my hand.

"How do you feel, Mr. Smith?" asked Rob.

"Fine, thanks. They let me out about an hour ago. I'm feeling just fine, Rob. The Doctor at P.H.S. said my head must be made out of pig iron."

They made appropriate noises.

"I'm sorry. I didn't mean to interrupt your conversation. I'll come back later."

"No. Sit down, Okey. You'll be interested in hearing what Rob has to say. Bring him up to date, Rob. "

"Well, I was just telling Mr. Parks that the people are treating me funny."

"No, not that. Tell him what happened before that. "

"You mean the phone call?"

"Yes. "

"Well, O.K. The night you got hurt, Mr. Smith, I came back from Ramah Navajo reservation. We had been over there helping them on a rape investigation. I had the late night duty, here at the office. About 1:00 a.m. the phone rang and the call was from the police in Hastings, Nebraska. They said some old woman was found in a boxcar, in the railroad yard, and they thought she might be a Valenci. They said she was hurt pretty bad and might die. She was suffering from malnutrition and exposure, and she appeared to have been beaten severely."

"Who is she?" I asked.

"We don't know that yet."

"Tell him what you did, Rob. "

"Well, I asked them how they knew she was a Valenci. They said some doctor in the hospital up there told them he had worked in Valenci at the P.H.S. a few years ago, and that he knew she was a Valenci from the way she talked. They said he even thought he had seen her before."

"Wow, that's a real coincidence, if it's true."

"It's not as unusual as you might think, Okey." Howard explained. "We've had a lot of young doctors through here. Sometimes we have four or five at a time. They're always fresh out of medical school and usually they only stay here for about a year."

"So you don't know who the doctor is?"

"No. The only people I've talked to are the Hastings police, and they just relayed what they had been told."

"What did they want you to do?" I asked. I didn't know where this conversation was leading, but I was in no hurry to change the subject.

"They wanted to know if we have any old ladies missing."

"Well, do you?"

"No. Certainly none that I know about."

"Since then, Rob has checked pretty carefully. If he says there aren't any missing, then there aren't any missing," said Howard.

"Well, anyway, I told them I would call them back. Then I put in a call for Mr. Parks. Mrs. Parks answered, and she said the two of you were up on the mountain somewhere near Big Rock. So I called John Perez. He came back from Ramah with Casper and me. He got out of bed and got dressed, and came over and took charge of the office. I got in the Patrol Wagon and went to see if I could find Mr. Parks and you."

"It's a good thing he did, too," Howard injected. "Otherwise, I never would have gotten you out of that hole."

"I didn't know you were up there that night," I said, remembering Luke's visit to my hospital room and what he had said about Rob.

"We loaded you and the corpse, too, into the back of the wagon and brought you to P.H.S."

“Yuck. Me and a corpse sharing a bed.”

"You shouldn't mind," said Howard, "the corpse was an old friend of yours."

“What do you mean ‘a friend of mine’? Who was it?”

"Larry Denti. The guy in the cell, the wild-eyed one who doesn't exist?"

“He was a no-good bum," Rob said with considerable feeling."

"Well, get on with the story. "

"When we finally got you in the hospital," Rob continued, "I came back to the office here. It was almost dawn, and I was afraid John Perez was going to be mad as hell because I left him here to finish out my full shift."

"Now here comes the part I really can't understand," said Howard.

"I walked in to the office and there sat Chester asleep at the desk."

"The pride of the police force, old Chester himself," said Howard.

"Well, when he woke up he was mad," said Rob. "He said John Perez awakened him at two-thirty in the morning, and asked him too take over the office. He said he came down, and as soon as he got here, Perez took off somewhere without any explanation at all."

"It gets more peculiar," said Howard. "When I got to the office and heard the story, I drove over to John Perez's house. His wife said he came home in the middle of the night, packed a bag and left."

"Left for where?" I asked.

"Left for Hastings, Nebraska!"

"You’re kidding. Hastings? Why?"

"I wish I knew," said Howard.

Chapter Thirty-Seven

"It was a very busy night for all of us." Again, I thought about Luke's story, which I had once rejected as ridiculous.

"Then yesterday is when all this other stuff started," continued Rob.

"You may as well tell him about that too." Howard directed.

"People started treating me funny."

"What people?" I asked, puzzled.

"The old people. John Perez's wife has been all over the Pueblo talking to the old people. I found out that much. Now the old people are treating me funny. "

"This is about where we were when you came in, Okey," said Howard. "Now, explain to both of us what you're talking about, Rob."

"Well, that's just it, I can't. It doesn't make any sense. They're simply treating me funny."

Rob was unable to articulate exactly what change had occurred. Whatever it was, it was making him very uncomfortable. I looked at him for a while and then made up my mind, Rob was a damn good man. Luke Ring had lied to me, for sure.

"Let me add to the confusion," I said.

"Be my guest," Howard responded, without enthusiasm.

"I had a visit from Luke Ring while I was in the hospital."

Howard interrupted me in an angry tone. "I told that sonofabitch to stay the hell away from you."

"He didn't bother me, but he did give me a message. "

"What big threat did he make this time?" asked Rob.

"He said you were the one who told him to rough me up the other day in the Pueblo, and, that you were the one who hit me over the head on the mountain."

Rob leaped to his feet, and, with a loud angry statement in Valenci, started for the door.

"Rob! Sit down!" Howard ordered.

Rob's face was black with anger. The veins in his neck stood out in hard ridges. He sat down on the front edge of the wooden chair.

Howard turned to me. "Now let's get this straight right now. Do you believe what Luke said?" he asked.

"I told Luke he was full of shit."

"You didn't answer my question." Howard wanted there to be no doubts left on this subject. "Do you believe what Luke said?"

"When Luke told me the story, I didn't believe a word of it. Then, just now, when I learned Rob was on the mountain that night, I had a brief moment of doubt. While you two went on talking, I resolved that doubt. I am now absolutely certain that Rob had no connection with my injury or with Luke Ring. Is that direct enough?"

Howard turned to Rob. "Does it satisfy you?"

"Yes, sir. I'm glad Mr. Smith knows I didn't hit him over the head. Now can I go?" He started out of the chair again.

"Hold on, my friend. Just where is it you're going?"

"I'm going after Luke Ring. I'm going to kick his ass clear up to his shoulder blades."

"That's what I thought. So just sit right where you are. I don't want you off somewhere half-cocked and adding to the confusion. I want Luke Ring, but I want him in condition to talk. Cindy!" he called through the closed door.

"Yes, sir?" she opened the door.

"Cindy, get all the other deputies in here as quick as you can. Then put in a call to the police in Hastings, Nebraska. Tell them I want to speak with someone who knows the details on a telephone call that was made to us about an old woman in the Hastings hospital. Got that?"

"Yes, sir. Mr. Parks. Oh, there's somebody waiting out here to see you when you have time."

"I'm too busy to see anybody now. Tell them to come back later. Who is it anyway?"

"He says his name is John Denti."

Howard looked at me and then at Rob. The antique octagonal wall clock counted out five seconds before he finally spoke.

"Tell him I'll see him in just a few minutes. Now get busy with those calls."

She closed the door.

"I wonder where he showed up from? John Denti is all I need to make this day complete," said Howard. "I suppose he's here to find out what happened to his dead brother."

"Can I go get Luke Ring now?" Rob tried again.

"Can you do it without losing your cool?" Howard directed an even look at Rob.

"I won't harm a hair on his ugly head."

"O.K. Then bring him in. But if you mess him up, you're fired, and I'll personally kick your butt all the way to the Federal Courthouse in Albuquerque."

"I'll treat him like a member of the family."

The door opened as Rob reached for the knob. Cindy stuck her head in the room.

"Mr. Parks," she said, with an exasperated look on her face. "That man that said his name is John Denti has left. I told him you were busy with Rob and Mr. Smith and that you'd see him in a few minutes. Then I put your call in to the Hastings police. He suddenly got all excited and said he would see you some other time. He almost ran out of the office. I tried to get him to stay. I'm sorry. "

"Don't worry about it. That's the least of our worries. He's a screwball. He'll be back if he has anything on his mind. Now, get to work on those calls. Rob, you can get moving too, and remember what I said!" he yelled as Rob hurried out of the office.

Moments later the phone rang and, Cindy had her head back in the door again.

"Ready on your call to the police in Hastings, Mr. Parks."

Howard picked up his phone. I followed enough of the conversation to know that the old woman was still alive, but the balance of what was said made no sense to me. Outside the building a truck engine started, died and started again. After what seemed an eternity, Howard replaced the telephone on the cradle. "Well, I'll just be damned," he said with a puzzled look on his face.

"What did they say?"

"They've identified the old woman."

"Who is she?"

He stood up and walked across the room to the window. He stared out the window for a time and then turned back to me. "Her name is Celestina Gaiule, and get this, she's Rob Gaiule's grandmother!"

"You've got to be kidding!" I knew he wasn't.

"And if that weren't enough, they thanked me for sending 'our man' up there so promptly to help them make the identification. I can only guess 'our man' is John Perez. They said he arranged to have her moved to P.H.S. here in a few weeks when she's strong enough."

"She' s going to live then?"

"They say she's going to pull through, but she came awfully close to buying the farm."

"Is Perez still there with her?"

"I don' t think so. They said 'my man' left about an hour ago. They assumed he was on his way back here, but he didn't tell them where he was going. He just made the arrangements and left. When Rob gets back, I'll give him some time off to go and see about her." Howard re-crossed the room and sat down behind his desk. He had the capacity to absorb and integrate the unexpected faster than anyone I had ever known.

I wasn't so well endowed. It took some time for my brain to get back in gear. When it did, I came up with a startling idea.

"Howard, do you know Rob's grandmother?"

"Yes and no. I don't know her well. I've seen her a few times, but that was several years ago, before she left here. Come to think of it she went to Chicago, or Detroit, or one of those places out there where you live. Not many Valencis have gone into that part of the country. Why did you ask?"

"Do you know Rob's grandfather?"

He settled back in his chair and made a steeple with his hands and fingers.

"Actually I know him pretty well. He is a fine old man. He got a wacky idea about seeing the white man's world, so he just up and took off for the East. I'll say this for him. He is well respected around here. I've never heard anyone say anything but good about him. I certainly like him. I think he is some sort of religious leader, but I never have known exactly what his job is supposed to be. What are you getting at?" He was talking with me but his mind was working somewhere else.

"What does his grandfather look like?"

"Look like? Well, the last time I saw him, that's been quite a while ago now, he was about Rob's height but a good bit thinner. He had long hair, down to his shoulders, and snowy white. I'd guess he is in his seventies or maybe older. He had a round wrinkled face. I still don't get it. What are you driving at? What difference does it make what Rob's grandfather looks like?"

"Tell me one more thing. Did he have a small scar across his lips?"

"I think so, now that you mention it."

Suddenly his attention was all on me. The penny had dropped. "Wait a minute! Are you thinking what I think you're thinking?"

"Well, I don't know what you think I'm thinking, but you told me that not many Valencis ever migrate into my part of the country. Now, just tell me one more thing, before you start to ask questions. What does Rob's grandmother look like?"

"She's a fine looking old woman, no bigger than a church mouse. For an old lady, her face is one of the prettiest I've ever seen. She always seems to have a smile for everybody. That's about all. Like I told you, I don't know her well, but what I do know about her, I like. Is that what you wanted to know?"

"In a way, yes. Howard, I've got a screwball hunch. Suppose Charlie was really Rob's grandfather, and the woman I hunted for and called Liawu is his grandmother?"

"I thought you said this Liawu woman is dead. Didn't you say you saw her body? Did this Charlie cellmate of yours have such a scar?" The questions came in a machine gun burst.

"One question at a time please. Yes, he had such a scar, and I said I saw a body. It was an Indian woman, and I just assumed it was Charlie's wife. Now I'm not sure. For one thing, I thought she looked too mean to be married to Charlie. For another, she looked too big to be his wife. Look," I said uncertainly, "this whole thing is the strangest tangle I've ever been in. I got railroaded into trying to do a nice old man a favor. Since that very minute, my life seems to have changed. Every time I think I understand what's happening, it all changes. Now, suddenly, I have a hunch, a feeling, call it whatever you will. But I think there's an outside chance that the old woman in the hospital in Hastings, Nebraska, might be Charlie's wife."

"That's a pretty flimsy hook for the kind of web you're trying to weave. Still," he added, "I have to admit I play gut feelings and on very rare occasions one of them works out. Suppose you're right. What are you going to do about it?"

"I want to go to Hastings with Rob. I want to talk to the old lady myself."

"I should have guessed as much," he said. "And just exactly how do you figure on getting to Hastings? Rob doesn't have a car and if I remember correctly you don't have a car and what's more you claim to be broke."

"I'm going to get there the same way I got here. I'll travel on my thumb. You might be surprised how much territory I can cover that way. Rob can come with me if he wants to."

"I'm going to be more particular the next time I see some guy hitchhiking," he said. "Alright. You take the keys to my car and drive up to the house. Pack your gear. I'll have one of the boys bring Rob and me up in about an hour or so, as soon as we get a line on Luke Ring. Tell Betty what's happened and tell her I said to fix something for you and Rob to eat on the road. I ought to have my head examined, but I'm going to let you two guys borrow my car for your wild goose chase." He tossed his car keys across the desk, and then swung his desk chair around to face the wall. "Now get the hell out of here."

"Cindy!" he shouted, "where are all my deputies?"

Chapter Thirty-Eight

It took less than five minutes to pack the clothes Howard had loaned me into his suitcase.

"You have to eat before you leave," Betty Parks ordered. "I'll feed you as soon as I finish fixing your food for the road. Now, quit twittering about. In fact, just sit down." She bustled back into the kitchen.

Forty-five minutes later, they arrived in the patrol wagon. Betty was still in the kitchen stuffing food into an oversized cardboard box.

"Did you find Luke Ring?" I asked as they came through the door. I felt extraordinarily cheerful in anticipation of our big trip.

"Yes," Howard replied, looking tired.

"Rob found him." He sank down on the couch.

"Well, what did he say, or has he talked yet? You didn't forget your promise and scalp him, did you Rob?" I laughed.

"Luke Ring was dead when Rob found him," Howard said simply.

"Somebody cut his throat," Rob added with a sick expression on his face, "and then they stuffed his mouth full of dirt."

I deeply regretted my smart-alecky question to Rob. Luke Ring's death didn't bother me particularly.

"I was going to let Rob go with you, since it is his grandmother in the hospital up there." said Howard. "But now we need all the deputies here. And let me set you straight on this," his words were directed more to Rob than to me," we're keeping Rob here because we need his help. We do not suspect he caused that bastard's death. Do you get that?"

"Yes, sir," I said.

"You do have a driver's license don't you, Okey?"

"Yes, but it's my wallet and my wallet is back at the place where I worked in Chicago."

"Oh, for crap sake! Well, it's too late now. Try not to get picked up, but if you do, then have them call me. I'll dream up some excuse for you. Damn it Okey, if you're going to Nebraska then get the hell out of here!" he exploded. "Here, you may as well take my gasoline credit card as long as you have my car."

"I'm on my way, and thanks, Howard. "

"Yeah, sure. Okey," he added in a quieter voice, "be careful. We've got a killer on the loose, and it's just possible you might he on his list. I don't give a damn about you, but I wouldn't want anything to happen to my car." He tried to smile.

Chapter Thirty-Nine

It was three o'clock in the afternoon when I left Lava. Twenty hard driving hours, 1300 miles, sixty gallons of gas and sixty gallons of coffee later I walked under the brown sandstone archway that spanned the entrance to the Hastings Memorial Hospital. It smelled like all hospitals; the waiting room was crowded with anxious people.

"May we help you?" The receptionist had smiling eyes. At least, I thought she did. I was too sleepy to be certain. "I would like to see a patient named Celestina Gaiule, please. My name is Smith. I'm a friend of the family."

"Mr. Smith, she is not allowed any visitors except family. She is still very, very weak."

"I'm also from the police department in Valenci, New Mexico. We are investigating her assault. I really need to talk with her." I was getting pretty good at making up lies.

"You may stay only a minute or two. Mrs. Branscomb, will you show this policeman to Room 487? He is only to stay for a few minutes. Don't let him wear her out."

A very severe looking Mrs. Branscomb, and I rode the slow elevator to the fourth floor, and then walked down a quiet corridor.

"Mrs. Gaiule," I called softly as we stepped into the darkened room. One small lamp glowed over the bed. Her eyes were closed and the visible part of her face was covered with stitches. She opened her eyes halfway and looked at me. Her poor, wounded face might have once been pretty but now the part that wasn't bandaged or stitched was withered into a thousand creases. Someone in the hospital had tied her long thin white hair into a pigtail. Only her head showed above the sheet. She was so tiny that her body barely made an impression in the bed.

Nurse Branscomb stepped out into the corridor and allowed the door to close behind her.

"Mrs. Gaiule, my name is Okey Smith."

She continued to look at me. I wasn't sure whether she was seeing me or not. It was likely, after what she had been through, that she would not want to talk to anyone, much less a total stranger. I had to go directly to the point if I were to get through to her.

"Mrs. Gaiule, a few weeks ago I was in a jail cell in Chicago with a man. I have reason to believe that man was your husband. Please forgive my bluntness, but did your husband die in a Chicago jail?"

She looked at me for a few moments longer and then in a whisper asked, "Why do you want to know?"

"Because, if that man were your husband, he left a message for you. He told me I was to tell his wife exactly what I saw and what he said."

"What was this message?" she whispered. Her eyes never left my face.

"I'm sorry, but first you must tell me if he was your husband. The message was meant for one person only."

"What was this man's name?" I could barely hear her.

"I don't know his name. I called him Charlie but that wasn't his name."

"Then how can I answer your question?"

"I was told by an undertaker that his name was Taaiyalote Alowish and that his wife was called Liawu. Later, I learned that those names were probably not real names."

She stared at me for a time almost as if she could look directly into my soul. Finally, she said softly, "I am Liawu. What message do you have to tell me?"

I believed her. I told her everything I could remember about his last hour. I even described Charlie's burning flesh. I repeated his exact words. When I finished, she turned her face away from me and for a long time she said nothing. Then I saw a small tear form in her eye and run across the wrinkles and scars and bandages.

I shifted from one foot to the other, uncertain what to do, or say, next. Then she turned her head back and fastened her gaze on me again.

"Did the smoke rise?" she sounded anxious.

I remembered how old Charlie had been so very careful to blow the smoke from his flesh toward the ceiling of the cell.

"Yes. The smoke rose. "

"Can you find our son?"

This was too much. If John Perez had told the truth, her son had been killed in a drunken car wreck. Her grandson, Rob, was her only surviving descendant.

"You have not spoken. "

Her words brought me out of my black study. There was nothing to do but plunge ahead with the whole awful story.

"I'm sorry, but your son is dead, Mrs. Gaiule. Rob, your grandson, is the only one left alive."

Her lips started to move. For a moment I thought she was making an effort to speak to me. Then I realized she was doing just as Charlie had done for weeks on end in our cell. I was too crude, I thought. I should have waited until tomorrow when I wouldn't be so tired and inarticulate. She's slipped over the edge. I hesitated for a moment longer and then turned to leave.

"Wait! Do you know this son of my son?" came her whispered voice again. I quickly turned back.

"Yes. I do. I met him a few days ago. He is a fine young man. He works as a policeman in Valenci. He wanted to come up here with me, but because of his job he couldn't.

"Has he taken himself a wife?"

"I'm sorry. I don't know. I don't think so, but I never thought to ask him."

"Anglo, you have done well. You have done as my husband asked you. Now, hear my words. You must be the one to get the 'key.' I will tell you where to find it. But you will not give the son of my son the 'key' until he has taken a Valenci wife. Do you hear me?"

"I do. "

"Until you are certain he has taken a Valenci wife, you must protect the 'key.' There are those who would try to change our way. I believe you are not one of them."

"I'll do the best I can, I promise you. What is the 'key', Mrs. Gaiule? And, where is it?"

"On the wall, there among trash is the 'key.' When this son of my son takes his wife, you will give it to him. Only then will he understand and then he will reward you."

She looked at me for a second or two longer and then closed her eyes.

"But. I don' t understand what you mean, Mrs. Gaiule."

I stood there frustrated by what she said. I wanted her to explain, and I wanted to go to bed and sleep for a week.

"You'll have to leave officer Smith. You've been in here much too long, sir," said Nurse Branscomb at the door.

I walked out of the room without any argument; my questions temporarily unanswered.

I had to find me a dry sack and a cup of coffee before I keeled over. Tomorrow morning would be soon enough to come back and get the rest of the answers. First on the list would be to find out who treated her so terribly.

I left Howard's car in the lighted hospital parking lot. At least it wouldn't be stripped when I got back to it. A dozen cheap hotels surrounded the hospital grounds. I picked out the closest one, registered under Howard's name using his gasoline card and went directly to my room. There was no telephone in the room but there was a pay phone at the end of the hallway. I sat on the edge of my bed and checked my pockets again. Howard's credit card and $14.45 was left out of the twenty the Lambs had given me. The room, a front street special with giant poinsettia wallpaper, cost $18. Should I call Howard and tell him what I had learned and failed to learn, or should I wait, get a night's sleep and go back for the rest of the answers from her tomorrow? What had she meant by "on the wall among trash is the key"? What wall? What trash? I was asleep before I thought up any more questions.

Chapter Forty

At 9:30 the next morning, feeling more like a human being instead of a zombie I again appeared in the corridor outside Mrs. Gaiule's room.

"Hi, cowboy. What may we do for you?" asked a cheerful young girl in a pink and white striped uniform.

"I came to visit with Mrs. Gaiule. Am I too early?"

"Is she the elderly lady in 487?"

"Yes."

A peculiar expression replaced the smile on her face. "Will you wait one moment, please? Doctor Clinebell will want to speak with you."

I stood and watched nurses cruise the corridor. The hospital disinfectant odor was not as the night before but the noise level was much higher. Everyone seemed to be on a mission. Moments later a white-jacketed man hurried purposefully down the corridor toward me.

"I'm Dr. Clinebell. Are you the policeman who was in Room 487 last night?" Doctor Clinebell was a thin, horse-faced bald man who looked as if he smelled something unpleasant. A stethoscope hung around his neck like a rubber noose. Steel and wood implements protruded from his breast pocket.

"Yes, I'm the one."

"Come with me." He commanded and strode off like a sergeant major leading a parade.

"Is there something wrong?" I hurried along behind him. "Has something happened to Mrs. Gaiule?"

"Step in here, please." He held open a door and looked at me as if I were the thing that smelled bad.

I walked into a small office without any windows. Two men sat on folding chairs on either side of a green metal desk. A third man stood behind the desk. All three had thin black lines for mouths. Cigar smoke had replaced ninety percent of the oxygen in the room.

"Here he is. He's the one," squealed Clinebell.

"Thanks, Doc. We'll take it from here. Come in please, sir, and sit down over here." The 'sir' had an ominous ring to it.

He directed me to a straight back chair in the middle of the floor. He sat down behind the desk; flanked by the other two hard-eyed men.

"What's this all about?" I asked. "Has something happened to Mrs. Gaiule?" The three of them stared at me as if I were some new kind of disease carrier.

"Please tell us your name, sir." He tilted back the desk chair and rolled a pencil between his hands like a child making a clay snake.

"Tell me who you are first. What business of yours is who I am?" I knew damn well they were cops. I could smell cop all over them.

"We are police officers. Here is my identification," he said, as he temporarily freed the pencil snake and flashed me a brief glimpse of a leather folder. "My name is Petersen, Detective Lieutenant Petersen. This gentleman is Sergeant Marston and this is Detective Burke. Now that you have been introduced, it's your turn to tell us your name, sir." Again the 'sir' was drawn out with unpleasant emphasis.

"Okey P. Smith."

"May we see your identification, Mr. Okey P. Smith?"

I reached for my wallet and then realized I didn't have one. My pockets gave forth only the gasoline credit card with the name 'Howard Parks' on it and the one five dollar bill I had left from the hotel and breakfast. Damn! Why hadn't I made up some sort of identification card?

"I'm afraid I don't have any identification with me."

"Let's see that credit card," said Detective Burke as he plucked it from my hand.

"Lieutenant, this credit card belongs to some person named Howard Parks," he reported.

"Well, well," said the Lieutenant. "Maybe we'll just check to see if it's stolen. Hang on to it. Now, Mr. Okey P. Smith, do you live in Hastings?"

"No, I don't. I'm just here to see a lady in this hospital."

"What is your address, then?"

Well, here we go. "At the present, I have no permanent address. "

"Are you employed, Okey P. Smith?"

"No. But I have friends who will vouch for me. You still haven't told me what this is all about."

"All in due time, Okey, boy. Now you say you have friends in Hastings who will vouch for you?"

"Well, no. Not in Hastings exactly."

"Well, where are they then?"

"In Valenci, New Mexico, and in Chicago."

"You mean to tell us that no one around here knows you?" He raised his eyebrow in mock surprise, and looked at the other two cops.

"Not that I'm aware of."

"Well now, isn't that just something? Well, let's change the subject, Mr. Okey P. Smith. How did you happen to be in Room 487 last night?" His gaze was fixed on my face.

"She's a relative of a friend of mine. Has something happened to her?"

"That's twice you've asked that question, Okey P. Smith. What makes you think something might have happened to her?'"

"I'm sure you don't have me in here to pass the time of day."

"He's sharp. Okey boy is real sharp." commented Sergeant Marston.

"We're to understand then that you came here from somewhere out of town to visit Mrs. Gaiule who just happened to be a relative of a friend?"

"That's right."

"What do you think?" He directed the question to both Burke and Marston.

Marston removed the cigar from his mouth and blew a slow string of smoke toward the ceiling. "He's lying. He's the one," came out at the end of the smoke string.

"I agree, " chimed in Burke.

"Okey P. Smith, you are under arrest for vagrancy. You have been found wandering about at odd hours and in odd places without any proper identification, and you have no visible means of support. You've also been pretending to be a police officer. But, most of all know that I expect to re-arrest you later on today and charge you with the willful, deliberate, and premeditated murder by suffocation of Mrs. Celestina Gaiule."

Chapter Forty-One

I was rapidly becoming a certified expert on getting in jail for something I didn't do. The King of the Slammers, that's me. I'll probably spend the rest of my life in one jail or another. A parade of gloomy thoughts marched through my mind as I was led in handcuffs, through the front door of Galesburg's Disneyland.

"Lieutenant Petersen, if you'll just check with Howard Parks, the head man at Law and Order in Valenci, the one whose name is on that credit card, he'll set you straight about me."

"Absolutely. You can bet your cowboy boots that is precisely what I intend to do. But first, Mr. Okey P. Smith, we are going to book you and mug you and print you and find you a nice cozy room all for your very own. You won't have to share it with anyone because you are the only murderer we have in custody today. Now if you will just step this way we will introduce you to your home away from home in Hastings."

I smiled for the mug shot. It might help break the monotony for some future criminologist as he plowed through scowling faces day after day. Lombroso's theory might become fashionable again and I would be the exception that proved the rule.

I knew as soon as they printed me they would find out about my stay in the Chicago jail. I hoped the FBI rap sheet would also show that the prosecution had been dismissed.

Shortly after twelve o'clock, just in time to miss the noon feed, they finished processing me through the Hastings style bureaucratic machinery. I was alone in my own private room. Detective Lieutenant Petersen certainly kept that promise. Now maybe he would keep his other promise and call Howard. I lay down on the top bunk. The cell was hot. I was tired and thoroughly disgusted with my life. The single recessed light in the ceiling shined directly in my eyes. It seemed as if time had telescoped. I was back in another cell ten feet by six feet by eight feet. I closed my eyes to block out the light. Poor Charlie, I thought, what a hell of a way to die. Why am I thinking about 'poor Charlie'? Poor me is who I better start to think about. What if they don't call Howard? Before long, when he doesn't hear from me, he'll get worried about his car and send out a stolen car bulletin with my name on it. Oh, well, what's auto theft compared to murder? Murder, murder, murder, who's got the murderer? We've got the murderer, said Detective Lieutenant Petersen and his name is Okey boy. We've got the Okey boy vagrant and the Okey boy car thief and . . . Crap! The hospital will have Howard's over parked car towed in. I'll get out of here with five bucks and they'll want fifteen to get it out of hock. I've committed something worse than murder, I've committed over parking. Hang the man high, and use my stethoscope for the noose, said Horseface Clinebell, M.D. I bet his wife is named Clarabell. Clarabell Clinebell runs the tow-in lot. She appeared in riding breeches, wearing dark glasses and clutching a Thompson sub-machine gun in her hands. I could hear the medals on her uniform blouse clank as she walked….

"Wake up, Smith..."

I awakened from a fitful nap in this steam room cell. Reality flooded back in on me. Petersen stood at the cell door. It was wide open.

"OK, Smith, or whatever your real name is, get your shit and get out of here before I change my mind." He was standing in the open cell door with a sheaf of papers in his hand.

"Why the hell didn't you tell us you are an undercover policeman? And, 'Mister Smith,' in case you've forgotten your manners, the next time you go into somebody else's jurisdiction for an undercover job; you damn well better let them know you're working their territory."

He was more than boiling mad. He threw my commitment papers, my mug shots and my fingerprint cards onto the lower bunk and stalked angrily out of the cell. I picked them up and tore all but Howard's credit card and my five-dollar bill into small pieces as I followed him out of the building.

Howard really must have read him the riot act. I wonder just what all Howard told him. He sure was burned.

Chapter Forty-Two

To be outside again was like being in Heaven. I walked around for twenty minutes breathing in the cold fresh Nebraska air. When the jail stink was gone from my nostrils, I called Howard from a pay telephone booth in a drugstore. He told me that Detective Petersen let him know that an unknown assailant who visited her room during the night had smothered Mrs. Gaiule to death with a pillow.

"Okey, your hunch is paying off. Follow through on it. Go on back to Chicago instead of coming here. "

"Why? I don't get your point."

"You found out from Mrs. Gaiule that she didn't let that key thing get into the hands of the bastard who beat her and stuffed her into the railroad car. It's a reasonable bet that it's still in her digs in Chicago. Go on back up there and go over that apartment with a fine-toothed comb. You know a whole lot more about Valenci now than you did the first time around. I believe there's a chance you'll find it this time. "

"O.K., Howard, I'll give it another shot, but don't expect too much."

"And, Okey..."

"Yes?"

"Whoever it was who killed Mrs. Gaiule might have the same idea. Watch out. And Okey, would you please try to stay out of jail. I hate telling lies to policemen."

"Yes sir! No more jail, I hope. Anything else?"

"How are you fixed for money?"

"I'm tapped out. I've got five dollars and your gas card. Is that enough for a first class passage to and from Chicago together with a few nights at the Hilton?"

"Funny, funny. You should take this act on the vaudeville stage. I'm going to wire you a few bucks out of our budget for crime investigation. Try not to spend it all in one place. Seriously Okey, whoever that guy is, he means business. You could get hurt bad. Be careful!"

"As soon as that money gets here, I'll be on my way. Don't worry about me; I can take care of myself. I'll keep you posted on what's happening. Thanks Howard, for getting me off the hook here in Hastings."

After the connection was broken, I realized I forgot to ask him whether they caught Luke Ring's murderer. It didn't matter. I'd find out when I got back.

The car stood unmolested in the hospital parking lot. I gassed it up using the credit card, and headed for the Western Union and Chicago.

Chapter Forty-Three

My first impulse as I drove into the outskirts of Chicago was to go straight to the Lambs' house and tell Dorothy and the Professor all that had happened. Miss Dorothy had been floating through my mind throughout this whole adventure. Oh well, at least I'm not too old to dream. Upon further thought I decided the Lamb visit could wait. The first order of business had to be to search through the Gaiule apartment as quickly as possible.

It was ten minutes until eleven p.m. and as dark as the bottom of a coalmine when I parked in front of the run-down apartment building. The wind was cold and there was the feel of snow in the air. I had almost forgotten such miserable weather existed. A week in the Southwest is damn poor training for winter life in Chicago. The street was empty of pedestrians. Only one other car, a dilapidated pick-up truck, was parked on the same side of the street.

I rang the bell of the manager's apartment. No one answered. I tried knocking. Still no answer and no light showed under the door. I decided to go on up to the apartment to see if I could get in without the manager's help.

Six flights later, I stood puffing in the darkened hallway outside the apartment. How the hell do people jimmy an apartment door? It looks so easy in the movies. On impulse I pressed the doorbell button. The bell rang and I heard movement inside. A moment later the door opened and light streamed out into the hall. A fat man clutched a woolen bathrobe around his bare middle and stood in the doorway glaring at me.

"You sure as hell took your good sweet time getting here," he exploded.

"You expected me?"

"Oh hell no. No, I didn't expect you. That's the reason I call a T.V. repair man, so I can stand around not expecting him."

"Well, here I am, at last. Sorry for the delay," I said brightly.

"Where's your damn tool kit?"

"Too heavy to carry up six flights. I diagnose the trouble and then step down to the truck for parts."

"Well, get at it. Irv Kupcinet will be on soon, and I don't want to miss him."

"Lived here long?" I asked as I stepped around him and walked inside.

"I moved in last week, not that it's any damn business of yours. The set is over there. Hurry up and fix it."

I glanced toward the elephant size television set. I know absolutely nothing about electronic equipment except that before the things work, they have to be plugged in to the power. From across the room I could see that his set was unplugged.

"I think I can handle this repair, but I'll need a screwdriver and a tape measure or a yardstick."

"A what?"

"A screwdriver and a straight edge of some kind. I need to level the rubilator. Look around and see if you can find a ruler. Of course, I could always go back down to the truck, but you said you were in a hurry to have it fixed." If he were like most people I know, he would have to hunt all over hell to find a ruler. That ought to keep fat boy out of my hair while I tried to spot the 'key.'

"Well, that's the damndest thing I've ever heard. How long a ruler?"

"The longest you have. I'd really prefer a yardstick."

He left for the kitchen muttering under his breath. As soon as he was gone, I turned the television switch to the OFF position and then plugged in the set. I turned the volume down low and turned the set back on. After a moment a picture appeared. The across-the-room diagnosis proved to be correct. The only thing wrong with his TV was that the stupid operator forgot to plug it into the wall socket. I turned it off again and gazed around the room. Nothing looked the same. The apartment manager had taken all of her stuff out before the bathrobed clown moved in. I sat on the floor next to the television set and played with the dials while I continued to look around the room.

"On the wall among trash," she had said. I looked at the walls. They looked the same. The same gawd-awful wallpaper hung in tatters. The same bad pictures from Woolworth's hung in place. Then I saw it. On the wall, next to the front door, was the 'key'. I sat looking at it. It was so very obvious now. It was also very obvious why I hadn't known what it was when I saw it on my first visit to the apartment.

"Here's your damn screwdriver," said the fat man as he came back into the room. "I can't find no ruler."

He handed the screwdriver to me. I stuck it into the back of the TV set and rattled it around. After a few minutes I muttered, "I think I have it," and turned the set on again. Seconds later the tube flickered and came to life.

"Well you took your good sweet time gettin' here, but it looks like you fixed it fast enough. There couldn't have been much wrong. How much are you going to clip me for?"

"If I charge you what I am supposed to for a complicated middle-of-the-night job like this, it could be pretty expensive."

"Yeah? What do you mean 'it could be'?" he asked suspiciously.

"I haven't logged this call in yet, so maybe you and I can make a little deal? As long as you don't tell the boss, I sure as hell won't tell, right?" I winked and poked his belly with the screwdriver.

"Yeah. Well, maybe. What you got in mind?" He smelled a chance to put one over on my boss and save himself a wad of money at the same time.

"I've been looking around your living room here while I worked on your set. I sure do admire the pictures you got on the walls. Give me one of them pictures and two bucks and we'll call it square."

"You got to be kidding. T.V. repairmen don't take no damn pictures for pay. What's the gimmick?"

"No gimmick. You see, I'm an art student. I work on T.V. sets to pay my tuition. We study these pictures like you got in my class at school. I can use one for my homework.

He knew he almost had something for nothing. He was going to con me. The pictures didn't belong to him, they came with the apartment, but he was still suspicious.

"Well, I don't know. Which pitcher you want?" he asked.

"You pick it out."

"Are you kidding? You mean, whichever one I want to give you, you'll take it?" He was no longer suspicious. He knew he had a certified sucker. Quickly he looked around the walls of the room.

"That's right," I said and smiled. "I like almost all of them."

"O.K. I pick that one there. The one with the stupid looking cow on it."

I tried to look disappointed.

"Come on now. That was our deal," he said quickly, "any pitcher I picked. And that's the one I pick. You can't back out on me. That's the one."

"It sure is," I thought.

I took the picture from the wall. It was in a cheap dime store plastic frame.

"What about my two bucks?" I held out my hand.

Reluctantly he fished two crumpled one-dollar bills out of his wife's pocket book.

"So long, sir. Anytime you need us, just call. Remember, 'Fast and Efficient Service' is our motto. "

I walked quickly out the door and along the hallway to the stairs.

"Hey," he yelled after me. "Hey, put that damn pitcher under your coat before you go by the manager's apartment."

I resisted the temptation to ask him why and hurried down the stairs, through the cold and into the car. I was elated. I had the 'key.' I didn't know why it was the 'key' and I didn't know what it meant, but I knew, at long last, I had it.

The 'key' was an exact duplicate of the petroglyph I had seen in the cave on the cliff in Valenci. It was a picture of the sun, and a cow, and a group of little men dancing or digging a hole or something. After staring at it for a few minutes, I removed it from the frame. The figures were painted on soft leather. I examined it a few moments longer and then folded it up, and put it in my jacket pocket.

Chapter Forty-Four

It was too late at night to call the Lambs. I was still all worked up about having the 'key.' Some sort of a celebration seemed to be called for. I took the suitcase out of the car trunk and put the empty picture frame in it. Then I tossed the suitcase onto the back seat. To drive around the streets of Chicago was the only celebration I could think of. In spite of the cold the car motor turned over easily. I flicked on the headlights and started to pull away from the curb. Suddenly there was a loud racket on the passenger's side. Someone pounded on the window. Still hanging onto the steering wheel, I hit the brakes and leaned over to see who it was. It was a woman. She was yelling unintelligibly and making excited gestures. I started to tell her to get lost when the door on my side flew open, and someone lunged into the car and landed like a ton of cement on top of my bent over body. My right arm was jammed under me, and my left arm was trapped between whoever it was and me. My face was pushed into the car cushions. The way he had me wedged in, I could hardly breathe.

"Get the suitcase! Get the damn suitcase!" The man's voice roared in my ear. I heard the back door of the car open.

I struggled to sit up or turn around, but I couldn't move an inch. Both arms felt like they were pulled out of joint. He had me pinned down tight.

"What's going on? Who the devil are you..." I mumbled into the seat cushion.

"I got it, Benny! Benny, I got it! Come on, let's get the hell out of here!" squawked a female voice.

"Get in the truck!" the elephant on top of me trumpeted to his mate.

I tried to thrash around but all I could move were my feet. Then I heard a truck motor start and, as quickly as it came, the weight was off of me. The door of the pick-up truck slammed. Tires screamed as it sped around a corner and was gone. I sucked air into my collapsed lungs and tried to sit up. My arms hurt like hell.

When I finally got the car rolling again and turned the corner where the truck had disappeared, I knew it was useless to try to chase them. The street was long with many cross streets and, as far as I could see, it was empty. Whoever they were, they got the suitcase, my dirty socks and underwear and the empty frame but I still had the 'key.'

I drove aimlessly through the streets trying to arrange my thoughts. I didn't know the make or the year of the pick-up. I didn't see the license number. I saw the woman only briefly and then through a dirty car window. The man had never let me turn my head. All I knew about him was that he weighed a ton, he smelled bad and the woman called him "Benny." If it were only my suitcase they were after, then I would never see it or them again. Ordinary thieves would throw away the suitcase as useless junk, once they had searched it. If they were after the 'key' though, they were going to be mightily confused and disappointed, and I had a good chance of meeting them again. Before that could happen I ought to hurry back to Valenci, give the 'key' thing to Rob. I ought to forget this whole episode and get on with my life such as it was. That's what someone with good sense would do, but Bentura had made me mad. He smothered that defenseless old woman and he pushed me around. I was sure the lummox who sat on me while the woman took the suitcase was Bentura. Now, more than ever, I wanted a good look at this thug Bentura. I also wanted to wring his damn fool neck.

At an all-night diner with an outdoor telephone booth, I placed a reverse- charges call to Howard Parks in Lava.

"Did something go wrong again or have you bought stock in AT&T?" he asked when I identified myself.

"Yes and no," I said. "I'll make it brief. I'm in Chicago and I'm pretty sure I've found the 'key.' But right after I found it I was mugged by someone called "Benny." I didn't get a look at him, but the odds are good it was Bentura. He got your suitcase and all the stuff in it but he didn't get the 'key.' When he discovers it's not in your suitcase, he's bound to make another try for it. If I can get a good look at him the next time around, we'll know for sure who our murderer is. I won't take any chances with the 'key' though. I'll hide it up here in Chicago in a place where he'll never find it."

"Why do you think he is going to be able to find you again, and, if he does, what's to keep him from killing you?"

"I'm going to plant myself out in the open in a place where he knows a lot of people. If he makes any effort at all to find me, he'll succeed. As for killing me, I'll just have to be careful. Howard, I want to see that bastard's ugly face, and I figure this is the best way to do it."

I talked and talked some more until he finally agreed to the plan. He cautioned me in no uncertain words to take as few chances as possible with Bentura. One more killing wouldn't get Bentura in any more trouble than he was already in. He had demonstrated clearly that he didn't mind killing anyone who stood in his path.

I hung up and then placed a second call. The telephone rang six times before a sleepy, female voice answered.

"This is the Lamb residence."

Chapter Forty-Five

"Dorothy, I mean Miss Lamb? Dorothy? Is that you?" It was a stupid question. Who else would answer her phone in the middle of the night? I don't know why I got so excited just hearing her voice.

"Yes. Who is this, please?"

"It's me, Okey. Okey Smith. I'm back in Chicago. Listen, Dorothy, I need to put a car in your garage for a few days. I haven't time to explain, but I promise you there's no trouble. If I came out to your house right now, would you be willing to bring me back to town, tonight?"

"You mean now? In the middle of the night?"

"Yes. It's very important." I put as much urgency in my voice as I could.

"Well, I don't know. I suppose I could, but what's this all about? When are you coming?"

It took only twenty minutes to make the drive. Traffic was almost non-existent outside of the downtown area. As I pulled into her driveway, she was climbing out of the jeep. Its exhaust pumped clouds of blue vapor into Chicago's already polluted and bitter cold night air.

"Now what's this all about? We thought you were in New Mexico. When did you get back? Whose car is that? Why are you back in Chicago?" she strung together in a half curious and half exasperated voice.

"Let me go in the house for one minute to go to the bathroom and to get warm. I'll explain the whole thing as we drive back downtown."

"Don't you make a lot of noise in there, Father is still asleep," she shouted, as I walked toward the house.

I went through the kitchen and into the hall. The house hadn't changed. Books were still stacked everywhere. I grabbed a fat one entitled "Ethnographic Studies of the New Hebrides" and placed the 'key' between its pages. Then I took the book into the library and hid it behind a row of dusty books on the top shelf. If Bentura found it there he would deserve to have it.

Outside, Dorothy waited impatiently in the jeep. When I climbed in she growled at me and then drove and grumbled while I told her parts of the story.

I did not tell her I had hidden the 'key' in her house. What she didn't know, she couldn't tell.

"It seems to me that all I ever do is take you back to skid-row. I had hoped to keep you out of that awful place, but here we go back to it again." The expression on her face would curdle milk. Even so, I thought, she was pretty as a speckled pup.

"I don't like going back there either, but I have to go back. That's where they found me the first time and that's where they'll look for me again. If I'm ever going to catch up with this guy Bentura, I'll have to use myself as bait. He thinks I have the 'key.' He's tried for it several times before and missed every time. He'll try for it again, but this time I'll be ready for him."

At my request she let me out at LaSalle and Madison. I didn't want anyone on the row to see her or her jeep.

"Okey?" She leaned toward the open door.

"Yes?"

"Okey, you be careful, real careful ... please?" I wondered if I heard something more than sisterly concern in her voice.

For once I was sure I knew where I was going and what I was doing. Three nights later I wasn't quite so confident.

Chapter Forty-Six

No one will ever convince me that God enjoys hearing seventy-five hungry, hopeless men sing "Love Lifted Me." Singing was a far-fetched euphemism for the mumbling, coughing, shuffling, and scratching going on around me. All of us assembled in the room knew we had to endure a tub-thumping sermon and one more song before we could eat.

The Right Reverend Dr. Garniss Fetterman, Pastor of the Blessed Arms of Jesus Mission, maneuvered his arthritic bones and his shiny black suit onto the low wooden platform in the front of the stuffy, hot, crowded room.

I had picked this end-of-the-line mission as the place where Bentura could most likely find me without even working very hard at the project. Privacy was unknown in the Arms of Jesus. We all washed in one room, we all endured Reverend Fetterman's endless sermons in one room and we all swilled slop in the same room. If anyone, anywhere on the row, should ask about me, someone would surely have seen me here. Bentura would have to make his next try for the 'key' on territory I knew as well, or better, than he did. My wandering thoughts were interrupted by the start of Reverend Fetterman's harangue.

"Our text this evening, -huh, is taken from the Book of Revelation -huh where it is written in eighteen -huh verse fourteen --huh 'And the fruits that the soul lusted after are departed from thee, -huh and all things which were dainty and goodly -huh are departed from thee, and -huh and thou shalt find them no more at all. Blessed be –huh the name of the Lord! "

Reverend Fetterman had developed his public speaking style in Kentucky or West Virginia. Nowhere else on earth do preachers grunt 'huh' after every other phrase. I felt right at home.

I looked around the room and saw rows and rows of faces-not people, just faces. I focused on one face across the aisle from me. I couldn't see a smile or a frown or any other human expression, which might give away the secret that a real human being lived behind the mask. I wondered if anyone still lived in there, and, if' he did, whether he would ever come out again. Then I decided that he might be one hell of a lot better off hiding in there than he would be out here with me where I was probably going to get my ass kicked again.

The good Rev. Fetterman clanked on ,"And I say to you brethren -huh that you are like the souls -huh who lust after flesh and hard liquor -huh..."

No one in this room had lusted after flesh for years, I mumbled to myself. If you split one pint bottle of real store-bought hard liquor among the whole crowd, it would kill every one of them. If Fetterman wanted to list relevant sins, he ought to preach against indifference, or, at least about Sneaky Pete, lighter fluid and Sterno. He might even say a few words about loneliness.

A thousand years later, I tuned in again to hear him say, "And as we close I want those of you who have never known –huh the sweet blessing -huh of Jesus huh to come kneel down at the altar –huh rail with me. . ."

He's about to wind down, I prayed. Well torture one more song and then we can troop down to the basement and eat.

"Sowing in the morning..." our voices weakly bounced off the dingy yellow plaster walls. The sole decoration in the room was a picture of a pasty-face Jesus with a lamb in his arms. He looked as blank and tired as the rest of the men in the room.

Bringing in the 'sheep' instead of 'sheaves' ought to be the name of the song. I wondered if we were going to have meat tonight? Probably not, we had S.O.S. last night. That meant navy bean soup and day-old bread for the flock tonight.

There was a remarkably refined group gathered around the dinner table. Only three of the regular guests passed out during the meal, and, for a change, not a single new man vomited into his plate. 'Count your blessings, count them one by one,' I sang under my breath.

After another mercifully shorter prayer meeting, we lined up for the mandatory shower baths. Each night we had to bathe, whether we needed it or not. Under the careful eye of Brother Garniss, we peeled off our clothes and hung them on a row of wooden pegs along the wall. Then we were given a paper-thin sliver of gritty soap and were lined up and led in to stand under a cold-water shower. Some of us chose to lie down and sleep under the shower. We dried with a dishtowel and then, back in line again, we received a fulsome dusting of our private parts with flea and lice powder. From a laundry hamper, we were issued a ragged, short, hospital nightgown, and it was off to beddy-bye. For breakfast tomorrow, those of us who live through the night, will get weak black coffee and dry untoasted bread. One thing about all this luxury though, it is very good for the figure. There was not a fat man in the room. We were all shabby, unshaven, grey ghosts.

I had another top bunk. That was good. Theoretically, the stink of old age, garlic, gut winds, and decay is a little lighter higher up-if, and when, the ventilators worked. They hadn't worked since I arrived.

During the daylight hours the three days I had been back on the row, I walked the streets poking my face into one bar after the other in order to be seen. That isn't as easy as it sounds. A long time ago, the man who decided how everything should be decided that saloons should be dark. Only neon light, never sunlight, should glow inside a bar. It's hard as hell to distinguish one face from another under blue and red neon lights.

During my travels I learned one thing well. Skid-row saloons vary from their uptown counterparts only in the odor. Uptown, when you sit at the bar, you can't smell the disinfectant blocks in the urinal.

Outside of one bar, on the second day, I thought I saw the cops pick up Shulsey Dan. There was no sign of Half-Witt. No one paid the least attention to me. I was invisible. If I had wanted not to be seen, then everyone on the street would have known me.

Walking the street with no purpose except to be seen had given me plenty of time to think about the 'key.' I finally worked it out in my mind that Old Charlie had been some sort of a hereditary custodian of the 'key.' He wanted it passed on to his oldest son, and Mrs. Gaiule had thought that was where it ought to go, too. This father-to-son succession must have been going on for a long time because Howard had said those petroglyphs were very old, over a thousand years old. No, wait a minute. That's not what he said. He said no one knew how old they were. That drawing on leather couldn't be a thousand years old. I hadn't examined it carefully, of course, but I knew darn well it wasn't that old. But when I thought about the paradox of why have a drawing of a carving, and, why pass it on and what did it mean, I remained at a loss for any kind of answer.

"Hey, cowboy," came a shout from the night man standing in the doorway of the mission dormitory.

I snapped awake.

"Hey, cowboy, " he shouted again, and flicked the ceiling lights on and off. There was no doubt he had called me. Wearing the clothes Howard had given me had brought more than a few sarcastic comments about cowboys from the clowns who worked at the Arms of Jesus.

"Knock it off! Shut them damn lights off!" and whistles joined other comments, hand claps, and boos from the other troops whose sleep was being disturbed.

"Go to hell, you damn deadheads!" he shouted without interest in the protests.

"Smith! Git your worthless ass outa that bunk and git over here right now when I call you!"

This was it. The lull was over. This was what I had been waiting for. My fish had risen to the bait. I slid down from the bunk. As I walked to the door, the excitement, or the open back of the hospital gown we slept in, made a shiver go down my spine.

"Cowboy, get your clothes on." He spat on the floor and hooked his thumbs into his hip pockets. His place in the world's pecking order was firmly established. When the Rev. Garniss Fetterman went home, he was the boss.

"Why?" I asked.

"Cowboy, when I tell you get dressed, you get dressed. If I wanted you to know why, I'd tell you why. Now move your ass!"

As soon as I got my gear off the peg I discovered that someone had re-arranged the few things in my pockets. If that someone were looking for the 'key,' and I was sure he had been, he didn't find what he wanted. My uninvited visitor wasn't an ordinary thief, because my two-dollar TV repair fee was still in my pocket, but he had put it back in the wrong one. Since he hadn't been able to steal the ' key' from my clothes he would have to try to get it from me directly. I wondered how he persuaded the Arms of Jesus night man to let him search through my clothes? A pint, or two dollars would be a good guess.

The night man had his feet propped up on the desk, and was painstakingly mouthing his way through a Donald Duck comic book when I returned.

"O.K. I'm dressed. Now, what the hell do you want?"

He laid the open comic book on his legs, and looked at me.

"There's a man wants to see you, cowboy. He said he had to go and make a phone call, so he went down the street. He's gonna take you someplace, and give you a job. If you have any more stuff back there, or if you sneaked something into the dorm, go on back in there and get it.

"Did he ask you to tell me to do that?"

"Don't get smart with me. You stew bums are always so everlastin' damn suspicious of anyone who tries to do you a favor."

You're giving whoever he is, his two dollars worth, I thought.

The street door rattled. The night man put his comic book on the desk, stood up and limped to the door.

He tried one more time before he opened the door. "You sure you ain't got nothing else back there you want to take with you?"

"I'm sure."

The door rattled again.

"All right, God damn it, hold your horses. " He threw the bolt and cracked open the door. The chain latch was still fastened. He looked outside through the crack and whispered to the person outside. His whisper was so loud it could have been heard for half a mile in the middle of a tornado. "He ain't got a damn thing on him. You seen it all." He closed the door, removed the chain and opened it wide.

Chapter Forty-Seven

I don't know whom I had expected, but certainly it was not the man who walked through the door of the Arms of Jesus.

"Okey, dear boy, I've searched for you ever friggin' place," said Romeo 'Grease Ball' Lillard, the king of the Dirty Movie Palace. He held out his arms as if he intended to embrace me. His fat ugly face tried to smile. The effort was weird but wholly unsuccessful as a smile.

"What the hell!" I exclaimed.

"I know you are pleased and surprised," he cut me off, "and well you might be. You weren't very nice to me, not coming back to see me when you got out of the friggin' jail. But all is forgiven dear boy. All is forgiven." He put his fat hand on my shoulder. "Come along now lad, come along with me. I have saved all your old things for you, and I have your old job ready for you again."

Stunned at this unexpected turn in events, I obediently followed him out of the mission and into the street.

He chattered away about how glad he was to see me. My brain was in a whirl. This isn't what's supposed to be happening. This made no sense at all.

His battered old Cadillac car was parked at the curb. "Get in, boy, get in," he urged. I got in.

He started the motor and pulled into the light traffic. He headed west on Madison. A police ambulance with blazing red lights screamed past us in the night.

"Now let's you and me have a little chat, dear boy," he said as he rounded a corner and headed North.

"O.K., I give up. What do you want, Grease Ball? Didn't you have enough fun kicking me in the head?"

"What I want, is for you to tell me about your vacation out West. Did you have a good time out there with all them friggin' Indians?

"Lillard cut the crap. What the hell do you want?"

"All right, since you insist on doing business right now, Mr. Smith, let's get down to brass tacks." The light from an all night used car lot momentarily illuminated his face.

"I trust you noticed that because of my absence at your friggin' trial, you are now a free man? Well, did you ever stop to wonder why I wasn't there?"

"If I didn't know better, I'd say you had an attack of conscience. But since that's impossible, suppose you explain it to me."

"While you were in jail, I received a message from an old associate of mine. He told me that you had come into possession of some information. He also told me it was information that could prove to be of considerable value to you, and to me too. Under those circumstances it wouldn't have done either of us any good if you had been convicted and had been required to serve a sentence, would it?"

I added it up quickly. It made sense. Half-Witt had said that when he was out of jail he sometimes worked with Lillard. Poor, stupid Half-Witt believed all that crapola I had made up about what Charlie said to me about a treasure before he died. He had passed it on to Grease Ball, who had believed it too. Then out on the street when I told Half-Witt I was looking for an Indian named Bentura, he decided that it had to do with that imaginary treasure. Two-to-one he and fat boy Lillard had located Bentura and associated themselves with him. Well, the three of them deserved each other. One thing was certain. Lillard believed the 'key' represented money. Lillard didn't give two whoops in hell about what happened on an Indian reservation. But, if you waved money under his fat nose he salivated like Pavlov's dog.

I decided to play dumb a while longer. "Grease Ball, get to the point, what do you want?"

"All right, Smith. It still is 'Smith,' isn't it? Well, Smith you have information I want. If you choose to share it with me--that is, with my associates and me, it will work to our mutual advantage-yours and ours. Now, what about it boy? Shall we all be friends and work together?"

"Why do you think I have any information you could possibly want? I don't know a damn thing about dirty movies."

"Oh, come now, let's not beat around the friggin bush, Mr. Smith," he emphasized the 'Mr.' "I'm sure you realize that we arranged to borrow your suitcase from you the other night. We also took the liberty of examining your meager clothing at the mission. Unfortunately, for us, we found nothing that could tell us what we wanted to know. That means you have the information we want but it's in your head. So you see, friend Smith, we're more or less forced to seek your cooperation." His smile would have put a chill in the heart of Attila the Hun.

The Cadillac pulled to the curb and stopped in front of a non-descript run-down brick apartment building.

"Shall we go in, Mr. Smith?"

"Why not?" It was too late to back out anyway.

We climbed the creaky wooden stairs and stopped in front of a door on the second floor. The wallpaper in the corridor was water-stained and peeling. More burlap backing than nap showed in the remains of a maroon hall runner.

"Who lives here?" The place stank like the fumes from a garbage pail.

"Your very good friend and my old associate, Mr. Maitland Jerome Witt."

"Half-Witt? Half-Witt is named 'Maitland Jerome'?"

I had guessed right. Half-Witt and Grease Ball Lillard, what a combination! Now if Bentura were only a part of it.

“I have heard him referred to in that derogatory manner, yes."

Grease Ball knocked. A woman opened the door. We walked through the doorway past her without speaking. As soon as we entered the room I saw Howard's suitcase jammed against the wall behind a dilapidated overstuffed chair. The TV set boomed out an old Carole Lombard tearjerker.

Grease Ball looked around the small room and turned to the woman.

"Turn that crap off. Where's that friggin' half-wit?" he roared.

"He went out to get us some beer. He said he'd be back in a minute," she didn't care one-way or the other what Lillard wanted. Her eyes never strayed from the T.V. set.

"Dammit, I told him to stay here. Where's the big Indian? Where's Benni?" He shouted to be heard over the TV clatter.

"How the hell should I know? He left, just took off after you called. He was in a hurry and he sure as hell didn't say where he was going." She slid back down in the chair in front of the ten-inch television screen.

Grease Ball turned back to me.

"It seems we're going to have to wait a while, Mr. Smith."

Now I knew for sure, the third man was Bentura. I looked at the woman. I was sure she was the one who helped steal my suitcase. She had not looked at me once since we entered the room.

Thirty minutes later the apartment door opened, and Half-Witt shuffled in with a carton of beer in each hand and one under his belt.

"God damn it, it's about friggin' time you got here you little creep. Where's Benni?" asked Grease Ball.

"I don't know, Mr. Lillard. After you called and said you didn't find nothing in Okey's clothes, he took off. So I went out to get us some beer," replied Half-Witt.

"Hey, Okey buddy," he smiled a toothless grin at me.

"Pay attention to me. Did he say where he was going?"

"No. He just said 'Hoch'ob,' or something crazy like that, and stormed out the door.

"When is he coming back?" persisted Grease Ball.

"I don't know. Pretty soon now, I reckon, Mr. Lillard, Is the deal still on?"

"The deal is on. Our good friend, Mr. Smith, has agreed to cooperate fully. Isn't that right, Mr. Smith? "

"You told it right, Grease Ball. I'm with all of you one hundred percent."

We settled down to drink Half-Witt's beer, watch Carole Lombard, and wait for the return of Bentura.

Chapter Forty-Eight

The first light of dawn was only minutes away. Grease Ball was asleep on the couch. Half-Witt and the woman were in the bedroom. I dozed fitfully in the overstuffed chair. "Benny" who had to be the man I knew as Bentura, had not returned. Theoretically, we still waited for him, but realistically it looked as if my big effort to find him had gone to waste.

It was not a completely wasted effort, though. I had learned a few things during the long night with these characters. I was now certain that neither Lillard nor Witt knew anything about the death of Liawu or Luke Ring. Bentura was still the most likely suspect. Of course, I was assuming a connection between their deaths. It was possible, too that the Indian who we thought had hanged himself, Larry Denti, was one of Bentura's victims.

Then there was that old Indian lady in the empty apartment, who the hell was she, anyway? Had Bentura killed her?

Grease Ball began to snore. Grease Ball was a three hundred pound zero. He wasn't vicious enough to have killed anyone. Neither was Half-Witt. They were small time hoodlums who only got into this thing because they thought Charlie knew about a buried treasure. That was the joke of the year. Charlie and Liawu were so dirt poor they could barely keep from starving. Nobody starves when they can lay their hands on money. As a matter of fact, there aren't any rich Valencis. The whole tribe lives a hand-to-mouth life. If there were a buried treasure, Charlie and the other Indians would have dug it up and spent it on themselves a long time ago. I started to speculate about how the Valencis could add a little quality to their lives with a treasure. Oddly enough, everything I thought of was something I wanted myself.

A siren wailed in the street. Lillard woke up instantly.

"What's the matter, Grease Ball?" I asked. “Don't you have a clear conscience? You think those cops are after you?"

"Fuck you, Smith." He flopped back and in a few seconds was snoring again.

He's not so anxious to be my friend when he's sleepy, I thought. Maybe people show their true nature when they are sleepy.

I dozed off too.

At 9 o'clock in the morning Bentura still hadn't returned. Grease Ball and Half-Witt were at each other's throats. Grease Ball blamed Half-Witt for allowing Bentura to slip away and Half-Witt blamed Grease Ball for leaving him alone with the big Indian. The woman wisely stayed in the bedroom, out of harm's way.

I decided it was time for me pull up stakes. I had wasted enough time. I was ready to go back to Valenci, and I didn't want these two clowns and their girl friend following in my wake.

"I bet I know what's happened to Benni,”I said.

Grease Ball reacted instantly. "All right, smartass, what? And while you're in such a talkative mood, tell us exactly what the hell you did learn from that friggin' old Indian jail bird.”

"Grease Ball, I wish I did know something more than I’ve told you. The only thing I know is that the old man told me that years ago he buried some money. I figured it had to be where he lived, in New Mexico. So I went out there and tore up his whole damn place. I couldn’t find a thing, not one damn thing. So I came back to Chicago to see if I could locate the old man's wife. I figured she might be able to tell me something. But she's gone and nobody seems to know where. You stupid bastards don't think I would be back in Chicago, dead broke, and living in a damn mission if I had found a pile of money, do you?"

They looked at each other unhappily. It was patently obvious that they believed me. No one, with money to spend, would have lived in the Arms of Jesus.

"O.K., Smith. What were you going to tell us about Benni?" Grease Ball finally asked.

"The way I figure it, is that last night when Benni found out from you that I hadn't gotten anything from the old lady's apartment, he went out to look for her himself. By now, he's probably found her and gotten what he was after. The three of us will never see him again."

"Yeah. That's the way I see it too, Mr. Lillard," injected Half-Witt. "That damn Benni has done gone and skipped out on all of us."

"The dirty fink left us holding the bag," I added. "And, the hell of it is, that I thought I was getting in on a big thing. The only reason I played along with you guys last night was because I thought you could tell me something. Boy, was I ever wrong. You two clowns are just as dumb as I am."

"All right, Smith, lay off. I've had enough of you to last me a lifetime." Grease Ball had surrendered. Now all of us were certain that Bentura had left for good.

I administered the coup d' grace. "I don't know about you two guys, but I'm going to get my gear, find me a place to live and try to forget this whole stinking mess. Hell, I might even get me a job. How about that Half-Witt? You want to join me in a job hunt?"

"Huh? Oh, no thanks Smith. I'm doing alright on my own."

"Well, gentlemen, if that's it, I'll be taking my leave. I believe you have some things of mine?" I stood up and eyeballed the suitcase.

"Where are you going to be, Smith? We might still work something out. Benni might have had an accident or something," Grease Ball mouthed the words but he didn't believe them. He was certain that Bentura was gone for good, and with him had gone Grease Ball's grand dream of buried treasure.

"I'm going to be at the same place I've always been when you wanted me-the west end of Madison Street. I've still got a few bucks, so I'll sleep in a cage joint tonight. Maybe Vladimir Borrilli will give me back my old dishwashing job again. Or, how about you, Mr. Lillard? You still need a good man to run your 'art' films?"

They sat silently with their chins dragging on the floor while I picked up the suitcase and walked out of the apartment. They didn't even say goodbye.

Chapter Forty-Nine

At the corner I hailed a taxi. "Where to, buddy?" I gave him the Lamb's address. As soon as I was seated in the cab, I opened the suitcase. Everything was there. Nothing had been taken although it was obvious that it had been thoroughly searched. As the taxi wound its way through the traffic, I tried to figure out what really might have happened to Bentura. There were several possibilities. He could have been arrested or had an accident. Neither was likely, because he would have gotten word to us one way or another, unless he were dead. There was the possibility, which I immediately dismissed, that he abandoned the project. No, he wouldn't, not after killing two or maybe even more people. No, Bentura wasn't ready to quit. But why had he waited almost three days and then agreed to have Grease Ball and Half-Witt bring me into the plan? Without a doubt, Bentura had seen the 'key' when he searched Mrs. Gaiule's apartment the first time. If it meant nothing to him then, it would have meant nothing to him the second time around. Even if he had known that it was the 'key,' I seriously doubted that he would have known about the connection with the cave on the mountain. Very few people had seen the petroglyph in the cave, and I was willing to bet that Bentura wasn't one of them.

"Here you are, mister. That'll be two and a quarter," the taxi driver announced our arrival at the Lamb house.

I dug into my pocket and paid him. Two dollars and fifty cents was all I had left and over fourteen hundred miles to drive back to Valenci. Money or not, I had made up my mind to get back to New Mexico as fast as I could. That was what I should have done four days ago. To my disappointment, the Lambs were not at home but the house was unlocked. I left a note thanking them, removed the 'key' from the book and the car from the garage and started the long drive to Valenci.

Hours later, dust boiled through the air and the car was covered with grime. I was tired. My back hurt from the miles behind the wheel, and my face was blistered by the wind whipping dust through the open windows. Chicago had been cold, snowy, and miserable. Kansas was cold, dusty and miserable.

On the highway, somewhere around Liberal, Kansas, I finally figured out an explanation of why Bentura might have left us. If I were correct, then my decision to hurry back to Valenci with the 'key' was exactly what he expected me to do. The more I thought about it, the more I knew my guess was a good one. Bentura actually believed there was a treasure. He used Grease Ball and Half-Witt to help him find me just as I had unsuccessfully tried to use them to find him. He dumped them as soon as he discovered they were no longer useful. He saw the contents of my suitcase and nothing in it had meant anything to him. When Lillard called and told him he had found me, and that there was nothing my pockets, Bentura obviously concluded I had the information in my head. He knew then that all he had to do was go back to Valenci and wait for me to arrive. I would be sure to lead him directly to the treasure. When I had, he would do what he did best, he would dispose of me and the treasure would be his alone. It made very unpleasant sense.

Of course, several important things were wrong with Bentura's plan. The worst mistake was his assumption that there was a treasure. That was nonsense, because no treasure existed. Unfortunately that nonsense must have been the basis for at least two homicides. His second mistake was in assuming I would know what the 'key' meant. I didn't have the foggiest idea what it meant. His final mistake was, of course, to have assumed I would lead him to the non-existent treasure. Even if I believed there were a treasure, and I didn't, I wouldn't be dumb enough to try to find it all by myself. No, Bentura figured me all wrong, I thought. All I wanted to do now was get the 'key' thing into Rob Gaiule's hands. Once that was done, I would have kept my promise to old Charlie and I could get the hell out of Valenci.

I would hitchhike someplace and get me a job. Damn the Indians and their stupid ‘key’ anyway. Double damn Bentura, whoever he might turn out to be. While I was at it, damn me too, for having made up that stupid story about a treasure in the first place.

It was night when I drove through Gallup and turned onto the road to Valenci. I had only sixty miles, more or less, to go. Half an hour later I passed the "Welcome to Valenci – The Land of the Giant Sky” sign. It seemed as if it were a hundred years ago when I first saw that sign. Three miles further down the road I noticed the lights of another vehicle coming up behind me at a high rate of speed. I was driving too slowly because I was exhausted, but that guy is really coming on fast, I thought. Moments later his lights nearly blinded me. Then came the sound of grinding metal and my car lurched sickeningly toward the edge of the highway. The damn fool rammed me! He must be crazy or drunk! I gripped the wheel and smashed down on the accelerator. His lights dropped back for an instant and then they came on again, faster than before. At the very last moment, just in time to avoid another collision, he swerved into the opposite lane and passed me. It was a pick-up truck, and it was going at break-neck speed. The tidal wave of air as he flashed by engulfed my car and almost caused it to go off the road again. I watched as he raced down the highway ahead of me. If it were possible, he seemed to be gaining speed. He had frightened me badly. My arms and legs were trembling. I couldn't still them even though the danger to me had passed. Suddenly from far ahead I saw the truck's brake lights come on and then they swung violently to the left. Suddenly everything went haywire. His lights flashed across the landscape in a wild zigzag pattern and then were gone.

"He wrecked!" I shouted to an unhearing world. It took me another full minute to get to the place where he had gone off the road. The pick-up truck was in a field beside the intersection of the highway and a dirt road. It was upside down, the front wheels still turning slowly and the horn was blowing. Smoke rolled from under the hood. The truck was on fire.

I jumped out of my car and ran down the path newly created by the truck wreck. Flames were now visible and growing stronger by the second. I looked in the upside down truck cab and no one seemed to be there. Both windows were wide open, but there was no sign of the driver in or around the wreck. I walked back and forth along the furrow made by the wrecking truck and searched for anyone who might have been inside. The whole twisted metal wreck was on fire. The light from the flames illuminated the desert with an evil red glow.

"Hey, down there, are you O.K.?" came a shouted voice.

"I'm O.K. but I can't find the driver," I shouted back across the roar of the fire. A man clambered down into the field. He was an Indian I had seen several times in the Pueblo.

"What happened?" he asked as we searched again along the path between the burning truck and the highway.

"I don't know. This guy came up behind me like a damn maniac and slammed against me. Then he roared by and all of a sudden he was out of control and wrecked.

"Do you suppose he was trying to turn onto that side road? Maybe he hit a rock and had a blowout."

More cars had gathered and groups of people stood on the highway watching the fire.

A familiar figure pushed his way through the crowd and moved quickly toward us. It was Howard Parks. I heard a siren crying up the valley from Valenci.

"Okey, are you all right?" he shouted.

"I'm fine, but I am sure glad to see you." I shook like a watch spring as I answered him.

"What happened? Where's the truck driver?"

I described the events leading up to the wreck. As I told him about it, John Perez and another deputy arrived in a patrol car.

"Get some of those men," shouted Howard, "'and spread out across here. Hunt for the driver. He may be seriously injured. When you find him, call me. Don't move him. Look for any tracks you can find. "

Volunteers for the search poured down from the highway.

"Okey, do you feel like driving on home by yourself?" Howard asked.

"Yeah, sure. I was sort of shook there for a while but I'm OK now. Sorry about your car. I'll go on, unless you need me here."

"No, but we'll have to be here for a while. Betty is in Ramah, spending the night with some friends, so you'll have to let yourself in. The key is over the door.

"Thanks, I sure could use some shut eye. I'll make a pot of coffee for you before I turn in."

"Forget that. You hit the rack. I'll talk with you in the morning. Now take off. You look like the north end of a south bound mule."

I pushed my way through the crowd, climbed in the car and slowly drove down the highway toward Valenci. The pickup truck was still burning, but I didn't look back.

By the time I arrived at the Parks' house, I was too tired to move. I sat in the car for a long time before I finally pulled myself out of the door and dragged up the front steps.

Chapter Fifty

Howard let me sleep in late the next morning. At ten o'clock, when I finally walked into the kitchen, there was a note on the table.

"Okey -When you feel like it drive down to the Law and Order office. We need to talk. Howard."

I fixed some coffee and scrambled an egg. Jumbled scenes of the burning truck, the lights swinging wildly across the desert all mixed up in some crazy way with Liawu in her hospital bed kept racing through my mind.

Howard looked up when I walked into the office an hour later.

“Okey, did you know that there was a dead woman in that wreck last night?”

"Oh God, no!" I said and sat down heavily.

"For crying out loud, I didn't say she was killed in the wreck. I said there was a dead woman in the wreck. There was, but she had been dead for a long time. The doctor at P.H.S. says she may have been dead for as long as three weeks." Then he laughed. "You sure look green. If I didn't know better, I'd say you have a weak stomach.”

“Well what is all this? How could there be a dead woman? I didn’t see anyone in the truck. Who was she?"

"We'd like for you to have a look at her. Then maybe we can answer some of those questions. You wouldn’t mind, would you?" There was a malicious grin just under the surface of his deadpan expression.

"I'd mind, but since I obviously have no choice in the matter, I'll do it."

"There's one more thing, Okey. This little tidbit really ought to interest you."

"What’s that?”

"At the wreck last night, just after you left, I saw that chipped heel boot print again."

"The one we tracked up on the mountain?"

"That very one. It may not mean anything, but I did see several just like it. Now, before we drive up to the hospital how about telling me about your Chicago trip?"

He propped his boots on the edge of the desk and tilted his chair back against the wall ready to listen.

I told him everything I could remember from the time I left Lava through Hastings and then Chicago and then back to the wreck. The only thing I left out was the description of the 'key.' I told him I had found it, but not what it was. That particular piece of information was only for Rob.

"That's quite a tale, Okey. You'll have to wait for a while to give Rob his 'key' thing though. He's not here. He's gone to Albuquerque to testify in a federal case."

As we rode to the hospital, Howard told me they had found no sign of the driver of the wrecked pick-up, unless the chipped heel boot prints belonged to him. The prints led off into the desert and then disappeared. He also told me it was a stolen truck. It had been taken from a parking lot in Gallup about two weeks ago.

Outside the office at P.H.S., a white-coated doctor leaned against the wall waiting for us.

"Where's the old woman's body?" Howard asked as we walked up the steps.

"In the ice box," he said and gestured toward the opposite end of the building.

"Did you do the autopsy yet?"

"Not an extensive one. There wasn't much left inside her. However there was enough for us to have a pretty good idea what the story is. She died of arteriosclerosis, about fifteen days ago. Maybe even longer. The reason we couldn't do more is because she had been embalmed. That's why the body was in such good shape."

"Then, she wasn't murdered?"

"Not unless you consider old age a murderer."

"Could you tell who had done the embalming job?"

"Not a chance, but I can tell you it was a real cheapy."

"Let's go have a look at her?'"

"As the Marine Sergeant says, follow me."

The doctor led us down the hospital corridor and into a small insulated room used to store refrigerated supplies and occasionally, dead bodies.

"I'd better warn you, she stinks pretty bad. Rub some of this Mentholatum under your noses. It'll help a little."

The corpse was wrapped in a black rubberized bag. It lay on a narrow rubber wheeled gurney that stood in the middle of the room.

"Open up the bag just enough so we can see her head and face. We don't need to look at the whole thing," Howard ordered. A small crowd of onlookers had gathered outside the door to watch everything we did.

The doctor pulled back the covering. It took a few moments for my brain to let my eyes look at her. When I did, I recognized her immediately.

"Who is she, Okey?" Howard knew from the expression on my face that I recognized her.

"She's the woman in that apartment over the pool room in Chicago! She's the one I thought the police would say I killed!" I was immensely relieved to learn that I had never been sought after as her murderer.

"Do any of you people out there in the hall recognize who she is?" He directed the question toward the gaggle of curious onlookers.

Every one of them knew her.

The small crowd at the temporary morgue door all nodded their heads yes when Howard repeated the question. “Are you sure you know her?”

“Sure do. Its Mora Denti, the witch," one of the uninvited visitors volunteered.

"That's her all right. You remember her, Mr. Parks. Her boy Larry is the one who killed hisself the other night," said a fat woman.

"Have any of you seen her other son, John Denti, in the past few days?" Howard asked looking around the gathering.

This time only a few muttered “no's” and negative headshakes were his answers.

"O.K., thanks folks. Doc, wrap her up," he said. "Come on, Okey, let's get back to the office. "

Chapter Fifty-One

We returned to the office in silence. When we arrived Howard had visitors so I sat down to wait with John Perez in the deputy's office.

"What happened to you that night that we heard about Rob's grandmother being in the hospital in Hastings? I know it's none of my affair, but I can't help but ask you why you went up there?" The worst that could happen is for him to tell me to mind my own business.

"I went to Nebraska to see her."

"What for?"

"To pay my respects." His answer was given in such a manner that I knew it would be a waste of time to ask for any more details. He had very politely told me to mind my own business.

We sat silently hunting for a new conversation subject. Finally, he came up with one. "Mr. Smith, will you stay with us long enough to see Lakoshi?"

"I don't know. When is it? What is it?"

"Eight months from today. It's the most important celebration in Valenci," he said. "It is a reenactment of the time when the ancient ones came up through the sacred lake and found this world. People come here from all over the country to see Lakoshi."

I remembered Charlie's words, "I am ready to make the journey up through the next lake and into a brighter world."

Since he seemed to be in the mood to talk now, at least about local color, I decided to try him out on another line of questions.

"John, do any Valencis still practice cremation?"

"Oh yes. A few of the old people believe in it, and have it done, I think. They say that when you die your spirit has to go up into the sky like the clouds. Do your people practice cremation?"

Tit-for-tat. I ask questions and then it's his turn. We weren't going to get far with this exchange. I decided to give it one more try.

"Did you ever hear of someone burning themselves so that the smoke from the burn would carry them to heaven."

He looked startled. "I don't know. I never heard of such a thing. People believe in all sorts of strange things. I never heard about that one though."

I changed the subject. "Have they found out anything more about who killed Luke Ring?"

"No. Not a thing. It's really funny the way he was killed, just when we wanted to talk to him. It was almost as if the person who did it knew we were on our way to get him. Luke Ring wasn't a very good man, you know, Mr. Smith. I don't think he will be missed much."

"John, I wanted to ask Rob something, but, since he isn't here, maybe you can tell me. Is Rob married?"

"Who? Rob Gaiule? Our Rob Gaiule?"

"Yes."

"Good heavens no. Rob isn't married. Why do you ask? Do you have some nice Anglo girl in mind for him?" he laughed.

"I'm afraid not."

"That Rob, he's something else. He really ran with a lot of girls when he first got home from the service, but then he met Evangeline Batina, one of the schoolteachers. I guess they're pretty serious about each other now."

Maybe I won't have to hang on to the 'key' much longer, I thought, but I wished he were already married.

"Is his school teacher girl friend a Valenci?" I asked.

"Yes. Of course she is. Why do you want to know?" His face broke into a big smile. "In case you are interested we still have lots of pretty girls here. Would you like to meet one?"

Before I could think up a joking response, two deputies crashed through the outside door with a happy drunk in tow. John left me to help them pour the drunk into a cell. I realized I had gained some understanding of the meaning behind old Charlie's words and actions on that last night—"up through the lake" and "the burning flesh" and "the smoke from his flesh rising." Of course, I could never be sure, but it made a kind of strange sense. One thing I knew with absolute certainty. Old Charlie hadn't been crazy. He had been very different from anyone I had ever known, but being different doesn't make a man crazy.

Howard appeared at the door. "Come on in. I've just got a couple more things to do and we can go home."

As we walked into his office, I asked him again about the woman's body.

"We found her just after you left. She was about twenty-five yards away from the edge of the highway. As best we can figure it, she was in the bed of the truck, and when it flipped over the first time she must have been thrown out. The truck rolled at least two more times before it stopped. Her body was wrapped in a heavy woolen blanket. I guess the driver brought her all the way from Chicago in the back end of that truck. He couldn't have had her up in the cab with him; she was stiff as a board, and she stunk to high heaven."

"Do you have any idea yet who was driving the truck?"

"Not yet. We can guess, of course, and the best guess has to be her son, John."

"Bringing her back here for burial?"

"Maybe. When we catch him we'll ask him."

"Why only 'maybe'?"

"Well, he surely waited a long time to bring her home, if that's what he had in mind, don't you think?"

I thought about it. It was just one more strange thing in a long list of strange things I had encountered since I first laid eyes on old Charlie.

Chapter Fifty-Two

The long warm New Mexico spring day was ending in a beautiful display of changing colors on the Taaiyalote mesa. Howard and I sat on his front porch.

The season's earliest mosquito circled for a landing on my neck.

"Did Rob ever solve the problem of why people were treating him funny?" I asked Howard, as I swatted in vain, at the elusive bug.

"I've tried to get him to explain what he means, and all he can tell me is that people act like he knows something, and that they know he knows it, but that it is something not to be talked about. The problem is he doesn't have a clue to what the conspiracy is about."

"That's the damndest thing I've ever heard. Does everyone in the tribe treat him that way?"

"No, just the older people. The younger ones and the kids treat him just like they always have-they're his friends when he's not working, and when he's in uniform they treat him like a cop."

"And how do they treat cops?"

"Not the way we'd like to be treated, I can tell you that. They throw rocks at the patrol truck and make faces at us-after we've already gone by, of course. Put it this way. When we're on duty, we are not universally loved and admired."

"Speaking of unloved people, do you have any more information about our mystery man, Bentura?"

"I've asked everyone I know. I've run out of people to ask. No one has ever heard the name Bentura. The truth is, we're up that famous creek without a paddle. Frankly, unless and until he makes another move, we aren't going to be able to do much more than we have done."

"You mean unless he commits another crime?"

"That's exactly what I mean. I don't like to admit it, but until he catches himself, we're not going to catch him."

"Do you think he's going to catch himself?"

"Well, now, I'll tell you, Okey. I have the notion that most people who commit crimes go out of their way to get caught. It isn't just the stupid ones either. The smartest of the bunch will pull some damn fool trick, something that he would never do if crime were a totally rational process. That apparently stupid mistake traps him every time."

"For example?"

"For example, a burglar leaves his wallet with his driver's license in it at the scene of the burglary. Now you take that very same guy--ordinarily he wouldn't misplace his wallet in a thousand years. It's the same process that makes people confess to a crime when we don’t even know the crime has been committed."

"Why would a guy try to get caught? That doesn’t make sense, does it?"

"Maybe it's some unconscious need to confess his sins or, now don't you laugh, maybe he needs love and we're the only ones left to give it to him."

"Love? Come on now, Howard – love?" I couldn't keep the grin off my face.

"Yes, love, you smiling jackass. People need a certain amount of love, just like they need a certain amount of air and water. Call it love or attention, or what you will, but whatever it is, we all need it. If we can't get enough of it one way, then we'll get it another. Committing some outrageous crime is not an unusual way of getting that attention.“

"You’re realty serious about that, aren't you?"

"I sure as hell am. I've seen it happen too many times. Some faceless man will suddenly explode. He just can't stand being alone and unnoticed any longer. You can call it what you want. For lack of a better word, I call it love. It's a horribly distorted version of love, though. "

"Do many lawmen agree with you?"

"Hell no. The few I've ever told it to, look at me about like you did a few minutes ago. So I keep my theory to myself. That doesn't change my mind, though.

"Anyway, if they don't believe it, it's their problem, not mine." He grabbed up a magazine and buried his face in it.

"Howard," I ventured after a few minutes. "I can't get John Denti off my mind. Are you going to hunt for him?"

He looked up from his reading. "Well, so far as we can tell, he's dropped completely out of sight. The Valenci won't talk about him at all, and none of the Anglos have seen him around either."

"Do you think he had anything to do with this?"

"This what?"

"The murders, and all the screwy things that have happened to me."

"Truthfully, I'm not sure. Sometimes I think he might actually be your mysterious Bentura character, and other times I remember him as nothing but a neer-do-well bum. Even before he was banished, the people didn't pay much attention to him, except when he got drunk and tore up the place. To answer your question, though, yes, we're still trying to find him. " His eyes drifted back to his magazine, and I started a complicated day dream that seemed to involve Dorothy Lamb and enough money to burn a wet mule.

Chapter Fifty-Three

The sun was gone and the fantastic all-night star show would soon commence. Venus shone like a spotlight in the western sky.

After a time, I broke the silence again. "Do you think we could go back up on the mountain where we took that first hike?"

“I don’t see why not. Do you have some special reason to go back?"

“No, nothing special, I'd just like to see all those petroglyphs again. "

"They are well worth another look. If you want to go when I'm busy, just take the car and go."

"You're a real sucker for punishment. Don't you remember what happened the last time you loaned me your car?"

He smiled and put his feet up on the porch railing. "I remember all right, you hillbilly cretin. If you so much as get another speck of dust on my new car, I'll jack up the jail and put you under it."

He was all set to elaborate at length on this theme when we were interrupted.

"Hey, Howard, you gonna play ball for the ‘Lava Big Nine’ this year?" came a voice out of the dusk at the front gate.

"Hell, no! I've got enough trouble without springing a new hernia. Come on up here Sam. I want you to meet somebody." The man at the gate had on the largest cowboy hat I had ever seen. He grinned, opened the gate and rolled up the front walk like a sailor on shore leave.

"Sam, this is Okey P. Smith, from back East somewhere. Okey, this is Sam Powers. Sam's our resident expert on all things agricultural. He works for the BIA., when he isn't goofing off or playing ball -which isn't often."

"What is it you do for the BIA?" I asked.

" I'm sort of a county agent. That's what I'd be called in your part of the world. Most of my time I spend filling out totally useless quadruplicate forms for bureaucrats in Washington. One of these days the damn government is going to drown under a sea of onionskin. I wish to hell they'd just let me do what I'm trained to do."

"Sit down, Sam before you get all steamed at your employer. Where've you been? I haven't seen you for six weeks."

Powers squatted down on the top step. "Yeah, I know. I've been over at Grants trying to set up sheep quotas. They've overgrazed the land in the valley again. What's been happening around here? Nothing, as usual?"

"Nothing much, " Howard said carefully. " Sam, did you ever hear of a man named Bentura?"

"Bentura? Old Bentura? Why, hell yes. I just saw him this morning. Why are you interested in Old Bentura?"

I started to blurt out an answer, but Howard cut me off with a look and continued to talk as if nothing very important were being discussed.

"Who is he, Sam? What do you know about him?"

"He's a medicine man. Hell, he's my number one man with the Rio Grande farmers. If I didn't have his help, I never would get anything done over in the valley. Now, what gives? What's this all about?"

"Sam, while you were gone..." Howard proceeded to fill him in on the events of the past few weeks.

"Whew!" he said when Howard finally finished. "You've had a hell of a poor introduction to our part of the world, Okey."

I couldn't contain myself further. "Where can we get our hands on this Bentura character?"

"Hold it right there, my friend." Powers interrupted me. "You're barking up the wrong tree. Old Bentura has been with me every single day for the last five weeks. You'll have to take my word for that of course, but I can guarantee you he isn't your man." The stainless steel look on Power's face indicated clearly that he was not going to allow his friend's name to be tarnished.

"But, that name-Bentura?"

"Bentura is known all over the country East and North of Albuquerque. He's an important and influential man. I don't know who this character is you're looking for, but, whoever he is, he's stolen that name. He isn't the real Bentura. Hell, if somebody called himself President Roosevelt and held up a bank, nobody would think the real President Roosevelt did it, would they?"

I was defeated. Howard looked disappointed too.

Powers continued, "If this guy who calls himself Bentura is a Valenci, then he's stolen that name from another tribe altogether. There aren't any Valencis named Bentura and the real Bentura isn't a Valenci. He isn't the man you're after, either,"

I shook my head in resignation. One of our few leads had been the name and now we knew that even the name had been stolen.

"Thanks, Sam. You've saved us a whole lot of time and trouble. We could have wasted days looking for someone named Bentura and he wouldn't have been who we wanted at all."

"Don't look so glum, Okey," Howard commiserated after our visitor left. "Look at it this way, now we know the name Bentura is a phony. This jerk we're after heard the name somewhere and took it because it belonged to someone of importance. We know a lot more about our man now. We're learning how his mind works."

"Sure," I said, "I guess we're doing just fine." But I didn't really believe it.

Chapter Fifty-Four

Two days passed before I decided to act on Howard's offer to use his car to go to see the petroglyphs.

"Why in the world are you going up there?" Betty Parks asked when I told her what I proposed to do.

"Just an urge to see those petroglyphs again. I won't be gone too long. It's only a few miles back from the road."

"I swear you men are all alike. You get more like Howard every day. Go on, get out of here, I'm busy."

I drove the car to the same place where we had parked before at the base of the mountain. The air was cool, the sun was bright, and the sky cloudless. I moved slowly up the steep path to the first point where the petroglyphs could be seen. I found a big flat rock and sat down. The view across the valley was spectacular. Subtle colors of a thousand shades and hues glowed in every rock face, sand hill, and mountain. Now that I knew what to look for, I could see more ancient ruins at the base of the mountain. From here it was easy to see that there had been many small groups of buildings scattered throughout the valley and not just one large pueblo. The crumbled walls of the kivas were clearly distinguishable from the other ruins because of their circular shape.

Having caught my breath again, I stood up and cautiously made my way along the narrow path at the edge of the cliff. The real reason I had come back here was to see the petroglyph that was the original of the 'key.' I couldn't shake the notion that if I looked at it long enough I might unwind its riddle. The face of the mountain grew steeper. The path along the ledge seemed more vertical and much narrower than I remembered. If my foot slipped and I fell it would be a long way to the bottom. I inched along a few feet further and then stopped. A sound of some sort came from ahead. I listened intently but heard nothing more. A loose stone falling could have made the noise. I edged along a few more yards. Damn this trail, I thought, it's one hell of a lot narrower than I remembered. At one place my face was pressed against the rock, my toes were on the path, and my boot heels and fanny hung out in thin air.

I grabbed hold of the roots of an old weathered juniper snag and pulled past the very dangerous point to a spot where there was enough room to sit down. Howard had brought me along an easier path. My knees felt as if they were made of foam rubber. I wished I had paid more attention to Howard's route. If I had, then I wouldn't be fumbling around out on this ledge. The sun was still hot and bright, but, much lower in the sky. The shadows in the valley had lengthened perceptibly. I knew if I were going to look at that petroglyph and get back home in time for supper, I should get a move on.

Fortunately, the path opened up again and there was more walking space. With each step, thin sandy soil billowed up and covered my boots and the legs of my trousers. Prickly pear cactus with bright yellow blossoms grew in bristly clumps on the edge of the path. I moved several hundred feet up the mountainside before I got tired again. I looked for another resting place. I was surprised and disappointed to find I would poop out so quickly. Maybe I should have waited for Howard before trying to come back up this high. I squatted down on the path and leaned back against the cliff face. My breath came in gasps. Fully five minutes passed before I felt energetic enough to start up again. I started to pull myself erect, and that's when I saw the print in the sand-a heel print with a little notch in it, identical to the one Howard had shown me the night we tracked Larry Denti. Very carefully I stooped back down and stared at the print. I knew nothing about how to estimate the age of footprints. This one might be fresh or it might be old. The maker could have been up here this very day or he might have been here months or ever years ago. Then I thought, “it might belong to the man who had attacked me.” I remembered that Howard said he had seen a similar heel print at the pick-up truck wreck.

Larry Denti sure as hell hadn't made that wreck site footprint unless he came back from the grave to make it. As I sat there speculating, a light breeze sprang up and the heel print blurred ever so slightly. Its sharp edges became rounded and softer. And then I realized it couldn't have been made as long ago as the day of Larry Denti's death. It wasn't even made yesterday. It was fresh, very fresh.

I knew I should immediately climb back down the mountain. To remain up here with evening rapidly approaching would be more than foolish. To remain on the mountain in the company of a known killer would be the ultimate in foolishness. But, as usual, my curiosity far outweighed my caution. I elected to be foolish. If I could slip very quietly just a little bit further up the path, I was sure to be able to see the entrance to the cave. If old ‘Chipped Heel’ were there, I could get a good look at him, find out who he is, and quietly leave. If he weren't there, I could take a quick peek at the petroglyph and then hurry on home.

I moved as quietly as I could. I planned ahead of each step exactly where to place my foot on the path to insure the least amount of noise. I tried to keep as close to the cliff face as possible. Just beyond a big rock, the trail made a sharp left turn.

Maybe the cave entrance was around that corner. I dropped to my hands and knees, and crawled to the bend. With exaggerated caution, I stopped and listened. There was no sound. I crept forward again until I could see around the turn. Nothing. I got to my feet and walked carefully to the next bend. For the second time, the trail turned sharply to the left. I repeated the performance by dropping to my knees, crawling, listening, and looking. This time there was something around the corner but not what I wanted. The something was a very large and smooth boulder, higher than my head. It completely blocked the trail. I could see no way around it. On the left side the cliff towered vertically at least a hundred feet to the crest of the mountain. On the other side was the valley, three hundred feet straight down. The boulder blocking the path was too unbalanced to climb over. I had sneaked up on a lousy stinking dead end.

I felt like a fool. The sun was directly behind my back causing my shadow to fall along the path and halfway up the boulder. I walked forward a few yards and the shadow climbed higher on the rock. If I could climb like my shadow, it wouldn't have been a dead end. In disgust, I turned to leave. Not more than three steps later my foot caught under a juniper root hidden in the path. I lost my balance, staggered and crashed heavily, my entire weight on the trapped foot.

Intense pain flashed up my leg, and I almost blacked out. Finally, I struggled around onto one knee and slowly pulled my injured foot out from under the root. The pain was fierce and the ankle started to swell almost immediately. What kind of a mess had I gotten myself into? I would never be able to negotiate that cliff face on my own with my injured foot. I didn't think it was broken, but it was badly twisted. There was nothing to do but sit down and wait until it felt better or until someone came to get me. That was a joke. The next person up here might not come for days. I dragged myself back against the path-blocking boulder and looked out toward the west. The sun shown directly into my eyes and wiped out the world in a dazzling golden glare. I closed my eyes to cut out the blinding light.

Either I passed out or I fell into a heavy doze. I would never know which. When I came back to life, the sun was below the horizon. Night would soon be here.

The sound of a familiar voice rang out. "It's a great place to take a nap, Okey, but maybe you'd better come back and see it again tomorrow. It's nearly supper time."

"Howard?" I couldn't believe my ears.

"Who the hell do you think it would be? Get up you lazy bum. Wait a minute--have you hurt yourself?"

"I'm afraid so. My ankle is hurt."

"Let's see it," he said and squatted down beside me. "That doesn't look too bad. Betty got worried when you didn't return on time, so I came up to see if anything was wrong. How the hell did you get all the way off on this end of the mountain?"

"I was looking for the cave. That one with the funny petroglyph in it."

"Good God, Okey, that's over a mile in the opposite direction. You sure are some outdoorsman."

"If I'm that far off, how in the world did you find me?"

"I picked up your trail at the car. It was like following the tracks of a drunken sailor through snow."

"Howard, there is something important to tell you." I described the heel print to him.

He grew very still and listened intently to what I was saying about the print and about how I figured it was a fresh print.

"Okey, let's get you down from here as fast as we can. When we get back to Valenci, I'm going to round up enough men to search this whole area. I want that guy and I want him tonight."

"Look, why don't you leave me here. I'm perfectly all right just where I am. You can go to Valenci and be back with your deputies in less time than it would take to get me down with this lousy foot. "

He looked down the mountain trail and then back at me.

"I think you're right. You're reasonably safe here if you don't try to move around in the dark. Now listen, Okey," he had made up his mind. "Stay against that boulder. Keep your back to it and don't take your eyes off this trail. I'm going to leave my pistol with you. If anyone, and I mean anyone, comes along the trail, you make them identify themselves. If it isn't one of the deputies or me, make whomever it is sit down and wait until we get back here. If they won't wait, then threaten to shoot them. If that doesn't work, let them go. Understand this, I don't want you to actually shoot anyone unless he directly attacks you. Do you understand all that?"

"I certainly do. Go on now, before it gets too dark."

"We'll be back. Keep off that foot, and don't worry. Everything will be OK."

I sat stiffly erect with my back to the rock and my eyes glued to the trail. Howard looked at me for a moment and then disappeared around the turn. My fingers played with the pistol. Whoever you are, Mr. Chipped Heel, please, please don't come back here tonight, I prayed.

Chapter Fifty-Five

One hour passed; then a second hour. It was pitch dark. A full moon should be in the sky, but the boulder blocked my view to the East. When Howard left me alone I fingered the pistol as if it were a string of prayer beads. As more time passed, I relaxed and soon the gun was on the ground by my side, largely forgotten. Old Chipped Heel is miles from here by now. I decided Howard and his deputies were coming on a wild goose chase. Nevertheless, when I heard the sound of approaching footsteps, I grabbed the pistol and experienced a huge surge of adrenalin.

"Okey? Hey, Okey. Are you there?" came a voice from around the turn.

"Who is it?" My hands were shaking.

"It's me. Rob. Rob Gaiule. Howard says you have his pistol. Please put it down, I don't want to get shot."

My sigh of relief could have been heard in Gallup. "I'm back here, Rob. Come on around. I won't shoot you." I laid the gun down in the dirt again.

He came gingerly around the corner. When he saw I did not have the gun aimed at him, he walked toward me rapidly.

"How's the foot?"

"I'll be O.K. What's the plan? What are we going to do?"

"We aren't going to do anything. Howard says for us to stay right here. I brought a First Aid Kit and some coffee for you. We didn't have time to get anything else. Here, let me put some tape on that foot. "

The coffee was hot, black, and good. As I drank it, Rob filled me in on the plans. John Perez and two part time deputies were stationed at the base of the mountain. Two of the regular deputies and Howard were working their way along the cliff face. One hastily recruited volunteer was stationed at the mouth of the valley to stop anyone who might try to come out. They assumed there was little likelihood that anyone other than the search party and me would be in the area-anyone except Chipped Heel, that is.

"Do you think it will work? Do you think they'll catch him?"

"If he's still up here, they'll get him. The trouble is, he's had, at least, a two-hour head start. He could have walked a long way in two hours."

"Why don't they have a deputy over on the other side of the mountain?"

"Three darn good reasons. First, there wasn't time enough to get anyone over there. Second, we don't have the manpower, and third it's in the wrong direction from the highway. We assume the man came here in a car. If he did, then he wouldn't want to get too far from it. If he went in that direction, he would have almost fifty miles of rugged country to cross before he came to a road and then he would still he almost a hundred miles by highway away from the general area where his car is likely hidden."

"It sounds like you really know this country."

"I ought to. I was born here. This is Indian country, Okey. Remember, we had it first."

"My history books say Coronado discovered it, so you must be mistaken."

"If we'd had a decent set of immigration laws, we never would have let Coronado across the border," he laughed.

We finished off the coffee and sat quietly staring into the night.

"Rob, how much has Howard explained to you about what I'm doing here in Valenci?"

"Well, he's told me some, but, of course, I can't know how much he hasn't told me."

"I think it's time for me to share with you almost everything I know."

"Almost? What's with 'almost?' "

"I made a promise to your grandmother, in the hospital in Hastings, only hours before her death, that I would not tell you everything unless and until you were safely married to a Valenci girl. However strange that may seem to you, I won't break my promise. John Perez has already told me you aren't married."

"Then before you start your story, let me tell you something John Perez doesn't know. I am married but it's sort of a secret. Evangeline Batina and I got married last October. She's a schoolteacher at the pueblo. We haven't told anyone because the school principal says people who are not married in the Christian Church, are living in sin and will not be allowed to teach in his school. We were not married in his Anglo way. Evangeline wanted to finish out this school year because she is so fond of the kids. I respect how she feels and agreed she ought to do what she wants."

"That surely simplifies things for me. By the way, congratulations."

"Thanks. Now, what's this story you have to tell me?"

In short form it would have taken a long time to tell. I chose to relate it in as full and complete detail as I could. I wanted Rob Gaiule to know his grandfather, as I had seen him. I wanted him to appreciate the dignity and great courage of his grandmother as I had seen her.

He said not one word during the entire lengthy monologue.

When I finally finished, it was almost midnight. A full moon floated directly overhead in the sky. The entire world seemed to have taken on an electric blue glow. Moonlight was extraordinarily bright in the clear air of Valenci.

"Where is the 'key' now?" he asked.

"At Howard's house, but he doesn't know it."

"Do you know what it means?"

"No. I wish I did, but I don't. The only thing I know is what I've told you--that a lot of people have a screwy notion that it has something to do with buried treasure."

"But you don't think so?"

"Think that there is a treasure? No. I don't. I do believe that your grandfather held some sort of a position of trust in Valenci. If that's true, since your father is dead, then you must now be the holder of that trust, whatever it is. My best guess is that the 'key' is some sort of a symbol of your inherited office. "

"I don't know, Okey. That's an interesting idea, but you've come at me pretty fast this evening. Right now the whole thing makes very little sense to me. "

"Rob, you commented to Howard once, in my presence, that the older people were treating you in an odd way. Do you suppose it has something to do with the 'key?' "

"They know something, that's for sure. John Perez went to that hospital in Nebraska and when he came back is when they started acting peculiar. I've asked him about it, and all he says is that he told everyone my grandmother said my grandfather was dead. John doesn't tell lies, Mr. Smith. When he says that's all she said, it's true. John is an important man. He may even be close to the Cacique in importance."

"Maybe the 'key' will mean something to you when you see it. Have you ever seen the petroglyph in the cave?"

"Not that I remember. I may have, but there are so many of them around on the hills, and no one really knows what they mean. I remember as a child making up stories about them but then when you get older you don't pay much attention to that sort of thing, but now I wish I did know more about them."

Chapter Fifty-Six

Each of us heard the noise on the path at the same instant. The noise was followed immediately by the sweep of a flashlight beam and a loud hail.

"We're around here, Howard," I called.

Howard Parks came around the turn with two Valenci men I did not know.

"Did you get Old Chipped Heel, I hope?"

"No such luck, I'm afraid. He apparently slipped away down the valley. Jake Lewis found his tracks and followed them all the way out to the Gallup Road. There were tire tracks where his truck had been parked."

"It's like trying to catch fog in a net." The disappointment was clear in my voice.

"He'll make a mistake sooner or later. I guarantee he'll be the author of his own destruction. We'll get him, Okey."

The four men took a long time to maneuver me around the narrow steep path, down the side of the mountain and into Howard's car. Before the cars drove off, I told Rob to come and get the 'key' as soon as he got back to Lava. Once he had the 'key' in his hands, my promise was fully performed.

On the road to Lava, Howard described the hunt. They found the footprints at several points along the cliff face but not once did they catch sight of the man. Nor did they find a clue as to what he had been doing on the mountain. Howard said he thought it unlikely that the phony Bentura, assuming he was old Chipped Heel, came to the mountain specifically to harm me. He had no way of knowing I was going to be there. We agreed that he must have had some purpose in being in such an out-of-the-way place but neither of us was able to guess what that purpose had been.

By the time I got my foot taped up at the hospital and arrived at the Park's house it was close to three o'clock in the morning. As soon as we were in the house I handed Rob the 'key.' He looked at it for a long time. Finally he shook his head. "I'm really sorry, Okey, but it means absolutely nothing to me. I was hoping it would jump out and speak to me."

"Well give it time. You're bound to figure it out sooner or later. "

"I'll come over later on today and we'll talk."

"If we can get Howard to describe to you the location of the cave with the petroglyph, we can go up there. Once you see the real thing then maybe the picture 'key' will make sense. "

"You want to go back up on the mountain after what happened to you last night?"

"If we take Howard's path instead of mine it's not much of a hike. I ought to he able to make it."

"We'll see, tomorrow. "

I was asleep before I hit the rack. All night long I dreamed about falling from high places. Somehow Dorothy Lamb was in that dream too.

In the early afternoon, Rob came to the Park's house, excited about a new idea. We went out on the front porch to talk.

"What's this great new idea?"

"You said your friend in Chicago is a Professor, didn't you?"

"Yes. He 's an archeologist. "

"Well, why not ask the Professor to look at it? The whole pueblo is covered up with 'professors' all summer long. They must know something about petroglyphs."

"I suppose I might, but how do we get it to him?"

"Last night you said you would never let it get out of your hands again. Have you changed your mind?"

"We can copy it, full size on the copy machine at the office and then mail it to him. In fact, I've already done it. Look here." He reached into his jacket pocket and pulled out a perfect copy of the 'key.'

"That's great. Professor Lamb will figure it out. We'll send the letter in today's mail."

Betty Parks joined us on the porch. "Have something to eat with us Rob."

"Thank you very much Mrs. Parks, but I have already eaten."

"Well, have a cup of coffee and sit with us while we eat. Howard!" she called into the bedroom. "Howard, your so-called 'breakfast' is ready. The very idea of breakfast in the middle of the afternoon!"

The telephone rang. "Howard!" she shouted, "answer that darn phone and then get out here to breakfast, lunch, and dinner. "

Several minutes passed before Howard strode angrily into the kitchen.

"Rob, you're here, good! Okey, you and Rob come with me."

"What's up, Howard?" He didn't get into the car as we expected, but walked rapidly up the street toward the BIA. hospital.

"That was Perez on the phone. He had two messages. Somebody stole Burton Santo's pickup truck. The second message is the crazy one. Doctor Gentry at the hospital called the office. They've managed to lose Mora Denti's body."

From a hundred yards away, we saw two white-coated doctors hovering anxiously outside the emergency entrance to the hospital.

"Parks, we just can't figure it. I went in there to get something and, by God, she was gone," fluttered the doctor who had worked on my injured foot. "I hope you realize that this kind of thing can get the hospital into all sorts of trouble."

We hurried into the cold storage room where Mora's body had been kept. Nothing else had been disturbed, but the body, rubber bag and all, was gone.

The cart stood gleaming white and empty in the center of the room.

"Has anyone touched anything in here since you discovered she was gone?" Howard barked at the doctors.

They looked at each other uncertainly. "I don't think so. When I discovered it was missing, I told Finesilver here, and he said to ask around. So I checked with the staff to see if someone had claimed her, or if it was some sort of a bad joke. No one admitted knowing anything about it, and that's when we called your office. Is body snatching a crime?"

"It used to be. You are absolutely certain that no one claimed the body, aren't you?" Howard asked.

"I checked the day book," replied Dr. Gentry. "No one claimed it. I wish to hell they had, but there are no entries. I checked that the very first thing."

"Well, get your whole staff together. Let's see if anyone here admits knowing anything about anything."

Chapter Fifty-Seven

Twenty minutes later the questions to the assembled and thoroughly embarrassed group had produced no useful information. The hospital was wide open twenty-four hours a day. At night the emergency entrance and the main door were always unlocked. The only locked spaces were the offices and the small pharmacy. Neither had been disturbed. The two patients in the wing next to where the body was kept had slept through the entire night and neither had seen anything.

"Well, boys, how do you figure this mess?" Howard rumbled at us as we walked back down the dirt street to his house. "First, the damn body shows up in a wreck, but it didn't die in the wreck. Not only that, but it had already been embalmed. Now it disappears into thin air. I'm beginning to believe Mora Denti really was some kind of a damn witch. "

"She's no more witch than I am. Whoever stole Santo’s truck took it," Rob said.

“Do you have any ideas, Rob?" Howard asked. He seemed unusually disturbed by all the things that had happened.

"Yes, I do, Mr. Parks. I think the man who took her was the same man who had her in the first place. I think he stole Santo's pick-up, and then went up there to the hospital and got her again."

"Who in the hell is he and what does he want her for?" I blurted out.

Howard didn't wait for Rob to answer any questions. He asked it over again for himself. "Who do you think it is, Rob?"

"John Denti. It has to be Denti. Nothing else makes sense."

"That's what I think too. He knew we were looking for him so he didn't dare show his face at the hospital to claim her body in the ordinary way."

"I still don't get it," I said.

"Alright, here's how I see it, Okey. I think the man you've been calling Bentura is really John Denti," Rob explained. "I think Denti is the man with the chipped heel print, too. He's the only person who has any logical connection with Larry Denti, Mora Denti, and Luke Ring. What's more, he's the only person I can think of who would want Mora's body. When he wrecked that truck the other night, he had to clear out of there fast. It was a stolen truck, and if he didn't take off you would have seen him when you drove up. Very likely he recognized the car you were driving as Howard's. He probably thought it was Howard driving. Of course, he might have thought it was you, if he's the man who took the suitcase from you in Chicago. In either case he had to hit the trail fast, and that meant leaving the body.

Now he's got it back again and he'll go on with whatever he planned to do with it."

"I'll buy that, at least for now," said Howard. " It makes as much sense as any other guess. How does it grab you, Okey?"

"If we could lay our hands on John Denti, we could find out quick enough."

"Rob, you seem to have worked this thing out pretty carefully. Do you have any idea where he might have gone with her?"

"I have a guess."

"Well?"

"When Okey here saw him, apparently he was trying to turn onto that dirt road that runs up the valley toward Big Rock, but he was going too fast and he wrecked. If he was on his way up there then, he might go back. I think that's where he's been hiding out and I think that's where he is now."

"That sounds right to me. Let's go have a look," said Howard.

"Mr. Parks, if we go up the valley, he'll see us, just like he did before. He can see ten miles down the valley from that mountain. As soon as he sees us coming, he'll get away again."

"What do you suggest?" asked Howard.

"Let me go in, alone, the back way."

"The back way? You've got to be kidding! That's a fifty-mile hike. That's what you told me," I said.

"Look, Denti must think the mountain up there is the safest place around for him. He can see anyone who tries to come up the valley. But, he might never think that someone would come the back way. Mr. Parks, if you'll block off the valley, I can flush him out for you. It'll take me about a day and half to make the walk. I can be there by late tomorrow evening. The first thing the following morning you cordon off the mouth of the valley. I'll come in across the mountain and either get him myself, or I'll flush him out for you to catch. One way or the other we'll catch the sonofabitch. "

"That's a pretty stiff walk, Rob," Howard said, but nevertheless he looked eager to try the plan.

"Yes, but we can do it," I said.

"We?" Rob said with genuine surprise in his voice. "What's this 'we' business?"

"I'm coming with you."

Chapter Fifty-Eight

We laid out a plan and a timetable. Howard would drive us to the drop point, south west of Ramah, that afternoon. We would carry enough gear for two nights in the wild. Because, even without my sore foot, I was sure to slow up Rob, the cordon across the mouth of the valley would not be established until noon of the third day. We agreed it was unlikely that Denti or Bentura or whatever else he called himself would be aware of the blockade, if the police were careful to stay out of the valley.

Rob and I were to make our way across country. When we arrived at the cliff, we were to try to locate Denti. If we could capture him without undue danger to either of us, we were to do so. If we could not, then we were to drive him down the valley into the hands of the police by raising enough hell to cause him to flee. Both of us were outfitted with pistols. Howard cautioned us again and again not to use the guns unless it were absolutely necessary to protect our lives.

We examined topographic maps of the area with great care. The region we were to traverse consisted primarily of broken sand hills and sparse vegetation.

The mountain and the cliff, where we assumed he would be found, was the dominant feature in the terrain.

"It won't be an easy walk. It's going to be long and it's going to be hot. By the way, there's a feeder stream to Big Rock creek that starts at about your half waypoint. That will be a good landmark for you even if there isn't any water in it. You should get to it about mid-morning, tomorrow." Howard pointed it out on the map.

"What about water? Are we likely to find some?" I asked.

"No. Not likely. I know the map shows intermittent streams but unless you have a hard rain, you won't see any ground water. Do you agree, Rob?"

"Yes. Those streams run above ground only after a hard rain. Sometimes, if you've nothing better to do, you can find subsurface water by digging in a dry stream bed, but we won't have time enough to fool with that. We'll carry our drinking water with us."

When all the gear was collected, it was a pitifully small stack. Two blankets, two ponchos, two flashlights, two plastic water bags, two whistles, some matches, a small first aid kit, a coffee pot, and two folding cups, and a hand full of food were the entire inventory.

"I sure hate to carry all this stuff in with us," Rob said, looking at me, "but I guess when you take an Eastern tenderfoot with you, you have to carry along a lot of extra, luxury items. Sure seems like a waste of effort, though."

"Where's the rest of our gear?" I said. "Where is our tent and some nice kitchen appliances? What about our cots and sleeping bags, and most important, where's the portable toilet?"

I knew from the looks on their faces that they weren't sure whether I was serious or trying to kid them.

"Oh, crap. Get on with it, Rob. Leave this dude at home. Next thing he'll tell us is that he needs to get his tuxedo pressed."

We loaded the gear into Howard's car, drove north toward Gallup, and then turned east. The sky was overcast when we arrived at the drop point.

Before he drove away, Howard leaned out of the car window. "Good hunting, boys. We'll see you day after tomorrow. Don't worry. We'll have that valley sealed up tighter than a drum when the time comes."

"Don't forget to write." I sounded more cheerful than I felt. Fifty miles didn't seem like much of a walk when I sat in a soft chair in Howard's office with a map in my hand. When I stood at the starting point and looked out over the desert I had agreed to cross, it seemed impossible. "Come on, Okey. Let's take a stroll," said Rob.

Chapter Fifty-Nine

We covered fifteen long hard miles before we stopped for the evening.

According to Rob, the first day's walk had been an easy one across open country. Easy or not, I was worn out when we quit.

"We're just about here," said Rob, pointing to a spot on his map. "Look. See that little gulley over there? I think it's this one here next to the elevation mark. We'll have to do better than this tomorrow."

"Roll up that damn map and let's eat," I grunted.

We ate in silence and then laid back on our bedrolls to watch the sunset.

"More coffee, Okey?"

"No thanks. One cup of your swill is enough to hold me this evening."

"What do you think of our country now?"

"The truth is that I really like it. I'd be happy to live here if there were some way for me to make a living. Tell me, have a lot of the Valencis left the Pueblo, or do they spend most of their lives here?"

"Some leave and go to work in the city, but they generally come back before long. Most of the ones who do leave go to the West Coast. I'll tell you one thing, if my grandfather hadn't died, he would have come back here, for sure."

"I don't mean offense, Rob, but the people here seem so poor. Why do they stay? They all seem bright. Couldn't they go someplace else and get jobs and raise their standard of living?" A heavy line of pink clouds remained in the indigo blue sky.

"Well sure, they could change it. I'm not exactly sure what you mean by 'raise it'."

"Come on, there's lots of ways. Look at all the things they could get. The women could use real stoves and washing machines, couldn't they? They could have cars and television sets and nice furniture. There are so many good things to be had. Very few people here seem to own half of what they need. They could even have indoor plumbing if the tribe had enough money to install a sewer system."

"You mean if we weren't such lazy welfare redskins, we would get to work and accumulate things like you Anglos do?" He didn't raise his voice and he didn't look at me.

"I'm sorry. I didn't mean it to sound that way. It came out all wrong. What I mean is, I like the Valencis and I want all of you to have all sorts of good things and not be so damn poor. That's all I meant."

"Poverty is relative, Okey." He sounded as if he had said all of this to me before. "There is a base line below which that isn't true. But once you're above that line, then it all becomes relative, and it becomes a question of values. If we were without food or without shelter, we would be poor. If enemies or disease laid us waste, then we would be poor. But, above that line, well, let me explain it to you this way. If we're hungry, if we have no food, we eat with our neighbor until we do have food. He won't regard it as an intrusion or a burden because he knows he can share with us if he gets in the same position. This isn't something we invented, though. A lot of you Anglos feel exactly the same way. Haven't you been a long time with Mr. Parks? Hasn't he shared his home and his table with you? Would you do the same for him? Or would you charge him room and board?"

My face flushed. "You're right. I have imposed on them much too long."

"No! No! You didn't understand me at all. I don't think you should be embarrassed. I think exactly the opposite. You are a human being. You need food and shelter and friends. You've only received what you need. That's what it's all about. That's what's important."

"Well, I'll pay them back. Maybe, when we figure out what the 'key' means, we'll find a treasure just like old Half-Witt and Grease Ball wanted. Then I can really repay Howard. We'll all be rich. You, Evangeline, the Parks, me, all of us, we'll have a ball." I was only half joking.

"Okey, you sure have a lot to learn about us, and about yourself too." He fluffed out his blanket on the ground. "Let's hit the sack, buddy."

I stretched out my bedroll and then lay awake for a few minutes. The sky was completely overcast. No stars were visible. The night was very dark. Maybe Rob is right, I thought, but what if we should hit the jackpot with that 'key'! Then I dropped off to sleep.

Chapter Sixty

The next morning I was awakened by a succession of rain drops splattering against my face. The blanket was already wet. I pried open my eyes and discovered it was dawn, but the sky was one solid storm cloud. The rain came down harder every new second.

"Better hurry up and roll your blanket before it gets even more soaked, Okey. We'll move out now and fix breakfast later when we find some shelter."

The rain came down in white sheets. It didn't soak into the parched ground; it sat on the surface until the puddle got big enough to run. As a result, the whole area became a mosaic of small streams. When I bent my head forward for my hat brim to shield my face, the water ran down my neck and back. Even under the poncho, I was soaked to the skin. We sloughed along through the new swamp for almost an hour before the rain let up enough for us to hear each other over the uproar.

"Are you cold?" he shouted.

"I'm pretty soggy. How long do you figure this mess will keep up?"

I was not only wet, I was freezing.

"I don't know. It's got to quit sometime. This is more rain than we've had all season. Wait a minute! Look! There's a shack. We're in luck, if the darn thing has a roof."

We stumbled and splashed the last few hundred yards toward a tiny box-like adobe structure. One small window opening was visible. The doorway was solid wood. Rain poured down harder than ever.

With rain streaming down his face, Rob came to a stop twenty feet short of the shack, stamped his feet on the muddy ground, and called out, "Someone is coming! Someone wants shelter!"

"What the hell are you standing there yelling about?" I choked out as I ran past him. We'll drown like rats out here. Come on, get a move on!"

It was a cloudburst. Standing under Niagara Falls couldn't have made us wetter.

I thrust my hands against the solid wooden door and reluctantly it gave way. I pushed past it and rushed inside. Two thirds of the roof was still on the shack.

Rob followed me through the door. Even with part of the roof missing, the single room was darker than the gloomy grey outside. It took a few moments for us to get the water out of our eyes and a longer time still for our eyes to adjust to the dim light.

"I'll build a fire and we'll dry out," Rob said as he uncovered the remains of a stone hearth.

"What the hell were you jumping up and down and yelling about out there?" I asked again. "No one has lived in this old shed for a hundred years."

"No people have lived here for a long time, but have you ever heard of rattlesnakes?

"Rattlesnakes?"

"They stay around old ruins like this. I just told them we were coning. They might not have heard our footsteps because of the roar of the rain. They don't care much for surprise visitors."

"Are you pulling my leg again?" I asked as I slid out of the dripping poncho.

"Nope." He piled up a few pieces of fallen roof timber and, before I got my shirt off, he had a small fire started. "I'm serious. Rattlesnakes pick up the vibrations of your feet. That's how they know you're coming. Usually they'll keep out of your way if they can. With the rain slamming down on the ground and the ground being so darn muddy, they might not have heard us. I was just announcing our arrival."

"You mean they still might be in here?" I gazed around the small room apprehensively.

"Probably, but don't worry. You won't see them. By now they've found a dry crack in the wall. They'll sit in it and have a good time watching us."

"Ugh! I hope they know we're peaceful."

Rob laughed. "Well, I don't know about me, but you sure don't look very war like. You look more like a drowned cat."

The rain continued to pour. Steam rose from our wet clothes that hung on sticks next to Rob's fire.

"Rob, I've been so damn busy getting my hide out of this storm that I had almost forgotten why we are here. Do you think we will make it to the cliff on time?"

"Not a chance. It's just unpleasant out there now. After a while it's going to be dangerous."

"Dangerous? What from, lightning?"

"No. Not lightning -water. The soil here doesn't soak up and hold water like it does back in your part of the world. Here, rain runs off, and runs off quick. With the amount we've had this morning we would have to cross a hundred fast moving streams between here and the mountain. We could be drowned if we tried to go on now. "

"But Howard will be there...."

"Howard Parks understands this country better than anyone I know," Rob cut me off. "He'll know exactly what kind of a mess we're in. We ought to be able to get out of here tomorrow. All this means is a one-day delay. "

"How will we cross those streams tomorrow?"

"With any luck, we won't have to. They'll be gone. I told you, the storm water runs off fast."

Within a short time we were dried out enough to start to work cleaning out a living area in the debris strewn shack.

"Who the hell would ever want to live out here?" I asked as I stacked up a pile of rusty tin cans.

"Sheepherders. You'll see them all over this part of the country. In the spring they bring big herds of sheep out here on the open range. Then they hire some old guy, usually a Hopi, to tend the sheep all summer long. Sheepherders are a strange lot, they like the extreme solitary life."

"I'm damn glad I don't have to do it. I'd go crazy out here." I commented.

"Oh, you never can tell," Rob replied. "You might even learn to live with yourself someday."

The coffee began to boil on the tiny fire. Rob was an experienced outdoorsman. His fire heated the room, dried our clothes, and boiled the coffee. We still had enough wood left for many more hours.

"Man, that's good. I would have given a million dollars for coffee like that in the slammer."

Chapter Sixty-One

"Tell me about yourself, Okey," he said leaning back against the wall. "Who are you?"

His question and the hot black coffee opened the floodgates. I told him about coalmines and jails, the navy, flop houses, and skid row.

"You've been so many different places and you've done so many things. You've led quite a life."

I experienced a rare moment of candor. "Rob, you don't understand. As old as I am, I still don't have two nickels to rub together in my pocket. I don't even own the pocket I'm wearing. The clothes I have on belong to Howard Parks. Hell, I haven't got a damn thing I can call my own."

"You keep talking about things. Why do you care so much about things?"

"What's so wrong about things? Your people sure could use a few more things. Truth is, it looks to me like all of you should spend more time thinking about things."

"You're partially right. We need some things. We need better education. We certainly need more intelligent relations with the federal government. We need better medical assistance. But all those things must come in such a way that they won't take over, and then destroy us. You Anglos are just like the Spanish Conquistadores. You want us to adopt your materialistic values and your God and your way of life, all on your terms."

"We're not talking about the same thing," I said. "You're giving me some kind of 'Indian Power' talk. It's alright with me if you choose to stay the same but..."

"Stay the same! Where did you get that idea? We aren't an endangered species. An Indian Reservation isn't a zoo. You have no more right to try to freeze us in time than you do to remold us into your own image. We are a nation. We have lived right where we are now for over a thousand years. In case you can't count, that's a long time before Columbus came. We have changed greatly over those years. Our nation has evolved just as much as yours has. We've grown too. There's a lot more of us now than there used to be. I'll have to admit, though, sometimes you puzzle us as much as we puzzle you. Just about the time we think we've figured you out, you put a new gang in office in Washington, and you change all the rules, and then you come on with some big new plan for our salvation. I'll bet you don't even know that your precious Declaration of Independence calls us merciless savages out to kill all of you without regard to age, sex, or condition. Did you know that? Sometimes I think that all of you Anglos are nuts."

I knew I didn't understand and I was too tired to think about it any longer. Anyway, the rain had stopped.

"Let's take a look outside, Rob. I've had enough sociology for today."

The formerly solid overcast was breaking up. Scattered showers could be seen in a dozen locations around the horizon, but the storm was over. Our problems weren't over though. There was water everywhere and all of it was running fast.

"I feel like I'm in the middle of a water maze. Do you suppose we'll be able to figure our way out of here?"

"Sure, we'll do it the Valenci way. We'll just sit back and wait until it goes away. We won't fight it, we'll outlive it." Then he grinned at me. "How about that, Okey. What would an Anglo do, form a committee, levy additional taxes, and build a bunch of new bridges?"

We wandered around the outside of the shack staring at the damage the rain had done. It was an incredible new landscape. New ditches, higher than a man's head, had been plowed. The sides of old arroyos had fallen into roaring brown water and had been swept away forever. Tons of woody debris sailed by on the rushing water. A petrified log that had been buried for a thousand centuries lay wet and exposed on the side of a new stream. Our sheepherder's shack had been built on a high place. That explained why it had lasted through all these years of storms. A collection of small animals occupied the hilltop island with us. Rabbits and ground squirrels hid under soggy sagebrush. Two skunks waddled around like pudgy, self-important matrons on an afternoon window-shopping excursion. If we had a boat, we could float all the way to the Gulf of California.

Evening came on slowly with no sign of retreat by the waters. When the sky faded from royal purple to black velvet, stars burst forth in unbelievable numbers. Light from the waning moon would blank out many of them later in the evening. In less than a minute, I saw a dozen shooting stars come from the same region of the sky.

I finally wandered back into the shack. Rob had already stretched out on his bedroll.

"Rob, I've been thinking about what we are doing. Do you know what John Denti is up to?"

"I've got an idea. I may be wrong, but I think he's after your imaginary treasure."

"I guessed that too. What I want to know is why he drags his dead mother around with him?"

He thought for a while before he answered. "It could be the other way around. You never knew Mora Denti. She was as rotten as a person can be. My father told me that she raised those two boys of hers, Larry and John, to have the morals of a mongrel dog. He said Luke Ring hung around with them all the time when they were growing up, and that was how he got to be such a bad one. Old Mora always claimed she learned to be a witch from the Navajos. To me that's pure bunk. I don't believe the Navajos would waste their time with her, but still she fooled some people. Larry and John were both great big men, so was Luke and that added to the problem. They were bullies, but, at the same time, they were mama's little boys. They did absolutely everything Mora told them to do. They were totally dependent on her to do all their thinking for them. John was by far the worst. Well, my point is this. I think he is still dependent on her. He needs her around him now just as much as he did before she died. I think he's a very sick, distorted, and probably insane man. I've been told that several years ago he and Larry stole some sacred jewelry or something like that. Anyway, whatever they did, I've heard the religious leaders declared them non-people. I figure that's when he became completely unglued. He had been taught a lot of the secrets of the tribe, and I've heard he even tried to sell them, too."

"What secrets? Wait a minute. That didn't come out right. I don't mean 'what secrets'; I mean what kind of secrets. Oh, hell, you know what I mean."

"I know what you mean alright, but, the truth is, I don't know what secrets. What I do know is that when you reach a certain age you are told certain secret information because you are presumed to be old enough to keep it secret or use it, or understand it or do whatever you're supposed to do with it. Since I'm not yet old enough, I've never been told what the secrets are about."

"When will you be old enough?"

"That's another thing I don't know."

"Do you think that might account for the way the older people have been treating you for the past few days? Do you figure in some way you are a part of one of their secrets?"

"That's the way it looks to me."

Chapter Sixty-Two

"Go on with your story about the Dentis.'

"Well, as I said, Mora was always the moving force. She made John and Larry do exactly what she wanted them to do. My guess is that she made them take her to Chicago because she decided she wanted something from my grandfather. Evidently, she was too old to finish the job. She died, but her power over the boys was so great that they refused to recognize her death and kept her body around to protect them while they were in the city. Then John brought her back here to help him find this hokey treasure of yours. As long as we're on the subject, I think John killed his brother, Larry, and his former friend, Luke Ring, too."

"Why do you think that?"

"Like I said, John was always the worst of the bunch, but he was Mora's favorite. I figure when she died the other two wanted to stop whatever they were up to. I think John got mad and killed them, rather than let them upset Mora's insane scheme. "

"What do you suppose happened to your grandfather's body? I presume John Denti was the man with your grandmother when she came to get the body."

"I don't know. Truth is that I don't think my grandmother was with him at all. I think it was Mora. When they failed to find anything on him, then they went after my grandmother. Clearly they failed to make my grandmother think they were her friends and protectors. As far as grandfather's body, I guess they just dumped him somewhere. Maybe on your skid row."

"One more body sure wouldn't make much of a stir there. He'd just be another unidentified stiff. Wait a minute, though, that wouldn't work. He had been embalmed. The cops see lots of guys that die on the street, but it's not likely they would miss the distinction between a dead bum and an embalmed body."

"I suppose that's true. Well, maybe they just dug a hole and buried him somewhere. I don't know. I do know that he wouldn't care. You had already helped his spirit through the lake and into the next world. After that, his body was just so much meat."

"Do you know why your grandmother and grandfather went to Chicago?"

"I've heard several versions, but the one I believe is the one my parents wrote to me while I was in the Marines. My grandfather told them he was getting very old, and before he died, he wanted to see the real white man's world. Apparently it had something to do with his wondering whether Valenci would be better off if it were more like the Anglo's world. He had a notion that he could change it all by himself if it should be changed."

" How?”

"Damned if I know. I haven't the faintest idea and neither did my parents. "

"Did he ever decide it should be changed?"

"No. My folks said he had somebody write a letter to them from Chicago and in it he told them they didn't know how well off they were. He said all he had learned was that he felt sorry for the Anglos and that they were the ones who needed help."

"Why didn't he go on home, then?"

"Apparently he got sick or something. We never did know what happened. It's almost as if he tried to disappear. We tried to find out, of course. John Perez went out to Chicago once to try to find them, but he couldn't. The very next thing I learned about them was when we found out about my grandmother being in Nebraska and then that story you told me about my grandfather in the jail. Now let's hit the sack. We've got a long day tomorrow."

I worried about rattlesnakes for a full ten seconds before I went to sleep.

Chapter Sixty-Three

Rob was awake and boiling coffee long before the sun rose. I rolled over in my soggy blanket and opened my eyes in time to see him fiddling with a small black stone. When he saw me staring at him, he thrust the pebble back into his jacket pocket and appeared slightly embarrassed.

"Good morning, Sunshine. Want some coffee? It'll be ready in a minute or two."

"Good morning to you. What's the little black rock for?"

"Oh, it's kind of a rabbit's foot. We could use some good luck today, don't you think? I say, old man, would you care for crumpets and caviar with your boiled coffee?"

"You are just the type who would eat crumpets and caviar for breakfast. If you don't mind, I'll have black coffee with my black coffee."

The air was cold, but through the holes in the roof, I saw the beginnings of a bright blue sky. That meant a hot day.

"I've checked all around outside. It looks like the water has run off pretty well. How's the coffee?"

"Wait till I chew it a while longer. Let me see that good luck rock of yours, Rob." I felt I could use some good luck too.

He reached in his pocket and pulled out a three-inch long black stone shaped like a fat black bear. It was smooth and had a glassy sheen. It had blue eyes made of tiny pieces of turquoise and tied on its back with a wrapping of rawhide, was a small turquoise arrowhead.

"It's a fetish," he anticipated my question. "It's supposed to be a bear."

"It's a fancy little thing. What's it made of?"

"Jet. It's not an old fetish. As a matter of fact, it's just one that was made to sell to tourists. But I like it. So I bought it from the guy who made it, and I carry it for good luck," he said, as he took it back and rubbed his forefinger on its nose.

"What do you mean 'an old fetish?' "

"The old people believe that if they find a stone that looks like an animal, then it is a real animal that was changed into stone by the children of the sun. All the natural powers of the animal are still present even if its limbs are stone. So if this living power is treated properly, and with great respect, and if you feed it sacred corn meal then the fetish will give help to its owner. If you get the assistance you asked the fetish for, then well and good. If you don't, then it isn't the fetish's fault. Either you offended it, by failing to feed it with proper ceremony or, what's more likely, you weren't of good heart when you asked for its aid."

"Sounds like either way the fetish wins. What kind of help is the bear going to give us?" I asked.

"This bear is named 'Clumsy Foot.' He will make us stout of heart and strong of will. Since his coat is the color of the land of night, he is the guardian of the West. In case you hadn't noticed, we are headed toward the West, and we will have to do some really hard walking tonight. So you'd better be good to old black bear here."

"If that bear doesn't work any better than my last rabbit's foot, you'll waste a lot of 'sacred' corn meal that could have been used for pancakes." I said.

Rob laughed. "You may be right, buddy." He put the fetish back in his pocket. "Let's get a move on."

We covered the rough terrain at a steady pace, stopping for a five-minute rest period each hour. The fast flowing water was gone, and the country looked as dry as it had before the rain. On some of the higher ridges, the red surface soil had peeled off and curled up into little cigar shapes that shattered into fine dust when I touched them. By evening we had covered twenty-five miles. That, plus the first day's walk, and the short distance we had covered before the rain on the second day, meant we were less than five miles from our objective-the cliff and its killer occupant.

"Rob, are we going to try to go on to the mountain tonight?"

"I was going to ask you how you feel about it. Do you want to rest here for a while, and then move on after it gets dark? Or, are you too tired?"

"Let me think about it for a while. I'm not sure. "

After we talked it over, we decided not to resolve anything until we had rested and eaten supper. We were in the shadow of a large overhanging rock and it would be a good place to camp for the night. I was tired, but not nearly as tired as I had been the first night.

"Will there be a moon so we can see where we're walking if we go on?" I asked.

"No, not until very late tonight. We've got old Clumsy Foot, though. He can see to lead us through the dark." Again Rob took the fetish from his pocket and rubbed its nose. "How about it, Bear. Should we go on tonight?"

"Well, what does he say?" It was crazy, but I really wanted to hear an answer to my question.

Rob sat and looked at the little rock bear in his hand for a few moments. Then he raised his eyes and winked at me. "Let's go on to the cliff and camp there tonight. We've got a little light left, and it shouldn't take more than a couple of hours longer.

We'll have to do some climbing. But, for some reason, I think we should try to get there tonight. O.K. by you?"

"Did Clumsy Foot tell us to go on?" I was only half teasing him.

"Sure," he answered, but his face was turned so I couldn't tell whether he thought it was a joke.

Chapter Sixty-Four

Traveling at night was much slower than we had anticipated. For the first three miles, twilight allowed us to move at a reasonable pace, but when the last light faded from the sky, we had to make use of our flashlights and were slowed considerably. More and more the ground was broken by gulleys, badger holes, boulders, and small cliff faces.

We walked up a long, sandy slope, which gradually narrowed and then ended at the bottom of a flat white rock. Rob sat down on the rock and turned off his flashlight.

"When we have climbed the rest of this hillside, we will be at the top of the mountain where the cliff is located. The moon will be up in about an hour. I think we should wait here until it comes up, and then we'll have enough light to work our way out on to the cliff. I don't think we ought to use our flashlights anymore. They show a long way, and, if he happens to be on the top of the hill, he'll see us for sure." He was almost whispering.

"Do you think we'll be able to handle him, if we find him? "

"He's out of his mind. He must be, hauling his mother's dead body all over the country and killing those people. So, it might not be too easy. Crazy people can be awfully rough."

"Howard made quite a point of not wanting us to use these pistols, didn't he?" I said, as I took out the gun, and aimed it at imaginary enemies on the horizon.

"Mr. Parks doesn't like guns. Neither do I."

He suddenly pointed to a glow on the horizon. "Here comes the moon. We'd better get on our way."

Reluctantly, I climbed to my feet, and we began to work our way up the steep, boulder-strewn, mountainside.

By midnight we had climbed to the top of the mountain. An hour later we had traversed the plateau and had arrived at the upper edge of the four hundred- foot high, almost vertical, cliff.

"From here on we've got to be extremely careful, Okey, it's a long way to the bottom. "

"I know. 'Watch that first step,' said the drunk. "

"What do you mean?"

"It's just an old joke. It's not worth repeating. What's the plan? What are we going to do now?" We were talking in whispers.

"We can't stay here; this spot is too exposed. As soon as it gets light he could see us. Let's climb down about a hundred feet and find a sheltered spot on the cliff face."

"In the dark?"

"The moon is bright enough. Come on, follow me."

A long half hour of bruised shins, skinned elbows, and whispered curses later, we had fumbled our way about seventy-five feet down the face of the cliff.

"Okey, this is a well-sheltered place. We'll roll up in here for the night."

"It looks good to me." Our temporary home was a shallow cave the size of a jail cell carved by Mother Nature into the mountainside.

"If we stay inside, he won't be able to see us when it gets light. We might even be able to spot him from that ledge out there. We're still much more than halfway up the cliff face, so we'll be able to look over a lot of territory when the sun comes up tomorrow. What's the matter with you, Okey?"

"This place. I've been here before." I looked around excitedly. "Rob! This is the place where your petroglyph is! Look there!"

Chipped into the stone at the rear of our little cave was the petroglyph. The sun face, the cow, and the dancing men, showed dimly in the soft reflected light from the moon.

Rob hurriedly walked to the back of the cave and stood staring at it. I wiped the sweat off my face with my handkerchief and laid it on the cave floor beside me. Then I stretched out my bedroll and flopped down, bone weary.

"Does the real petroglyph make any more sense than the drawing?" I finally asked him. He had been silent for a long time.

He sat shaking his head. "It doesn't mean one damn thing to me, Okey. Not one damn thing." He kicked his heel into the dirt floor.

"Maybe it means something to old Clumsy Foot, your little rock bear. He sure brought us straight to it in the black of the night," I volunteered.

Rob took the little bear out of his pocket again. "Thanks, Clumsy Foot," he said. "Now, if you will please, bring us a little more luck in the morning."

"That comes from both of us," I thought.

Chapter Sixty-Five

"The twenty-two named species of wood rats (Neotomas) are represented by seven species in North America north of Mexico. These rodents have adapted to a variety of swampy, semi-arid, and arid environments in the southern United States. One species, the bushy-tailed wood rat, Neotoma cinera, that lives in northern Arizona and New Mexico...is the only New World rat with a heavily furred tail...

"They build rather bulky houses that resemble beaver lodges. These are built on dry land, sometimes in crevices or under overhangs of cliffs... The habit of collecting things, particularly shiny objects such as tin foil or coins has given the wood rat the common names of pack rat, or trade rat."

The Audubon Nature Encyclopedia, Vol. 9, p. I647-8
Curtis Publishing Company (I965).

Chapter Sixty-Six

Kialutsi, a very important trader rat, had a busy night ahead of him. Not only must he visit his fifth wife, who would soon bear him many children, but he must also hustle to complete a new nest for his next bride-to-be. The place he had chosen for this new nest was the very same one his grandfather's grandfather's grandfather had used to found his noble line. How wise he had been, thought Kialutsi. The place is deep in the ground, safe from all but Snake. Badger cannot burrow through solid rock. Eagle and Owl will never see it. Coyote is too fat to enter its door. Oh, it is an excellent place. Man was here once, but that was so long ago that his smell has left forever. Only his debris remains; such a lot of debris, though. It was so hard and cold that it would never do for a nest. A nest must be made of the very best tiny sticks and soft grass. In the center of the nest must be a warm place for many babies. Kialutsi knew just the thing for the warm spot. He would use some of the wool from Sheep that could always be found around the hillside. Each time Sheep passed a juniper snag or a thorn bush he would leave a bit of wool for the nest builders. Sheep was a generous friend. What's more, Sheep never hunted Kialutsi. Kialutsi crept up the narrow passageway to the big room with its opening to the cliff. Something smelled. Something smelled bad. Something new was in the big room. Kialutsi investigated. It was Man. Two of the creatures, asleep. Beside one of them was a white thing. What was it? Kialutsi examined the white thing. It smelled of Man, but even so it was very soft. It would make a fine center place in a nest. Now there was no need to go outside where Owl might see him. Kialutsi took the white thing in his mouth and dragged it behind him down the passageway to his new nest. How fine it was. His bride would have to ignore the Man stink, but she would be glad to, when she felt how soft it was.

What could he give the Man creature in exchange for his white thing? Kialutsi would never take without giving. What could he give? He had a marvelous idea. Give the Man a piece of the Man's own debris. Very carefully Kialutsi gathered up a piece of the debris and carried it up the narrow passageway. Carefully he placed it beside the sleeping Man. He put it just where the white thing had been. Now he had his own debris, and I have a new soft lining for my nest. What a fine night's work this has been, smiled Kialutsi. My grandfather's grandfather's grandfather could not have done better.

Chapter Sixty-Seven

I awakened with the certain knowledge that something had changed. Something was out of place. I had dreamed I was a child again in West Virginia in my own bed, in my own home. That was followed by the kind of foggy unhappy feeling you have at the moment of awakening when you know all those things are only dreams and are gone forever. Through this maudlin haze came the realization that I was wrapped in a blanket, lying in a cave on the side of a cliff in New Mexico. Then came the sharp awareness that this was not the thing that was wrong, something else was out of kilter. I pulled up to a sitting position and looked around the cave trying to decide what had induced this odd apprehension. It was pre-dawn, only a light dilution of the blackness of the sky suggested the coming of day. I looked at Rob. He was still asleep. My gaze wandered to the petroglyph. It was still there, unchanged, the little men dancing forever in solid rock. I listened and heard nothing except my own breath and that of Rob. It was still. Some sort of night-dawn noises should have been going on outside, but I heard none.

This was foolishness! I lay back down. It was only because I was excited by today's impending manhunt and worn out by the long hike. It would pass, but sleep would not come. I lay awake and stared at the spider webs on the ceiling of the mountain vault. Minutes passed. The sky outside grew lighter. Rob began to stir preparatory to waking.

Without looking, I reached for my handkerchief. I had placed it on the cave floor beside me the night before. My fingers fumbled in the dust and sand of the cave floor. I couldn't find it. Irresolution kept me from sitting up and looking. Stubbornness kept my hand patting blindly around the floor. My hand lit on something cold. It was colder than the dirt. My fingers measured it. It was thin and flat and the size of a postage stamp. What had we dropped that felt like that? Reluctantly I picked the thing up and raised it over my face to see what it was.

I lay there for many minutes and looked at the object in my hand knowing that in one night my world had been radically altered.

In my hand was a small, bright piece of hammered gold. I sat up and called softly to Rob. "Wake up."

He awakened instantly, and sat up, still wrapped in his heavy blanket.

"What's wrong?" he asked, and looked anxiously at the cave entrance and then at me.

"Look at this." I handed the gold rectangle to him.

He turned it over a few times in his hands and then, without looking at me, asked where I had found it.

"Here beside me. I reached for my handkerchief and there it was."

I looked again at the spot and saw that my handkerchief was gone. I moved to see if I had rolled over it in the night. It was gone. Rob watched the performance without comment.

"My handkerchief is gone." Somehow this seemed of equal importance to the finding of the piece of gold.

"Hold still," he said sharply.

I sat very still and watched as he unwound himself from the blanket and then crept on his knees to my side.

"Look, there, in the dust, " he ordered.

I looked and saw tiny dusty tracks that led from a narrow opening in the rocks to my side, circled around, and then led back to the crevice. The tracks were wiped away where my hand had smoothed the dust. The gold had lain in the center of this spot.

"Trader rat," he said. "He took your handkerchief and paid you for it with gold."

We sat there looking at the gold. Neither of us wanted to voice what both of us thought. I finally broke the mood.

"Rob, this is hammered gold plate. It's man-altered gold. This isn't a piece of raw gold. If it came out of that hole then..." I didn't finish the sentence. I just broke it off and let it hang.

After a moment he took it up. "Then there is probably more where this came from. Maybe a lot more."

My mind was racing now.

"The 'key,' Rob. That's what it's all about. It really does mark a treasure. The 'key' is the key to hidden gold. Whoever has the picture can match it with the petroglyph and know where the gold is. We've got it made, buddy. We're rich!" As my excitement had risen my voice had grown louder and louder.

"Hold it down, Okey. Do you want him to know we're here?"

"To hell with him," I shouted gleefully. We're sitting on top of a fortune, and all you can think about is that jackass Bentura. Come on, let's dig in there and see what else we can find."

"O.K, but keep your voice down-please."

Rob seemed little moved by all this even as he helped me claw the dirt away from the crevice in the rock. In short order the dirt was gone, and we were scratching at a hole in the solid rock.

"Don't tear up your fingers on that rock," he said. "The only way you are going to get past there is with dynamite."

"Let me see if I can reach in," I said and laid face down on the cave floor.

My arm slid in, all the way to my shoulder, without coming to the end of the hole.

I withdrew my arm and sat up. "Shine your light down the hole," I suggested.

Rob dutifully aimed the flashlight into the crevice. The sides were illuminated a short distance and then nothing.

"It must open up again into a bigger hole about five or six feet from this end," he offered.

With more daylight in the cave and the dirt scraped away, we saw that the hole was not a hole in solid rock but was the broken corner of a large rock, closely fitted against a still larger rock.

"It's a rock wall. And, look see, it's man made," I speculated eagerly. "Look, you can tell. They've pulled those rocks together over the opening. Nature didn't close off this cave. Man covered it up!"

"You wouldn't have noticed it in a thousand years, though," Rob said, "except for that trader rat buying your handkerchief."

"I wonder how long ago it was built? It sure isn't recent."

"No, it's been here a long time, I think." Rob still hadn't joined in my excitement. He almost seemed to want to ignore what we had found.

Suddenly there was a loud shout from the entrance to the cave. "Hold it right there! Keep your hands away from those pistols or I'll kill you both."

Chapter Sixty-Eight

We sat dumbfounded for an instant and the voice came again.

"Leave your blankets and your guns where they are. Now slide back to the rear of the cave. I've got a gun and I'm not fooling. "

We did as he ordered. We could see him then, silhouetted against the clear morning sky. He had a shotgun slung in the crook of his right arm and it was aimed directly at us. In his left hand he held a long thin pole.

He was an old Indian man. His face was wrinkled and his hair was white. He wore the traditional Valenci headband, but his clothes were shabby and ill fitting.

He was bone thin.

"What are you up to, Hassigo?" Rob shouted. "Don't you know who I am?"

"I don't know who you are, and I don't care who you are. All I want to know is what you are doing here?" He raked both of our pistols across the floor and then over the edge of the cliff with the long pole.

"Put down that gun, Hassigo, before you hurt someone. Look at me! I'm Rob Gaiule. I'm a lawman."

Rob spoke slowly and deliberately as if he were talking to someone who was feeble minded.

"What's that name again?"

"I'm Rob Gaiule. I'm a deputy in the Valenci Law and Order. You know me, Hassigo."

"You ain't Rob Gaiule. I know Rob Gaiule. Rob Gaiule is as old as I am, maybe older. Who're you trying to fool? What's that in your hand?" As he spoke he was looking at the piece of gold in Rob's hand.

"My grandfather was named Rob Gaiule too. You remember him. I'm not trying to fool you, Hassigo. Please now, put down the gun." Rob's voice carried no emotion, but his eyes were alight with suppressed excitement. I was convinced the old man was going to shoot us. I started to feel sick at my stomach.

"Does The Secret Keeper know you're here, boy? He told me that no one knows this place except him and me. He even went away from Valenci to keep those damn Dentis from finding this place. I promised him I wouldn't tell a soul. I didn't either." He paused for a moment and his eyes seemed to glaze over. He looked as if he were reliving some scene from his past. Then he snapped back to the present.

"What are you doing here? Where did you get that gold?" He seemed more agitated than before. His last question was shouted, and he waved the pole around frantically in his left hand. The pole had some sort of pointed hook tied to its top end.

"Hassigo, my grandfather is dead. He told me of this place after he died. He sent this white man to tell me about it. This man is my grandfather's messenger from the brighter place," Rob gestured toward me. "Hassigo, listen, only you and I know of this place." Rob still had not shown the slightest emotion.

The words seemed to calm Hassigo. He lowered the shotgun slightly and looked directly at Rob for the first time.

"The Secret Keeper told me I can come once a year," he said in a singsong voice like a child reciting a poem. "Once a year and I can use my pole. I can fish from sun up until the sun re-lights the little sun on the wall. Then I must stop and not come again till the next year. I can keep what I catch but I must tell no other person. The Secret Keeper is my friend."

As he said these words he laid the shotgun and the pole on the dusty cave floor and squatted down with his feet under him. I was certain Rob would grab the shotgun. I looked at Rob, but he showed no sign of moving.

"He is my friend," continued the old man. As he talked he rocked back and forth on his heels.

"Hassigo, my friend, hear me. I am the son of Rob Gaiule's son. Your friend, Rob Gaiule, The Secret Keeper, has passed through the lake and into the brighter land. A few months ago my father also passed away in a car crash. I am of the blood of Rob Gaiule and now I am your friend." Rob explained this chain of events with obvious concern that the old man would listen and understand. He gave no hint that he was trying to subdue the old man or to get his shotgun. I was still too frightened to move.

The old man stared at Rob for a long time. We sat silently as he stood up, walked over and closely examined Rob's face.

"Yes. Now I can see. You are of The Secret Keeper's blood. You speak the truth. Today is my day to fish. I must hurry for the sun is about to rise. I will tell no one. I will keep only what I catch in the half day." Saying this, the old man picked up the pole and walked past us and to the back of the cave. He had left the shotgun lying on the ground at the mouth of the cave.

"Quick, Rob, get his gun!" I shouted. But instead of moving, Rob merely sat quietly watching the old man.

I still couldn't seem to make my legs move, and Rob didn't seem to grasp the fact that this was our opportunity to get the old nut's gun.

"Rob!" I hissed in a stage whisper.

"Hush, Okey!" he ordered quietly.

Chapter Sixty-Nine

We sat and watched the old man insert the pole into the trader rat hole in the rock, hooked end first. Then he lay down on the floor of the cave and ran the entire pole and half of his arm into the hole. From the movement of the muscles on his back I could tell he was waving the pole around in the hole. His face was a study in concentration. He paid us not the slightest attention.

After a few minutes Hassigo got to his knees and pulled the pole out of the hole. A small piece of gold sheet, slightly larger than the one I had found was impaled on the sharp hook at the end of the pole. He carefully removed the gold from the hook and dropped it into a small leather pouch hung around his neck like a necklace. Back into the hole went the pole and back down on the floor went Hassigo. This time it took almost ten minutes before he removed his pole. Sweat ran down his forehead and his thin white hair was plastered across his eyes and face. When he pulled the pole out, the hooked end was empty. Without any visible sign of disappointment he bent to his work again.

I couldn’t stand it any longer. "Rob, what the hell are we doing? Why don't we get his gun? That old guy is crazy as a loon and he’s got a shotgun." I had my voice back again, and I thought maybe my legs might obey me. Sick fear had been replaced by a sense of unreality.

"Hassigo," Rob said. "We must go now. We have work to do. Fish as you have always fished, and keep what you catch. Your promise to my grandfather is now your promise to me. Remember it!”

The old man looked at Rob. A great toothless smile split open his face. Then he nodded his head and bent to his work again.

Rob stood up. "Come on, Okey. Let's go find John Denti. "

We rolled our blankets into the ponchos and walked out of the cave. Rob's behavior still made no sense to me. Who gave a damn about John Denti when we had a fortune in our grasp.

The sun had warmed the thin morning air and the world was a dazzling white glare.

"I suppose you think you know what you're doing?" I finally growled as we climbed away from the cave entrance.

"Of course I do. We're going after John Denti, aren't we?" He seemed surprised that anything else could have been on my mind.

"Are you serious?" I exploded. "You can't be serious. That crazy old coot holds a gun on us, takes our pistols, and steals our gold, and you just walk away like it never happened. I've changed my mind. He isn't crazy. You're the crazy one!" I was shouting again.

"Okey, I'm sure there is enough gold there to keep you happy for the rest of your life, if that's what it takes. Old Hassigo hasn't removed but a tiny amount each year. He will take only enough to sustain him again this year. Now settle down and lower your voice. We have a job to do. We're after a killer, and neither of us can afford to get careless with John Denti. After we catch him and put him in the jail, we'll worry about the gold. O.K.?"

It suddenly came to me that I sounded exactly like a child throwing a temper tantrum. I was embarrassed at the way I was behaving. "I'm sorry, Rob. You're right. Of course the gold will be there tomorrow. I just forgot myself for a moment."

We climbed up the cliff face a few yards and took a position on a narrow ledge. We could see much of the rest of the cliff face from where we stood. Rob repeatedly cautioned me to remain concealed as we looked for Denti.

Try as I might, I couldn't work up any real enthusiasm for the manhunt. My mind kept going back to the gold. I ballooned it into a thousand and one day dreams.

A lot of them seemed to involve Dorothy Lamb and me.

Chapter Seventy

"How much do you suppose there is?" I said more to myself than to Rob.

"What?"

"I was thinking of the gold again. I wonder how much of it there is. How do you suppose it got in there?" I rapidly warmed to the subject again.

"I have no idea," he said in the voice used by teachers to dismiss students who persistently ask unnecessary questions.

We spent the next two hours moving slowly from rock to rock and ledge to ledge along the face of the cliff. There was no sign of John Denti. I tried manfully to keep my mind on what we were doing, at least enough to keep from slipping, falling, and breaking my neck. Shortly after mid-morning we stopped to rest.

"Okey," Rob said, "tell me again. Was my grandfather living like a rich man in Chicago before he died?"

"He certainly was not. He and your grandmother lived in a real dump of an apartment in the worst part of the city."

"Do you think he knew about this gold?"

"Well of course he did. He must have. He had the 'key.' He was very anxious that I pass it on to your father. Your grandmother was so anxious for you to have it that she must have known about the gold too."

I wasn't sure where such questions came from, or where they were going to lead.

"Do you think he was crazy-I mean insane?"

"No. Well, I'm not sure. He acted sort of crazy but I don't think he was. At least he was perfectly rational the night he died."

"What about my grandmother? Was she crazy?"

"Absolutely not! She was very badly injured when I talked to her, but she wasn't crazy, and she never had been. I'm certain about that."

"Well, then, Okey, how do you account for the way they lived? Why would two apparently sane people, who knew where there was a great pile of gold, live in apparent poverty?"

I wasn't sure, because of the expression on his face, whether he was asking questions or making some sort of obscure point.

"Damned if I know, Rob. Why do you think they did it?" I couldn't imagine people acting like that.

"I'm working on that, Okey. I'm working on it. I'm also trying to figure you out. Just exactly who are you, Okey? What do you want? I have the feeling you think you are one thing, when, in fact, you're something very different. Maybe someday you'll just tell me, and I won't have to figure it out for myself." He stood up again. "O.K., let's get going. If we don't find Denti before long, we will have failed our task." He moved away, crouching behind the rocks.

Chapter Seventy-One

I watched him for a moment or two, and then got up to follow. It was high noon and still we had found no sign of John Denti. The sun burned down, heating the rocks and the air until I felt as if I were climbing on the fangs in the mouth of hell.

"Rob, up there's some shade. Let's knock off for a while."

"I'm with you. Do you have any water left?"

"Not a drop. Do you?"

"About a mouthful. Here take a sip." He handed me the plastic canteen. I took a tiny amount of the warm water and held it in my mouth for a while before swallowing it. It tasted terrible but it felt good in my throat.

"I'm afraid we've had it. I don't think he's here." He sounded thoroughly disappointed. "We've been on a wild goose chase."

"I agree. Shall we start down the cliff to the valley and find Howard and his gang? I sure hope we don't have to walk all the way out to the road. Lord, it's hot!"

"Tell you what, Okey. Let's stay with it for one more hour. If we don't find him by then, we'll build a fire..."

"A fire? What's the matter with you? You couldn't be cold on a day like this."

"No," he smiled. "I'm not that strange. I don't want to walk out of here any more than you do. I figure if we get some smoke going, Mr. Parks might see it and drive on in. Then we can ride out with him, instead of walking out."

"How about that? Smoke signals. You tricky redskins beat all."

"I'm glad to see you have some of your distorted sense of humor back. For a while there, you seemed to be pretty uptight."

"Gold seems to have that effect on me," then after a moment added, "you know, Rob, that's the honest truth. That damn gold really does have a grip on my thinking. I can't shake it. It's like a bug with its head buried in my brain. A damn gold plated tick!"

"You're not alone. I've been thinking about it all morning too," he said, and shook his head sadly.

As we talked, my eyes swept the valley floor, far below us. The bed of the tiny stream that dug the valley meandered back and forth across its width. Dust devils stirred across the open spaces. A glint of sunlight caught my eye. Something reflected the sun back from the valley.

"Rob," I said, and pointed toward the glare, "what's that?"

"I can't tell. It's too bright. Let's move up on that ledge. Maybe we can see it better from up there."

We scrambled across the cliff face to another narrow ledge.

"It's a truck," Rob said. "It's somebody's truck and it's mired down there in the old dry lake bed. Some poor devil drove it up in there and got stuck. Look, the muck is up over the wheels."

"I thought you said there wasn't any water in the valley."

"There's no surface water, but in some places the water is very close to the surface. He may be stuck in quicksand."

"Well, whatever he's stuck in, he's really got her bogged down. Rob, look in the back of that truck! Do you know what that is?"

Chapter Seventy-Two

If Rob answered my question I never heard him, for suddenly the rock next to my head exploded with a skull-shattering roar. Pieces of stone cut into my check and forehead. Blood gushed into my eyes. Rob dived at my legs, and both of us tumbled on the ground. The next shot hit the rock precisely where my back had been one second before.

"Quick, in here," Rob hissed and rolled us both under an overhanging rock.

A third shot rang out. Whoever it was, he was above us and shooting down.

"He's got a rifle. It sounds like a big one. Hurry up and squeeze in here as tight as you can!" He inched further back into the slit.

"What the hell are we going to do?" I asked.

“There’s nothing we can do except lie right here. I don't think he can hit us, but he sure as hell can keep us penned up. It's a miracle you're still alive."

Another shot plowed a furrow in the dirt outside our hiding place. The flying dust and sand sprayed all over us.

"Did you see what was in the back of that truck?"

"It looked like the rubber sack that Mora Denti's body was in."

"That's what I thought, too."

For five minutes the only sound was the wind blowing across the face of the cliff. Then, the silence was shattered. "Hey, Anglo," came a voice from the mountain above us, "why didn’t you go back where you belong while you still had the chance? You'll never go there again." The question was followed by three quick rifle shots that slammed against our rock shield.

"It's Bentura," I whispered. "I've heard that voice before."

"It's John Denti. I know his voice. Well, that settles one thing -John Denti is the phony Bentura. We've found our man."

"The trouble is, it's like having a mountain lion by it's tail," I said, "we've got our man, but what can we do about it?"

"For the moment, not one darn thing. He's got us penned down tight. From where he is he can kill us the moment we move outside this hole. We've just got to wait here and hope that Mr. Parks and the others have heard the shots and are on their way."

"Do you think there's much chance that they can hear them?"

"I'm afraid not. The wind down in the valley can drown out a lot of sounds, especially when it's this far away. "

"Well, what the hell are we going to do then?" I repeated.

"Unless you have a better suggestion, we may as well see if we can talk him to death."

I did not have a better suggestion.

"Hey, Denti!" Rob yelled, "how come you're shooting at us?"

The answer came in the form of a bullet, which rang off our ledge and whined across the valley below. A crow swooped low to see what was happening on his cliff.

"Denti, you couldn't hit a bull in the butt with a banjo!" Rob yelled.

"What's that you said, you stuck up Little Secret Keeper? Are you making fun of me? Well, go right ahead, but remember, I'm going to kill you. I'm going to kill you and your nosey friend." Another shot followed the words.

"I don't think he likes us, Okey!"

“Hey, Keeper, are you afraid?" the voice came again. "Did you know your grandmother wouldn't tell me the secret? She was tough for an old woman, but I killed her just like I’m going to kill you."

“Denti, you're nothing. You don't exist. You don't even have a name anymore. You and your lousy dead brother are no longer humans. Both of you are big nothings," Rob yelled.

"Don't call me Denti. Denti is a stinking Valenci name. My name is Bentura. I'm no damn Valenci. I'm Bentura." He was silent for a while, and then he shouted,

"Hey, Keeper, I found your secret place. Do you hear me, Keeper? I found your secret place. It won't be a secret anymore. I'm going to kill you, Keeper and then I'm going to tell the Anglos about your secret place."

Rob looked at me. "He may be telling the truth. We made enough racket this morning. He could have heard us. "

I agreed with him. One of us had been extremely noisy. Beads of sweat rolled down my face. The air was like the breath from a blast furnace.

"Keeper? Don't you believe me? Too bad you can't go back to your Secret Place now and see what's left of Old Hassigo."

"What have you done to Hassigo?" Rob shouted furiously. For the first time he showed his anger.

"He's dead! He's dead! I killed him. His throat is cut and his dirty mouth is filled with a bag of Valenci gold."

"Why? Why did you kill that poor old man, you rotten sonofabitch?” I yelled.

"Well, well. Is that you at last, Anglo? I though the cat had your tongue. What's the matter, Anglo? Are you scared? You'd better be, because today you're going to die, Anglo."

"Denti, why did you kill Hassigo?" Rob yelled.

"He was one of those bastards who pretended they couldn't see me. Every year I followed him to find his secret place. But he was too smart. He wasn't like the old Secret Keeper. The old Keeper thought he could go to the city and hide from us. But we were too smart for him. We found him up there. You aren't smart, either. You and your dumb-ass Anglo friend led me straight to the secret place just like I knew you would. Now I have the secret place and I have Hassigo and I have you. Everybody will know me now."

Two more shots punctuated his harangue.

"You sure are good at making him talk," I said. "Now how about making him go away?"

"Any place particular in mind?"

"I've got one place in mind, but I'm not sure he would agree to it."

Chapter Seventy-Three

A magpie landed on our ledge and strutted back and forth until another shot tore into the ground in front of him.

"Okey, I've got an idea!"

"We sure could use one. What is it?" I caught some of the excitement from his voice.

"Let's not talk to him," he whispered.

"What the hell kind of idea is that?" I asked in disbelief.

"Let's be perfectly silent. Not a single word. Maybe if we treat him like a banished man, he'll get so upset he'll make a mistake, and then we can take him!"

"Well, why not? What we're doing now sure isn't helping things."

"Hey, Little Keeper," came Denti' s voice. "How come you're not like old Rob Gaiule? He would never have let me follow him here. I fixed his wagon. Did you know he died in a white man's jail house? But not you, you're going to die in the sun, Keeper."

We did not respond. My belly was sore from lying on my stomach. My rib cage felt as if it poked through my skin.

Ten minutes crept by and not another shot was fired. All I could think about was how much I wanted to live, and not die in this God-forsaken place.

"What's the matter down there? Hey, Keeper? Keeper, did you know I killed that yellow-bellied bastard Luke Ring? You want to know why? I'll tell you why. He found out I was going to tell about the secret place and he wouldn't help me. He claimed he was a still good Valenci. I killed him and stuffed his good Valenci mouth with dirt. What do you think of that, Keeper? Do you hear me, Keeper?"

We remained silent. My ear began to itch. A damned ant was crawling in my ear. I wanted to dig it out, but I couldn't move without the risk of exposing some part of my body to Bentura.

More minutes passed. The sun shone directly on us. I felt dizzy from the heat and lack of water.

"Hey, Anglo. Come on out, Anglo. I won't shoot you. You're no damn Valenci. You can be my buddy. We'll take the gold and drink every bar in Albuquerque dry. How about that, Anglo? You want to be my friend don't you?"

Silence.

Three shots broke the silence.

"Damn you sons-a-bitches, talk to me! I'll make you talk to me. You'll be sorry. I'll shoot you and string you out on barbwire just like my stinking brother Larry. You didn't know I killed him, did you? Well, I did. I've got his gun here to prove it. You hear that, Keeper. You're a stinking cop. I killed my brother, cop, what are you going to do about it, cop? Come on out and get me, cop!"

The ant ate his way through my ear and into my brain. My legs ached and my nose itched. The muscles in my back quivered and jumped. My kneecaps were bent around to the side of my legs. I didn't dare move and I couldn't speak.

More time passed. A weird looking toad jiggered by our hole. He cast a baleful eye at us, before moving on in search of lunch.

"Hey, Anglo. You found Mama, didn't you? Did she place a curse on you, Anglo? She is a powerful person. She told me I would be like her, and now I am. I'm an important person. I've got a powerful name. Now I'm going to destroy you and all the other damned Valencis. You talk to me Anglo, and you can be my friend. We'll make these damn Valencis see us."

My back was tied into a knot. Sweat rolled into my eyes. My neck hurt.

Suddenly the voice from the mountain changed into a singsong whine. “Mama, I'm going to stuff their mouth with dirt. They'll wish they had talked to me. Now they’ll never talk again. They'll die, Mama. We're going to make them die now, Mama!"

"Get ready, " Rob whispered.

Two shots slammed into the dirt beside us. We heard the sound of feet scrambling down the cliff, and then the voice was nearer.

"I'm going to tell everyone the stinking Valenci golden secret, the great Valenci golden secret. Anglos will come and then there will be no more Valenci. "

A moment later, the stumbling footsteps were directly above us.

"Talk to me!" Denti screamed and then leaped down in front of our hole. He was a huge man. His face was livid. Hair caked with dried mud hung down alongside his sweat-covered cheeks. His wild bloodshot eyes projected pure hate. Slowly, he twisted his mouth into a demented smile and raised the rifle to his shoulder. It was pointed straight at us. Then, suddenly his expression changed. A dazed, blank look replaced the fierce expression.

"Where are you? Where did you go?" he asked in a puzzled voice. He was only four feet away, and looking directly at us.

"Where are you? Keeper? Anglo? Oh…"

The rifle dropped from his hands, clattered across the ledge, and then fell over the edge of the cliff. He slumped to his knees, still staring directly at us. Big tears formed in his eyes and rolled down his face.

"They’re gone, Mama. They went away. Why do they all go away?”

He looked directly at the place where we lay watching him in disbelief.

"Talk to me," he whispered. "Oh, somebody -somebody please, please talk to poor John Denti." His mouth formed more words but the only sound was a long agonized moan. Very slowly he rose to his feet, turned and slowly and deliberately stepped over the edge of the cliff. He made not one single sound as he bounced and fell two hundred feet and ended his unhappy life on the rocks below.

A few moments later we crawled out to the edge of the cliff and looked down. John Denti's body lay on its back with its head turned to one side. His mouth was filled with dirt.

Maybe it was the sudden release from tension, maybe it was because I was exhausted or maybe it was the death of a fellow human being-whatever caused it, I sat on the edge of the cliff and cried like a baby.

Chapter Seventy-Four

Three bodies were removed from the valley that day. John Denti, Mora Denti and Old Hassigo. Rob and I carried old Hassigo down from the cave. We destroyed his long fishing pole, removed the pouch from his mouth and hung it back around his neck again.

Three bodies were buried that evening. John and his mama Mora were placed next to Larry, in a mountain meadow, just outside of Valenci. Old Hassigo was buried in the graveyard of the mission church in the pueblo. Howard, Rob, John Perez, and I were their only mourners.

As we left the little cemetery and walked through the dusty streets of the Pueblo, Howard and John moved on ahead while Rob and I dropped behind to talk.

"Okey, I am the only one, besides yourself, who knows where the gold is hidden. All the others are dead. I alone have the 'key.' I believe my duty is to preserve this secret and then, when I am ready to die, pass it on to my son and he to his son. The old Valencis know that my fathers are dead, and that I am now the keeper of their great secret. A vitally important thing has changed though. For the first time, an Anglo knows our secret. What will you do with your knowledge, Okey?'"

"I don't know. Maybe it would help if I knew why you plan to guard the treasure instead of digging it up and using it. Damn it Rob, look at all the things your people could have! You could build a real city here. You ask what I'm going to do. Let me ask you the same thing. What would you do if I dug up the treasure?"

"Do you have other questions?"

"No. That's it. That's what I want to know."

"We're both worn out now. Tomorrow we will talk. Too much has happened today. Tomorrow, we will both think with better minds." He smiled a totally weary smile.

Howard stood waiting for me at the door outside the Law and Order office.

"It's time to call it a day, wouldn't you say, Okey?"

"I sure would. I'm going to sleep around the clock. "

"By the way Okey, a letter came for you today. It's from your Professor Lamb in Chicago. It might be something important."

"I'll look at it tomorrow," I said. "Right now all I want is a thousand hours of undisturbed sack time and in a real bed."

Chapter Seventy-Five

The following morning, I took a long walk. My legs had grown so accustomed to walking they didn't know how to stop, and I needed time to myself to think before my meeting with Rob. I walked along the dirt street from the house and gazed out across the valley at the Sacred Mountain. My eyes drifted down the side of the black lava flow. I remembered what Howard Parks had told me when he first showed me this spot. He said the greatest blessing the Valencis ever had was that they had nothing the white man wanted. Rob had told me the same thing. I walked on through fields soon to be plowed and planted with corn and beans and squash. I walked beside the little shallow lake and watched a water snake glide around a patch of weeds. I turned west and walked across a broad stretch of desert land. Silver tipped grass, good for cattle grazing, and little barrel cacti with bright red blossoms grew in profusion. It was not an eastern meadow. It was a desert of sand and clay dotted with clumps of grass. The air was filled with the scent of sweet sagebrush. Thousands of minute, wild flowers flourished around the base of an old juniper snag. I looked again at Taaiyalote and saw the great, lonely pillars of sand stone that Valenci legends say once were the living son and daughter of a Cacique. They were turned to stone to appease the gods and halt the rising waters of a great flood about to destroy Valenci. Noah's flood might have occurred at the same time. My feet stirred up billows of red dust as I wandered back out of the desert and into the Pueblo. Two horses galloped across the road and into someone's yard. A pig wandered aimlessly down the street ahead of me. Children played around the houses and out in the road.

A pick-up truck loaded with Valencis on their way to Gallup sped past me. I guessed that, except for a few things like pick-up trucks, the sights and sounds and smells of Valenci had changed but little from what they had been eight hundred years ago. At least one lesson had impressed itself on me in the weeks I had been there, the Valencis didn't sacrifice the present in the hopes of the good times to come. They lived each moment and each day as it came. How would the treasure change all that? Beyond a doubt it would bring changes. But would they be for the better, as I had once been certain, or would they swallow up Valenci as John Denti had predicted? John Denti had been so sure the way to get his revenge was to tell the world about the treasure. Maybe he was right.

Rob and a woman who had to be his wife, Evangeline, were on the road coming toward me. She had long black hair that caught the light from the desert sun and reflected it back in a hundred iridescent shades and hues. Her face had something faintly Oriental about it. Maybe it was the set of her eyes or perhaps it was the structure of her cheeks. I wondered where the ancestors of these Valenci people migrated from. Did they really cross an ice bridge from Siberia? Could they have come from the East across the ocean to South America as some anthropologists thought? Or maybe the whole world started here. Perhaps, all of our ancestors came up through the water into a brighter place at this very spot. Maybe the mud at the edge of the Valenci River was the primeval ooze.

Chapter Seventy-Six

The three of us sat silently under a cottonwood tree beside the dusty road and looked at each other. Rob was the first to break the spell. "Okey, I lived in your world for a few years, and I saw what Anglos hold dear. Some of it is good. Some of it is not so good. But, to me, much of it is neither good nor bad. It is only different. It's yours. It's not ours. You must realize we have been in this valley for many centuries. We have developed our own laws, our own customs, and our own ways. Unlike you, we do not regard 'getting ahead' of others as a desirable thing. To us, it is bad manners to exalt one's own self over others. Let me give you an example: When I enter an Anglo's home for the first time, he takes me through each room in his house and shows me the things he had accumulated. In effect, I am asked to measure his worth as a human being, by counting his possessions. The higher the count, in quantity and quality, the greater the man is. This is not our way. We believe one person is no greater or lesser than another. We believe that people are important, not because of what they have, but simply because they are people. We believe every person has an equal claim to the sun, the rain, and the earth. Okey, I don't know where that gold came from, and I don't know how long it has been there. I do know that I don't want to see it used to destroy Valenci. I know there might be enough to build us a modern town. But the world is filled with modern towns. There is only one Valenci. It's not just some dirty little Indian pueblo out in the desert. It's a way of life. It's our way of life."

He paused for a moment and looked at Evangeline and then back at me again.

"Now I must know. What are you going to do?"

For a long time I sat and pondered how to give voice to all the things I felt. Finally, I just started talking in the hope that the words would come to me as I spoke.

"Rob, once you asked me why I kept my promise to old Charlie, your grandfather. I honestly don't know why. I guess I just drifted into keeping it. It wasn't a matter of honor or keeping a trust or a promise. I just wound up doing it. Then two kinds of things started to happen. People started lying to me and even trying to kill me. To make matters worse, I got my mind bent all out of shape when we discovered that pile of gold. The other side of the coin is that a group of complete strangers have taken me in and treated me like family. Out of a clear blue sky, I have real friends for the first time in a long dry spell." I paused for a moment to collect my thoughts and then plunged ahead again. "You say that many of my people have chosen to make the accumulation of things their primary goal. I guess you know that a lot of others want power- power to control events or things or other people. Well, I'm no different from all the rest. I've wanted those things too. As a matter of fact, the list of needs and claims and wants and desires I've gone through in my lifetime is endless. But out here in Valenci I've seen something different. Oh, sure, all you Valencis want shelter and food, and a sense of identity. And you want love, too. But once you have those things, you seem to be content. That really bothered me. You don't want more, you just want enough, and the hell-of-it is that I've come to like what I've seen. Now don't misunderstand me. I don't have any false illusions about trying to adopt the Valenci value system for my own life. I can't do it. I'm too much a product of my own culture, and I know it. But, on the other hand, I guess that I don't want to see my value system imposed on you. If, you choose to adopt it, that's O.K. by me. It's your choice to make. But if you don't want it, well then, no one, neither John Denti, nor I have the right to force you to accept it. I know now that if the outside world learned of the treasure, you would have no such choice. John Denti was right about that. But as long as the whole world thinks there is nothing here but Pueblo Indians making turquoise jewelry and dancing for rain, you may be lucky enough to be left alone. Well, not completely alone. You'll still get to entertain anthropologists and missionaries. But most of the rest of us will spend our lives never knowing that Valenci exists."

"So, Rob, the only way to answer your question is to say I guess I don't want to be the one who changes things. I'll be honest with you, though. Someday I might come to my senses and change my mind. Someday I might want that gold so much that I'll come and try to get it, no matter what the cost to Valenci. But, for now, I'm going to try very hard to forget the damn gold ever existed. "

"Okey, I… " Rob started to speak.

"Hold on, friend. You're not off the hook yet. Not by a long shot. I want my reward. Both your grandfather and your grandmother promised me a reward. I did what they asked me to do and now I'm ready to claim my pay. And, what's more, I know exactly what I want. I want your fetish, old Clumsy Foot, the bear. Don't worry, I'll feed him and I promise not to ask him to help me do the impossible."

Rob smiled wistfully as he reached in his pocket and got out the little black rock. He looked at it for a moment and rubbed its nose.

"Your reward may be greater than you think," he said as he handed it to me.

Chapter Seventy-Seven

"Where will you go now, Okey? What will you do?" Evangeline asked.

"I don't know. Maybe old Clumsy Foot here will lead me further west. But wherever it is and whatever it is, I'm going to start today- now."

We stood and looked at each other.

"Goodbye, Taaiyalote Allolowishkeh. Goodbye, Liawu."

"Goodbye friend."

I picked up my gear at the Park's house and told Betty goodbye. Howard drove me to Gallup. On the way, he handed me Professor Lamb's letter. We took our leave on Route 66 in the center of Gallup.

"Okey, we'd like you to stay on with us. You know that don't you?"

"Yes, I really do."

"Just keep this in mind. You've got a home now and you'll always be welcome in it."

"So long, Howard. Thanks for everything. I wish I ..."

"So long, Buddy. Hasta la vista."

Almost immediately Clumsy Foot and I caught a ride in an oil tanker truck-headed west.

After a few minutes of polite weather conversation with the driver, I tore open the letter from Professor Lamb.

"Dear Okey:

I received the copy of the petroglyph and I have examined it carefully.

In so far as I call tell, none of the figures suggest either the work of prehistoric people, or of the modern Valenci. It is not recent, but it may belong to the old, old modern period (1500-1700). The full-faced figure with headdress appears to be a Navajo sun symbol, and it is possible that the dancing figures are of the same origin. The animal you called a cow is probably a bison.

"While the particular juxtaposition of the figures in the petroglyph is somewhat unusual, I am certain that it is of no particular significance. These things were probably drawn for some long-since-forgotten ceremonial. They may even have been the idle doodling of a bored sheepherder.

"So Okey, don't waste too much time on that interesting little scratching. I'm afraid we'll never know what it stands for.

"When you get back to Chicago, be sure to come and see us. Dorothy sends her love.

Very truly yours,
Roscoe Lamb"

I smiled as I tore the letter into small pieces and sprinkled it out of the truck window into the wind that blows across New Mexico's deserts. It was quickly carried away in a cloud of red dust.

PART III

THE REPORT

COLONIAL UNIVERSITY
MACON, GEORGIA
Faculty Offices -School of Law

Chairman J. W. Tuttweiler Colonial University
Macon, Georgia
IN RE: Smith Manuscript
Dear Chairman Tuttweiler:

I have completed my examination and investigation of Okey P. Smith's manuscript and have reached the following conclusions:

1. Aside from Smith himself, the only person mentioned whom we can trace is Professor Roscoe P. Lamb formerly of our school who, as you know, is now deceased. Professor Lamb's daughter, Dorothy, who is mentioned several times in the manuscript, became Smith's wife several years after the events described in the manuscript are supposed to have taken place. They had no children. She predeceased Smith.

2. The police records in Chicago for the particular time frame in the manuscript include many hundreds of persons named "Smith." Twelve used the first name Okey."

3. Police records in Hastings, Nebraska, do not disclose any of the names found in the manuscript, but their records are not complete for the time frame about which we are concerned.

4. Hospital records in Hastings, Nebraska, fail to reveal any person as named in the manuscript.

5. The personnel records of the Bureau of Indian Affairs in Washington, Albuquerque, and Valenci reveal no such persons as are named in the manuscript.

6. The division of Law and Order at Valenci has had several non-Indian directors over the years. The person who fills this job is roughly the equivalent of a United States Marshal. One named Howard Parks occupied this office for

several years according to official records. He is now deceased, as is his widow.

7. The business establishments described in Chicago do not exist according to the City Directory of that city. However, I am told that many such amusement joints and missions blossom and die too quickly to be included in the directories.

8. Officials at the Valenci office of the Bureau of Indian Affairs assure me that the entire work has absolutely no basis in fact and is completely the product of Smith's imagination.

I am, therefore, forced to the conclusion that the probability is great that the Smith manuscript is not autobiographical, but is simply a work of fiction, which Mr. Smith authored at some period of his life and made no effort to publish. As to whether the manuscript should or should not be published under the imprimatur of the University as a work of fiction, I express no opinion. I would suggest that a representative of our English Department would be the appropriate person to make such a decision.

This has been an interesting experience for me; however, it will be nice to get back to the real world of the classroom again.

With kindest personal regards,
Andrew J. Duval
Professor of Law

--FINIS--